Annie Burrows has be...
romances for Mills & E...
have charmed readers w... ...g been
translated into nineteen different languages, and
some have gone on to win the coveted Reviewers'
Choice award from CataRomance. For more
information, or to contact the author, please visit
annie-burrows.co.uk, or you can find her on
Facebook at Facebook.com/AnnieBurrowsUK.

THE TROUBLE WITH THE DARING GOVERNESS

Annie Burrows

MILLS & BOON

First published in Great Britain 2024
by Mills & Boon, an imprint of HarperCollins*Publishers* Ltd,
1 London Bridge Street, London, SE1 9GF

www.harpercollins.co.uk

HarperCollins*Publishers*, Macken House, 39/40 Mayor Street Upper, Dublin 1, D01 C9W8, Ireland

With many thanks to Mills & Boon for making
my dream of becoming a published author come true.

Chapter One

'But I *lo-uh-lo-uh-love* him!'

Oh, dear, thought Rosalind, pausing with her hand raised to knock on the study door, from behind which came Lady Susannah's anguished protest. A protest which had now turned into a wild mixture of sobs and screams.

No wonder Lady Birchwood, Susannah's widowed aunt, had looked so distressed when she'd come, in person, to order Rosalind to get down to His Lordship's study and *'deal with the gel'*.

Since that was Rosalind's primary function in this household, she'd risen from her chair and come downstairs straight away. It was only now that she could hear how badly Lady Susannah was behaving that she hesitated, pondering how best to deal with her over-indulged and therefore rather pettish charge.

It sounded, from the few intelligible words she'd been able to make out before Susannah had become incoherent, as though Lord Caldicot was trying to put his foot down over the attentions of one of Susannah's suitors. Probably Mr Cecil Baxter, if Rosalind had to guess. It had been *Cecil says this* and *Cecil did that* for weeks now.

Actually, there was probably no point in knocking on the door, she reflected, lowering her hand. Neither of the people in that room was likely to hear it over the high-pitched wailing that Susannah was making now.

So she just squared her shoulders and went in.

The scene inside Lord Caldicot's study was pretty much what Rosalind had expected. Susannah was lying on the floor, thrashing about as she gave vent to her outrage, putting Rosalind in mind of a toddler who'd dropped her cream cake in the pond and seen the ducks devour it before anyone could get it back for her.

Yet she'd had the presence of mind, Rosalind noted wryly, to give vent to those feelings on the hearthrug, which was a soft, thick sheepskin, rather than on any other portion of the study floor, which had no carpet at all.

Lord Caldicot himself was standing behind his desk, ramrod straight as befitted a man who'd spent so much of his life in the military. He'd also selected the one sure defensive bulwark in the room, behind which he could duck, should Susannah take it into her head to start throwing things. He was no fool.

He did, however, look like a man who had almost reached the limit of his patience. Though his exasperated expression changed the moment he noticed her come in, to one of heartfelt relief.

'Take this silly chit back to her room,' he said irritably, 'and keep her out of my sight until you've talked some sense into her.'

Rosalind had been so pleased by the way he'd welcomed her arrival with such evident pleasure. But this tactless remark effectively doused her brief moment of joy.

Didn't he know his ward at all? Talking *sense* was never going to get through to Susannah when she was in one of these moods.

But then, of course, he didn't know her, did he? He'd been abroad, fighting for his country, when his cousin, the Fifth Marquess of Caldicot, had died and he'd become not only the Sixth Marquess, but also legal guardian of his predecessor's only surviving child, Susannah. From what Rosalind had gathered, since she'd taken on the role of something more than a governess, but not quite a companion to Susannah, everyone had thought that a bachelor, and a soldier to boot, would have no idea how to rear a girl child. So a succession of female relatives had taken turns to move into Caldicot Dane with her, to supervise her care. And all of them, without exception, had petted and cosseted the wealthy little orphan until she'd become almost unmanageable.

It was at moments like this, Rosalind reflected, regarding Susannah's flushed cheeks and thrashing limbs, that she was sometimes sorely tempted to take a glass of water and fling it into the girl's face. The trouble was that, if she were ever to succumb to such a temptation, she'd lose her job. Nobody, but *nobody*, had ever raised a hand to the girl. And for her to do so would result in instant dismissal.

Anyway, although Susannah was what some people described as *'a bit of a handful'*, this was by no means the worst position Rosalind had ever held. She wanted to keep this job. So she contented herself with merely imagining for a moment or two how Susannah would look, with cold water dripping down her face, before applying the only method that she'd ever found worked on her charge.

She went over and knelt down on the rug beside Susannah.

'I know, I know,' she crooned in apparent sympathy. 'He is a nasty brute. He won't pay any heed to your tears, you know. Come upstairs with me,' she said, holding out her hand.

'He has no right to say I may not marry Cecil,' said Susannah, abruptly, sitting up. 'No right!'

Ah. So that *was* what had brought on this latest storm.

'I have every right,' said Lord Caldicot, rather unwisely in Rosalind's opinion. Susannah had just stopped crying, sat up and begun talking. How she wished she had the right to advise him that the thing to do now would be to distract her, not reopen the argument that had started her off. But of course she didn't have that right. And it would never occur to him to *ask* her for advice. 'I am,' he persisted, 'your legal guardian.'

'You aren't!'

'I am.'

'No, you're not! I have trustees who…who…well, my aunts have always consulted with them, whenever I need something, and—' she gulped '—they let me have whatever I want!'

'The trustees,' said Lord Caldicot, firmly, 'acted on *my* behalf, while I was away fighting, and was not able to make those decisions in a timely manner. And let me tell you, young lady…'

Oh, no. Please don't, thought Rosalind.

'That had I been consulted,' he continued, impervious to Rosalind's silent plea, 'you would not have been indulged to the extent that nobody can now do anything with you!'

Well, on that score, she thought Lord Caldicot might have made a good point. Had somebody made any attempt to discipline Susannah, rather than passing her off to the next set of relatives when they'd started to find her temper tantrums tiresome, then she might not have turned out like this.

Had anyone stood by her, instead of walking away whenever she'd gone through one of her 'difficult' phases, Rosalind was certain she would have abandoned this sort of childish behaviour long ago. But nobody had. Instead, people blamed the girl for being unable to control her temper rather than wondering whether it might not be the end product of being alternately spoiled, then abandoned, by people who claimed to have her best interests at heart.

However, saying what he had did nothing to help matters. On the contrary, it provoked Susannah into sucking in a huge, indignant breath, then holding it for a split second, as though deliberating whether to use it to scream, or tell him exactly what she thought of his opinion and what he could do with it.

Rosalind took advantage of that pause to lean in and murmur into Susannah's ear, 'I shouldn't bother if I were you. Whatever you say now will only make him dig his heels in harder. We need to regroup and plan our next move. In private.'

Susannah's head swivelled in Rosalind's direction. She appeared to be considering Rosalind's advice.

It was touch and go. Rosalind could never tell which way Susannah's mood would swing, during one of these tantrums. But this time, to her relief, Susannah gave a decisive nod, got up, stuck her nose in the air and swept out of the room, without deigning to give her poor beleaguered guardian as much as a glance.

Rosalind didn't give her employer a glance, either, as she left the room and headed up the stairs in Susannah's wake, but not, she was sure, for the same reason as Susannah. Rosalind simply didn't dare. Oh, not that she was afraid of him, for all his martial demeanour—no, it wasn't that. It was worse. Far worse, to her mind. She was just scared that if she ever looked him in the eye, at a moment when he happened to be looking in her direction, then he might somehow perceive that she had a...well, that she thought he was...

No. No, she mustn't even *think* about the way she'd started to feel whenever she was in the same room with him of late. That would be to...to feed it. And she mustn't. No, she must starve that feeling. Or...or strangle it, or something. Because if he were to guess, or if anyone was to guess, that he made her heart flutter, and her pulses race, and her silly imagination run riot...well, they'd all think she was a complete ninny. Which was the exact opposite of the image which had landed her this position.

Lord Caldicot had hired her, on one of his infrequent trips to England, because, he'd told her, he thought she looked *sensible*. And *stern*. Attributes which, he'd said, Susannah's governess would need if ever she was going to make the girl fit to make her debut by the time she reached seventeen. He'd hired her because he believed she'd be able to make Susannah behave herself.

'*You look as if you have backbone,*' he'd said. '*Which is precisely what is needed, in my opinion.*'

If he knew that the *sensible* governess he'd hired was prone to silly, romantic, impossible daydreams...

Although she'd never had any before they'd all moved here, at the start of the Season, had she? On the contrary, she'd actually been a bit nervous about what it might be like to have a man permanently in residence, after having enjoyed living in a mostly female household for the previous five years. So nobody could justifiably accuse her of being *prone* to silly daydreams...

'I hate him!'

Susannah's bitter exclamation snapped Rosalind out of her reverie.

'And I hate Aunt Birchwood, too! She...she actually stuck up for Lord Caldicot,' said Susannah, shaking her head in disbelief. 'Said that even though Cecil was from a very old family, he is only a younger son, with no prospects, and that I ought to be aiming for a much more brilliant match.'

Having uttered her opinion of Lord Caldicot and her aunt's treachery in agreeing with him about Mr Baxter's unsuitability, Susannah flung herself face down on the bed and burst into another bout of noisy sobbing.

Rosalind, who had grown used to scenes of this sort since she'd come to work for the family, bit back the urge to sigh and went to sit on the most comfortable chair in the room while she waited for Susannah to calm down. It was right by the window and gave a really good view over the square, and the people wandering around down there.

She did not make the mistake of glancing outside, however. She'd done that once and Susannah had caught her doing it when she ought, to the girl's indignation, have been paying her attention.

It was safer to sit and look down into her lap, so that when Susannah eventually grew tired of weeping and sat up to find out why Rosalind wasn't fluttering about her, the way her aunts did, the way she thought everyone should when she was causing a scene, she wouldn't find her looking out of the window. There were several breakable objects stationed within Susannah's reach, and she had a remarkably good aim, even when she appeared to have lost control of all her other senses.

Then, all of a sudden, as was Susannah's habit, she sat up and turned to look at Rosalind.

'Stop scowling at me!'

'Was I scowling? I beg your pardon,' said Rosalind, mildly. 'I didn't mean to. I was just thinking, very hard and my thinking face must look so serious that you mistook it for a scowl.' It was probably why

Lord Caldicot had hired her, she mused. She'd been
determined, at that interview, not to take another job
where there was any risk of some male member of
the household thinking he had the right to take advantage of her.

She'd decided that since she was eighteen years of
age, it was about time she started to make decisions
about her future for herself, instead of relying on others to make provisions for her, so she'd signed on with
an agency. And when they'd sent her for the interview
for the post as Susannah's governess, she had asked
Lord Caldicot at least as many questions about what
she might expect if she went to live at Caldicot Dane,
as he'd asked her.

He'd leaned back in his chair, at one point, and
chuckled, remarking that he was beginning to wonder exactly which of them was conducting the interview. When she'd retorted that a girl had to be
careful, he'd nodded and said he liked the fact that
she hadn't backed down when he'd challenged her.
That his ward needed someone who wouldn't stand
any nonsense. That she seemed like just the kind of
person who could bring some much-needed discipline
into Susannah's life.

She supposed she did appear stern, when really
that was not her nature at all. She'd noted it on looking in the mirror recently. It was because of her thick
eyebrows. Perched as they were above a beak of a

nose, they couldn't help making her look decidedly formidable.

But then nobody would describe Lord Caldicot as classically handsome either, would they? His nose was not a beak, like hers, but neither did it look as though it had been chiselled out of marble. His hair was not wavy, flopping across his brow in a romantic fashion, or at least, he kept it cut so short that no waviness or floppiness dared to make an appearance. No, it was his eyes that had first made her think him...compelling, to her as a female. The clear intelligence in them. The way they narrowed, ever so slightly, when anyone said anything particularly fatuous. And then there was the way he behaved. With such *integrity*.

She didn't care what anyone else said. Rosalind could not fault him for only selling out, apparently with great reluctance, so many years after he'd inherited his title from his cousin. England was at *war*. He'd stayed at his post until it was time for him to supervise Susannah's come-out, in person, displaying, to her mind, the perfect balance between duty to his country and his family.

Then there was the upright way he carried himself and the air of...well, she couldn't describe it as anything but cleanliness. He didn't give off that sort of greasy, repellent atmosphere that had hung about the wealthy, titled men she'd encountered in her previous post. The men who'd regarded females, especially females in menial roles, as fair game.

'Thinking?' Susannah's face turned hopeful. 'About a way to bring Lord Caldicot round? So that he will let me marry Cecil?'

'Er...' Far from it! But the prospect that she might be was enough to make Susannah look in a better frame of mind. And she had persuaded her charge to come upstairs on the pretext of *planning their next move*, hadn't she? So it was only natural that Susannah would expect her to come up with a plan, wasn't it?

'I suppose,' ventured Susannah, 'that with all those books you read, you must have read about all sorts of ways of rescuing persecuted heiresses from the clutches of evil guardians.'

There were so many things wrong with that statement that Rosalind wasn't sure which misconception to deal with first. Susannah didn't need rescuing, for one thing—she needed to learn to listen to advice, even when she didn't like it. And her guardian wasn't evil, nor was he persecuting her. He just wasn't treating her with the sugary, flattering, doting manner that she'd grown to expect was her due, that was all. Trying to lay down a few rules, which was something none of her other relatives, so far as Rosalind, had observed, had made much attempt to do.

'In all the fairy stories I can remember,' Susannah

continued, while Rosalind was still debating the wisdom of saying what she really wanted to say, 'when the king forbids a suitor from marrying the princess because of some stupid thing such as he is merely a swineherd or something, the princess persuades the king to let him prove his worth by going on a quest.'

'A quest,' Rosalind repeated, trying not to laugh. If Susannah thought that anyone could persuade Lord Caldicot to send her Cecil on a quest to prove his worth...or to persuade him to do anything he didn't want, come to that! Didn't Susannah realise what kind of man he was? He was a military man, used to giving orders and having them obeyed instantly.

'Well, not a quest, exactly,' Susannah said, pensively. 'There aren't any dragons for him to slay, or, or magic lamps for him to find, not in London, these days...'

'Er...no,' agreed Rosalind, faintly, wondering what on earth must go on in Susannah's head for her to come out with such comments.

'But he could show... I don't know...loyalty, or bravery somehow, couldn't he? And persuade Lord Caldicot that he is not merely dangling after me because of my fortune.'

Ah...so that was what had caused Susannah to throw such a dramatic tantrum just now. Not so much Lord Caldicot's refusal to grant permission for Cecil to marry Susannah as the implication that he only wanted her for her fortune.

'He *loves* me,' Susannah protested. 'And I love him!'

Susannah reached for a handkerchief to dry her eyes and blow her nose, and began to look much more cheerful.

Rosalind didn't take much comfort from that, because Susannah now had that look on her face that she always wore when she was plotting something.

'You will just,' Susannah decreed, 'have to help us elope!'

She might have known it.

'But I thought,' Rosalind pointed out, 'you wanted to persuade Lord Caldicot that Cecil could be loyal and true...'

'Oh, yes, well of course Cecil could do all that,' said Susannah dismissively. 'But I don't see why I should have to wait while Cecil is changing Lord Caldicot's mind. And don't you think it would be romantic? Eloping?'

'What, climbing out of a window,' Rosalind pointed out, rather ruthlessly reminding Susannah of her fear of heights, 'at the dead of night?'

Susannah turned white. So badly did she fear heights that, the moment they'd arrived in London and she'd seen that her bedroom had a balcony overlooking the rear garden, she'd ordered Rosalind to swap with her. Even though it meant taking a much smaller room.

'It wouldn't have to be out of a window!' said Susannah. 'Or not one that was very high up...'

'Well, I suppose you could just meet somewhere as though by chance, during the day,' Rosalind mused, as though turning over the scheme with a view to making it happen. 'Oh, but then,' she said, regretfully, 'you wouldn't be able to take any luggage. Someone would be bound to ask why you were carrying trunks and hatboxes about in broad daylight...'

'I wouldn't need luggage,' Susannah scoffed.

'No? Oh, well, I suppose it wouldn't matter that you didn't have a clean change of clothes on the journey. I suppose the romance of it all would carry you through the unpleasantness of wearing the same clothes for a week...'

'A week! Why should I be expected to wear the same clothes for a week?'

'Well, I am not entirely sure how long it would take you to reach the border, but I do know that Gretna Green is in Scotland, which is a very long way away. And you would have to go there, you know, to get married, because you are still not of an age to marry without your guardian's consent in England.'

'How do you know that? Oh, from all those books you read, I suppose. But that is infamous!'

'What is infamous?'

'Having to travel to Scotland to marry without your guardian's consent,' she said petulantly.

'And only think,' Rosalind continued, warming to her theme, 'of how ill you get travelling in coaches. We had to stop three times for you to get out and walk up and down, just on the journey from Hertford when we first come up to London. And that,' she reminded Susannah ruthlessly, 'was in a very well-sprung coach. I don't suppose your...um... Mr Baxter would be able to afford such a luxurious one.

'And even if he could,' Rosalind put in hastily when she caught a militant look spring to Susannah's eye at the reminder that Cecil was not well-to-do, 'what with all that getting out and stopping, Lord Caldicot would be bound to catch you up before even one day was out.' She would guarantee it. There was no way he would permit Mr Baxter to spend a night with Susannah, thereby ruining her.

At that point, there came a firm rap on the door and Lady Birchwood's maid, Throgmorton, stepped in.

'Begging your pardon, Miss Hinchcliffe,' she said, sounding not the least bit apologetic, 'but Her Ladyship sent me to remind you that it was time to be getting ready.'

'Getting ready?' Susannah drew herself up indignantly. 'Aunt Birchwood cannot possibly expect me to go out tonight as though nothing has happened. How can she, or anyone, expect me to...to carry on as normal, to dance the night away, when my heart,' she cried, flinging herself backwards on to the bed, 'is broken?'

Throgmorton took a deep breath. 'Her Ladyship said to remind you that this is not just any ball. It is Almack's.'

'I don't care!' Susannah cried.

No. But Lady Birchwood did. And so would Lord Caldicot. A girl who cared about her reputation didn't shun Almack's without good reason, not after all the effort Lady Birchwood and several of Susannah's other female relatives had taken to obtain vouchers.

Throgmorton turned to leave the room, her lips pursed in disapproval.

Rosalind hurried over to the door, opened it and stepped outside.

'Tell Her Ladyship,' she said quietly so that Susannah wouldn't be able to hear, 'that I will do my best to make sure Susannah is dressed and ready within the hour. But don't, I beg of you, send her maid to attend her until I ring for her.' It would end in certain disaster if Pauline bustled in before Susannah herself had decided she was ready to change into her ball gown.

Throgmorton inclined her head very slightly before going away to relay the message to her mistress, in a manner calculated to remind Rosalind of her superior position in the household hierarchy. Throgmorton was, after all, the personal maid to a lady who was the daughter of the Fourth Marquess of Caldicot, the sister of the Fifth Marquess and cousin to the current holder of the title, even if her late husband had been merely the Earl of Birchwood.

When she'd gone, Rosalind mentally rolled up her sleeves. At the end of her interview with Lord Caldicot, he'd suggested that she take the job for a trial period and offered her a generous rise in wages if she managed to last a full quarter without Susannah driving her away with her tantrums. And, perhaps more significantly, without Susannah demanding her dismissal, the way she'd done with so many other hapless governesses over the years. Then, when he'd returned to England in readiness for the Season, he'd also promised her a staggering amount of money if she could steer Susannah successfully through her Season without her creating a scandal in one form or another.

He'd drawn her aside, not one week after he'd moved into Kilburn House with them. And, in the very same study in which Susannah had just been displaying the worst of her temperament, had said, 'Lady Birchwood may indeed have better connections than her sisters and no doubt she does have the entrée to the kind of places that matter to a girl of Susannah's rank, but…' He'd paused, lowering his head and toying with the paperknife on his desk. 'Well, she doesn't seem to be able to exert much influence over the girl.

Or at least, so far I have never seen her do so. Or attempt to do it. So…'

So Rosalind was going to get Susannah dressed and ready to go to Almack's, no matter what it took. And it wasn't just because of the bonuses, or at least, not entirely. It was because Rosalind could understand exactly why Susannah behaved so badly.

Almost from the moment she'd met Susannah, Rosalind had felt a sense of kinship with her. For Rosalind, too, had been treated poorly by her own family. They had made her feel unwanted and inconvenient, too. And she had often lashed out in frustration, as well. But, most importantly, it was because Susannah had asked her to stay with her through her Season. And Susannah needed someone who *would* stand by her, not flounce off muttering that she was impossible, just when she most needed someone to… to…*steady* her.

She closed the door and leaned on it, regarding Susannah thoughtfully.

'I was just wondering…' she said.

'Wondering what?' came Susannah's muffled response, since she'd rolled over to bury her face in her pillow.

'Well, if you intend to stay at home, how on earth you are going to contact Mr Baxter?'

Susannah went very still.

'I mean,' Rosalind continued, gazing up at the ceiling, 'you are going to have to tell him that although your guardian has forbidden the match, you are not so spineless that you are going to take it lying down, aren't you?'

Susannah sat up. 'Absolutely not! We will find a way!'

'Precisely so. Only...' she shook her head and sighed '... I cannot see how you are going to come up with a successful plan if you stay at home. I mean, I shouldn't think Lord Caldicot will permit Mr Baxter to call on you...'

'No. He wouldn't. He has forbidden me to even *speak* to him again! As though I could cut him, if I should meet him on a public street!'

'Ah. Well, don't you think that, should you stay here, weeping all evening, he might think that he has won? That he has defeated you?'

'Oh! Yes, that is *precisely* what he would think! But he shan't,' cried Susannah, leaping off the bed. 'Ring for hot water, Miss Hinchcliffe! I *shall* go to Almack's.'

Where, with any luck, Susannah's coterie of admirers would provide some distraction from her distress.

'You...you will,' said Rosalind, 'be careful, won't you?'

'What do you mean?'

'Well, if you make it too obvious that you are only going to Almack's to meet Mr Baxter and plan your next move, Lady Birchwood might report back to Lord Caldicot, and…well, then they might both do something…drastic, to prevent you contacting Mr Baxter at all.'

'Like sending me back to the country, I suppose. Yes, I wouldn't put it past them. But I am not going to give them *any* excuse for cutting my Season short.' She gave a peal of rather manic laughter. 'I will be the model of good behaviour, I assure you.'

Which was all that Rosalind could hope for. For tonight. And as for tomorrow…

Well, never mind tomorrow. She'd think of some way to survive whatever tomorrow threw at her, when tomorrow came.

And in the meantime, with Susannah out at Almack's, Rosalind would have the evening to herself. Peace and quiet, in which to read the latest novel she'd borrowed from the library.

Bliss.

Chapter Two

'The thing about women, Lord Caldicot,' Lord Darlington slurred, leaning forward as though uttering a confidence, 'is that they ain't like chaps.'

Michael didn't bother to reply to that inanity. Of course women weren't like men! It didn't take a genius to work that one out.

'Chaps, you see,' Lord Darlington continued, 'are like dogs.'

'Like dogs?'

'Yes. We stick together. Like a pack of hounds. Don't see hounds going off on their own when they're after a fox, do you? Eh? Loyal, that's what they are. Faithful. Women, though…' He shuddered, and took another gulp of wine. 'Like cats,' he said and belched. 'Can never tell what they're thinking.'

Michael suddenly remembered the waitress in that little tavern in Lisbon. The way she'd had to weave her way in and out of the tables, dodging the custom-

ers trying to either pinch or slap her bottom as she
served their drinks. He'd always been able to tell *exactly* what she'd been thinking. Her disdain for the
whole pack of them had been written all over her
pretty face.

'Walk alone, do cats,' Lord Darlington continued.
'Look at you with their calculating eyes, weighing you
up. Can't trust a cat. Like you can't trust a woman.'

It had been a mistake, Michael reflected as he
swirled the wine round in his glass, admitting to Lord
Darlington that he wasn't finding it easy to follow in
his cousin's footsteps. His esteemed cousin, the Fifth
Marquess of Caldicot, had always known he'd inherit
the title from his own father. The Fifth Marquess was
the sort of chap who loved all the pomp and the adulation that went with his rank, not to mention all the
endless paperwork that piled up on his desk every day.

Michael would warrant he had never had a moment's trouble from any of his sisters, either. Not to
judge by the way they kept on singing his praises.
That last part, about the Fifth Marquess's troop of
sisters, was all he'd admitted to Lord Darlington, but
that one admission had been all that it had taken to
prompt the elderly peer to launch into that ridiculous
theory about cats and dogs.

Give him a piece of open ground and a battalion
of men, Michael mused, with an enemy approaching
over the crest of the next hill, and he'd know exactly

what to do. Dispatch men to the flanks. Look for cover to conceal sharpshooters. Position the guns on the high ground. Form the infantry into a square...

Yes, out on a battlefield he could make plans, shout orders and be confident of gaining the desired result.

In Kilburn House, however...

He shook his head and sighed.

In a way, he *supposed* he could see what Lord Darlington was getting at with the dogs and cats analogy. He could admit that there were times when he did feel a bit like, well, a large bull mastiff, outnumbered and baffled by kittens. Though he was both physically, and legally, far more powerful than any of his female relatives, they...they somehow constantly managed to undermine his authority by being...well...either fluffy or striking out with their little claws.

All except that Miss Hinchcliffe, the young woman he'd hired to bring some discipline into Susannah's life. She was like a...like a swan, he supposed, if he was going to stick to comparing people to creatures. She glided along, looking down her long slender nose at the rest of them, totally unmoved by their antics.

No, not a swan...if anything she put him in mind of those magnificent eagles he'd sometimes seen, soaring above the Pyrenees, apparently effortlessly, making use of some mysterious power that enabled them to rise above the sordid realities that kept mere humans earthbound. Just as she rose above Susannah's tantrums and Lady Birchwood's fits of the vapours, or his own raised voice, with scarcely a flicker.

'Chaps,' Lord Darlington said, cutting through his own train of thought regarding the likeness of various members of the animal kingdom to his own female dependants, 'stick together.' He banged his glass down on the table. 'Like a pack of foxhounds.' As though to demonstrate the validity of that opinion, he threw back his head and gave a good impersonation of a hound baying when catching scent of a fox.

And all round the room, for no reason that Michael could determine, other men began baying, too. Or barking, or braying, or neighing like horses. The only man who showed no interest in joining in was a glassy-eyed youth who was sprawled on a chair with his legs splayed out in front of him, looking as though the only reason he hadn't slid down to the ground altogether was because someone had hooked the collar of his jacket over the chair back.

'See?' Lord Darlington waved his hand expansively round the room. 'That's why you join a club like this. Always have chaps to back you up! Even when they don't know why they're doing it.'

Yes, well…that wasn't exactly a great recommendation for joining, not in Michael's opinion. He neither wanted to behave like one of a pack of slavering hounds, nor had he any ambition to become a leader of such a brainless bunch of buffoons. He'd accepted

the invitation to dine here tonight because his predecessor had been a member, because he'd been told it
was an honour granted only to a very select few and
because it had therefore felt as though it was something he ought to do, now he held the title.

The only thing he'd achieved, by coming here tonight, was to confirm his belief that he didn't belong
with this set.

No, make that two things. It confirmed that he
didn't *want* to belong.

Was he ever going to feel like a marquess, rather
than just plain Major Kilburn? Was he always going
to feel this uncomfortable in civilian clothing? So...
other from the company he was now expected to rub
shoulders with? In the army, he might have had to undergo hardships, but at least he'd had the comrade-
ship of men he could trust and respect.

Cats and dogs, for heaven's sake! You couldn't divide people into two groups like that. People were...
people. Some were stupid, admittedly and some were
aloof.

And the ones in this room were just plain drunk.

All of a sudden he couldn't remember ever having
felt so alone.

'Another bottle,' shouted Lord Darlington, breaking into his musings, 'over here, waiter!'

'Sorry,' said Michael insincerely, getting to his feet.
'I have, er, something else I need to do...'

Lord Darlington grinned and winked. 'Of course you have. Of course! Women have their uses, eh? Can't do without 'em, in that respect!'

He made no comment, but left the room, mentally shaking his head. If that was the cream of English society, it was a wonder the country hadn't been overrun by the French years ago.

For the first time, he thought he could understand why his commanding officer had been so amenable to him selling his commission and returning to England, citing his need to find a wife and secure the continuation of his family line. The Colonel might even have meant what he'd said about England needing men of his stamp at home, as much as out on the battle front.

He paused on the front steps of the club to look up at the sky. The night was fine and clear. The air outside far more wholesome than the stuffy, overheated rooms of that so-called gentlemen's club.

Where to go now? He could go for a walk, he supposed, though the streets held no great interest for him. He supposed it was not a very patriotic thing to think about the capital city, but London, to his mind, couldn't compare with the bleak splendour of the Pyrenees, or the sun-baked plains of Portugal.

But he'd yielded to his family's increasingly impatient demands that he return to England. They'd pointed out that his ward was now of an age to make a come-out and would be wanting him around to steer her through the shoals of her first Season, and that while he was at it, he could do worse than look about for a bride for himself, too, and secure the succession.

They were right. He had put off that particular duty far too long already. But how could his cousin's girl have grown to the ripe age of seventeen already? It seemed only five minutes since he'd received the news that she'd been born. Less since he'd heard that his cousin himself had succumbed to a stupid fever and that Michael was now, legally, the Marquess of Caldicot.

And that was another thing, he mused as he set off down the steps. That girl, Susannah. He should have… He shook his head. It was no use now wishing he'd been more involved in her upbringing. Besides, any bachelor would have believed, as he'd done, that her female relatives would have a far better notion of how to bring her up. And she'd known them all, since his predecessor's sisters had been frequent visitors to the family seat, even after they'd married, whereas he was a virtual stranger. A sprig of a younger son, who'd only rarely seen the vast property that the Marquess of Caldicot could call home.

How was he to have guessed that they'd spoil her so badly that she could, at the age of seventeen, still think it acceptable behaviour to roll around on the floor screaming because he'd pointed out that Cecil

Baxter was not a suitable person for her to know, let alone marry?

He'd stood there, watching her in disbelief, reflecting that at the same age he'd already become a subaltern. He'd fought in battles. As for Miss Hinchcliffe, she'd hardly been much older when she'd turned up for that interview and impressed him with the strength of her character.

Thank God for Miss Hinchcliffe, the only one among them who never turned a hair when Susannah enacted one of her scenes.

Not only had she been spectacularly unimpressed by Susannah's antics today, but, in spite of Lady Birchwood's dire predictions, she'd coaxed the girl out of her temper and into an outfit suitable to make her debut at Almack's.

Where he ought to be, too, he reflected. Had he gone there, as Lady Birchwood and the rest of them had expected, he would not have had to witness the drunken idiocy of the men who he was supposed to now regard as his peers. But after that scene with Susannah he hadn't been willing to face the prospect of spending an entire evening enduring Susannah's pouts, while fending off droves of matchmaking mothers who wanted their spindly spotty sons to attract Susannah's notice, or worse, their giggly, vapid daughters to attract his.

And that was another thing. It was all very well

deciding he ought to do his duty to his family and find a suitable wife. But his idea of suitable did not stretch to girls just out of the schoolroom, no matter how impeccable their lineage. If he was going to live with a woman for the rest of his life, he had to be able to imagine holding a conversation with her, occasionally. That wasn't too much to hope for, was it?

At that point, he suddenly discovered that while he'd been in a brown study, his feet seemed to have carried him to the family residence in Grosvenor Square: Kilburn House. The house Lady Birchwood had insisted he host Susannah's come-out ball at the start of the Season, because it was the place from which *she'd* been launched into society as a girl. The place he was suddenly supposed to think of as home, but which still felt like his cousin's property. He'd only ventured inside a couple of times before he'd inherited it along with all the rest. And both times, after making his bow to his cousin, he'd been sent off to amuse himself in the garden.

His spirits lifted, just a fraction, as he remembered the time he'd spent playing there. The garden was a good size for a property in London, with paths leading to banks of shrubs where an enterprising young boy could make a den.

But as for the house… His spirits sank right back to where they'd been. It held no fond memories, as it did for the likes of Lady Birchwood, who'd run tame there as a girl. She still seemed to think that, even though she was a widow, she had a right to consider it as her house, not his.

Although, since Miss Hinchcliffe had somehow worked her magic on his troublesome ward, Lady Birchwood wouldn't be there, would she? In fact, the whole lot of them would all be at Almack's.

So the house would be empty. Or at least, empty of his female relatives.

Which meant that he'd be able to sit in his study, one of the only two rooms he'd so far been able to stamp his own personality on, with a book and a brandy. A pastime far better than carousing with a bunch of men who aspired to nothing more than being part of a pack, like so many sheep. Or searching in vain for a female who would meet both his family's, and his own, standards.

With a lift to his spirits, he began to mount the front steps.

Only to stagger back when the front door opened and Miss Hinchcliffe came flying out, so intent on fleeing that she didn't appear to have noticed he was there until she'd cannoned right into him.

He caught her by the arms just above the elbows to steady her. Or himself. And sighed.

'I thought,' he said, on a wave of disappointment, 'that you were made of sterner stuff. I never thought that Susannah would be able to drive you away, like she has done with so many of your predecessors.'

'Susannah?' Miss Hinchcliffe gave him a wild-eyed stare. 'I'm not running away because of Susannah. It is far worse! Oh, do let me go!'

He released her arms, but did not move out of her way, which was clearly what she wanted him to do.

'If not because of her, then…' He looked her up and down. She had a small case in one hand, from which something white and fluttery was trailing, as though she'd packed in a hurry. Her coat was buttoned up the wrong way and her hair was straggling out of a bonnet which was even now slipping down over one ear.

She gulped, dropped the case and pressed her hands over her face for a moment, then lowered them, to about the height of her throat, and gazed at him. Her shoulders drooped.

'I knew,' she said despairingly, 'I wouldn't get away with it this time.'

He felt the hairs on the back of his neck prickle. The way they did, sometimes, when the enemy had laid an ambush.

'Get away,' he said, 'with what?'

He might have known she was too good to be true. No woman who clung to a post managing a girl like Susannah could possibly do so unless she had some very good reason. Who was, in short, so desperate for work that she'd put up with anything. Why hadn't he realised this sooner?

'Let me see what you have in your case,' he said sternly.

'My case? Why should you be interested in that?'

'I want to see what you have tried to steal,' he said grimly, 'before deciding what to do about you.' He could hardly blame her for snatching whatever she could and making a run for it. He'd been tempted to get on his horse and make for the hills on many occasions, recently.

'I am not,' she said indignantly, 'a thief!'

'No? Then why were you leaving in such a hurry? And what exactly was it that you feared you wouldn't get away with? *This time?*'

Her eyes filled with tears. 'Well, I didn't mean to. Honestly I didn't. But all the same, it appears that… that I've killed him. I've killed Mr Baxter!'

Chapter Three

'Killed? Mr Baxter?'

His predecessor, the Fifth Marquess, would no doubt at this moment be expressing horror on hearing such news.

It just went to show how unfit he was to hold the title of Sixth Marquess that his prime response was that of envy. Yes, envy that she'd had the privilege of putting a period to the existence of that slimy worm who'd thought him gullible enough to grant him Susannah's hand in marriage.

He should have been the one who'd wrung that young man's neck, not the governess! He'd only managed to restrain himself from doing just that, earlier on, by reminding himself that one simply couldn't do such things in London. Particularly not in one's own house, with the female members of his family hovering outside the door.

'Did you wring his neck?' he couldn't resist asking her.

'What? No!' She looked horrified. 'I told you. I didn't mean to do it at all!'

'You just couldn't help yourself,' he said, nodding sympathetically.

'No! Well, yes, I mean...'

'Perhaps it would be better,' he said, extending one arm to the front door, 'to go back inside and tell me exactly what happened.'

She looked appalled at the prospect.

'In battle,' he mused out loud, 'chaps do sometimes kill people they didn't mean to. A rocket goes astray, or a shot ricochets, for example. I am sure you will have some equally plausible explanation as to how you came to *accidentally* kill someone in London.'

'I suppose,' she said morosely, all the fight appearing to go out of her, 'I would have had to explain to Grandfather why I had to leave this post as well, in the end. So there was never any hope of keeping it secret.'

'Secret?' The word dropped into his brain with the force of a bell ringing. 'Is there,' he asked, the moment he'd shut the front door behind them and they were standing in the hall, 'anyone else in the house? Could anyone else have heard anything?'

She looked at him with wide eyes. 'No. Well, that is, the male staff have all taken the opportunity to go to the tavern and the housemaids have all gone to bed. Oh!' She looked at him with a sort of wild hope in her eyes. 'Are you saying that it might be possible to hush this up? Hide the body, somehow? Perhaps...' Her face fell, abruptly. 'No, that would be *wrong*.' She wrung her hands. 'And yet,' she added, looking straight at him, 'if anyone could dispose of a body, that person must be you.'

'What? What sort of man do you think I am?'

'An intelligent one,' she replied without hesitation. 'A resourceful one! And...and possibly a *grateful* one.'

'Eh?'

'I mean,' she said, that wild light of hope gleaming in her eyes again, 'you must be jolly glad that Mr Baxter is no longer able to pursue Susannah, mustn't you?'

'Let us not,' he said drily, 'get carried away. There is a vast difference between wishing to put a bullet between a man's eyes and actually doing it.'

Her shoulders slumped again. She rubbed one hand over her forehead. 'Yes, of course, you are right. I don't know what I was thinking.'

He was thinking, all of a sudden, about the school of anatomy. They were always, so he'd heard, glad to have fresh bodies to dissect and weren't always fussy about knowing where, exactly, they came from...

But first things first. 'You still haven't told me how it happened. I mean, to look at you, one would never guess that you went round accidentally killing men on your evenings off...'

'I don't! I didn't!'

'And yet you said *this time*. As though you have tried to dispose of hapless males who strayed across your path on several occasions. And, also, you mentioned explaining your dilemma to your grandfather. *Again.*'

'Oh, but the other times were nothing like this! Oh, dear, how bad that sounds. What must you think of me?'

As she shook her head in a fashion that he could only describe as woebegone, he wondered—what *did* he think of her?

Well, for one thing, he'd always wondered what it would take to ruffle her feathers. 'The same as my family, I suppose,' she continued, despondently. 'That I am not fit to live in a house with...civilised people.'

'Not fit to...?' How could they? 'Your family? I didn't think you had any. When I hired you, you said you were an orphan...'

'Well, yes, of course I am an orphan. But everyone had parents at one time, didn't they? And mine were both from good families, to their own way of thinking, before they married each other against their respective fathers' wishes and got cast off, or cut off, or both, actually—'

'So, this grandfather you mentioned,' he cut in

when it looked as though she was about to veer off at a tangent, 'to whom you were about to flee...'

'He is my mother's father. He always steps in to rescue me when I get into trouble.'

'And he's had to do that frequently, has he?'

'More than he would wish,' she confessed, gloomily. 'But this is all beside the point, isn't it? Why are we standing about in the hall, talking about my grandfather, when there is a dead body...' she stopped, suddenly, and lowered her voice, 'in the back garden.'

Sensible as ever, he reflected with admiration. Even though she'd clearly had a nasty shock, she'd only succumbed to talking nonsense for the briefest of interludes before pulling herself together and getting right back to the matter in hand.

'Oh, you killed him in the garden, did you? What did he do?' he asked, realising that he was enjoying this encounter more than he ought. 'Surprise you while you were walking about with a lovely sharp spade in your hand?'

She glared at him. 'I wasn't in the garden at all. I was sitting in my room, reading, when he tried to climb in through my window.'

'The devil you say! I mean,' he corrected himself when her jaw dropped at the sound of his cursing, 'what cheek! Naturally you pushed him off your balcony.'

'I did no such thing,' she said with great indignation. 'I hit him with *Sense and Sensibility*!'

It was with great difficulty that he bit back a sudden urge to laugh. Instead, he asked her, in as serious tone as he could muster, 'Which volume?'

'Does it matter which volume?'

'I was just wondering which part of the story he interrupted. If it was a particularly exciting part, no wonder you got up and bashed him over the head with it.'

She gave him a look of exasperation. He supposed she was going to chide him for veering off the topic again and remind him that he ought to be worrying about the fact he had a body lying in his back garden. Which would be a pity. Because the dead man, clearly, wasn't going to go anywhere. But Miss Hinchcliffe might, if he didn't find more ways to keep her here talking.

He never could just talk to her, as a rule. She was always in the background, keeping decorously in her place. Which was all right and proper of course. He couldn't fault her for that. But he'd been feeling increasingly frustrated that he couldn't just strike up a conversation with her, when she appeared to be the only sensible person in the household. The only one he could imagine having anything worth saying.

'There are no exciting parts in *Sense and Sensibility*,' she said, gratifyingly engaging with his nonsense, rather than obliging him to be...well, sensible. 'It isn't that kind of story. And I didn't bash him with it,' she said indignantly. 'I threw it at him!'

'Hard enough to knock him clean out of the window? I confess to being impressed. You must be stronger than you look.'

'Well, he was off balance,' she replied modestly. 'With one leg half over the balustrade.'

'That's a very sporting thing of you to admit. Most men would have bragged about scoring a direct hit on the fellow's nose, or something of the sort. But you aren't a man, are you? You are a woman.'

'Have you only,' she said scathingly, 'just noticed?'

'No, of course not!' Far from it. But she worked for him. And he detested the kind of men who looked at female members of their staff in an impure way. So he did not do it. He *refused* to do it. 'It is just,' he continued, 'that you don't generally behave the way most other women do. Or at least, not the ones I've been unfortunate enough to have come across since I've sold out.'

Less than half an hour since, he'd been comparing her to an eagle, soaring effortlessly far above the turmoil created by his ward. But right his minute, he reflected, narrowing his eyes to examine her more keenly, she put him more in mind of a hen. Just after a fox had tried to get into the hen house, with her bonnet askew and her coat buttoned up incorrectly.

Though even if she did put him in mind of a chicken with her feathers ruffled, she was still a very impressive chicken to have fended off the marauding fox.

'I suppose,' he said, feeling rather more sympathetic all of a sudden, 'you must have been scared out of your wits when a man attempted to climb into your room, at night, when nobody else was in the house. No wonder you panicked.'

'Panicked? I did no such thing,' she said indignantly. 'I told you. He took me by surprise, and I just acted without thinking! I do tend to…er…go on the offensive when I feel threatened.' She started twisting her hands together, in what looked like an expression of remorse. Or possibly vexation.

'But then, if a woman ever shows the slightest sign of weakness when approached by a man determined on making mischief, like calling for help and hoping someone may hear, or worse, fainting, which would only serve to put her entirely in his power…' She paused, biting down on her lower lip, as though annoyed that she'd let it say too much.

'It sounds as though you have had plenty of experience with mischief-making men,' he said, examining her more closely than he'd ever allowed himself to do before.

She was tall, for a woman, and angular, with ferocious eyebrows and a nose which had put him in mind of the beak of some bird of prey. So not conventionally pretty. And she'd only been eighteen when she'd applied for the job as Susannah's governess. Which meant any experience she'd had of that nature must have happened before that. No wonder she'd scowled at him all through that interview. No wonder she'd asked so many questions about the conditions of her service.

How he wished he could find out what man had tried to take liberties with her, when she'd been scarcely more than a girl. He'd teach them to prey on defenceless females!

She shifted from one foot to the other. 'Well, not as bad as *this*.'

'What do you mean,' he asked, 'not as bad as this? Or,' he added, 'do you just mean that you do not make a habit of pushing men out of windows?'

'Of course I don't,' she said, looking agonised. 'And I didn't push this one, either. I told you—'

'Yes, yes,' he interrupted, in what he hoped was a soothing tone, 'you simply threw the book at him. Although I cannot help wondering,' he continued, finding himself inexplicably fascinated by Miss Hinchcliffe's hitherto unsuspected history, 'what you did to your previous victims?'

'Does it matter? Really? Should we not be concentrating on what we are to do about…*him*?' She gesticulated wildly in the direction of the servants' quarters, though he supposed she meant to point to the garden, where the body was lying.

'You are right,' he admitted, with regret. 'We should leave all that for another time. Though I cannot help wondering,' he mused out loud, 'why he was trying to climb into your window at all?' He'd heard some unsavoury rumours about Baxter. But he couldn't for the life of him see what the man thought he would achieve by climbing into the governess's room.

'I suspect,' said Miss Hinchcliffe, 'that he thought it must be Susannah's room. After all, it is the only room at the back with a balcony. He must have assumed it would be hers. And I also assume that it was with the intent to either seduce her or persuade her to elope with him.'

'Yes. That sounds about the sort of sneaky thing a fellow like that would do,' he agreed, feeling his lip curl. 'Also, it probably looked easier to get in that way, than by a window which was shut. You were sitting there with the window to the balcony standing open, I take it? If you were able to throw your book and hit him without breaking the window as well?' It occurred to him that his brain was beginning to clear. Had he had more to drink than he'd meant to, earlier on, that he'd been so muddled, up to now? It would certainly explain why he was comparing people to chickens and eagles.

Oh, and kittens, at one point.

And also why he was finding this encounter rather enjoyable, when a more staid sort of fellow would have found it shocking. But then, he reminded himself, he was not the sort of chap who ought, ever, to have become a marquess.

'Yes. Well, it is a very warm evening,' she reminded him. 'I was enjoying the breeze. And I think there is a nightingale...'

'He really did ruin your evening off, didn't he?' he remarked, leaning back against the wainscot and folding his arms across his chest. 'He absolutely deserved that you threw your book at him.'

'Well, thank you for trying to make me feel better. But actually *killing* him...' She shook her head, and tucked her hands under her armpits, as though unsure what to do with hands that had so recently behaved so badly.

'And you are sure that he is dead, are you?'

She paled and gave a stiff nod. 'First I leaned over the balcony railings and saw him lying in the bushes...'

'The bushes? But doesn't your balcony overlook the terrace?'

'Well, yes, but he'd climbed up at the side of the balcony. There is, as I noted, a drainpipe there, which must have offered decent handholds.'

'Of course, that explains it,' he agreed. 'Only, if he

fell into those bushes, they might have softened his fall,' he suggested.

'Well, yes they might, but I cannot believe that anyone lying at that precise angle could possibly be… be…' She petered out, turning pale.

He straightened up. 'So you didn't check him closely?'

'Well, I did go down to retrieve the book,' she said.

'To retrieve the book? Not to see if you could do anything for the man you'd just assaulted?'

'Well, it came from the library!'

'Of course. That makes all the difference,' he said drily.

'Well, it does! I couldn't just leave it lying on the grass. It would have been ruined! And it will have to go back, you know. So I just ran down and grabbed it, and fortunately it was lying some distance away from…him, so I didn't have to…see very much…' She swallowed, as though she'd just been obliged to eat something very unpleasant. 'And I put it on my dressing table,' she continued, 'with a note explaining that I'd had to leave in a hurry and asking someone to return it…'

'Never mind the blasted book,' he said, as a horrible thought suddenly struck him.

Her eyes widened at his second use of a curse word and she gave him the kind of look she'd so often used to quell his ward. Though, since he was not an impressionable girl, but a battle-hardened, seasoned veteran of many bloody campaigns, he felt only the mildest touch of shame that she'd made him forget his manners.

'Keep to the point, madam,' he said as sternly as he could, considering she was not one of his subalterns hauled up on a charge. 'Which is—how certain are you that Baxter is really dead and not just stunned, since you didn't look at him closely?'

'As I was saying, I went outside to retrieve the library book, once I'd packed my overnight bag, and piled all my other possessions into a heap on the bed, hoping someone would be kind enough to send them on later…only I don't suppose that would have been sensible, would it, once they'd discovered the body. Oh, how disordered my wits are tonight!' She raised a hand to her forehead. A hand which, he noted, was trembling.

'Take a deep breath,' he suggested, 'then tell me how you became so certain he is dead.'

'Well, for one thing, he had neither moved nor made a sound by the time I'd run round the bedroom pulling everything out of the cupboards and writing a note about the library book. And for another…' She gulped.

'Yes?'

'Well, there was blood. All down his front.'

He frowned. 'Blood? How the deuce…' He'd assumed the fellow must have fallen on to the paving stones of the rear terrace and that, therefore, there was nothing anyone could do for him. But this changed everything. If the fellow was just injured, he ought to be seeing if there *was* anything to be done. Without further ado, he stalked down the hall to the breakfast room in which there was a set of double doors that led out to the terrace, providing the quickest route to get to where Baxter lay. He heard her footsteps pattering along behind him. When he reached the double doors and paused to open them, she ran full tilt into his back.

He turned, steadying her by taking hold of her shoulders.

She blushed. Gasped. Trembled. But not, he didn't think, with horror. On the contrary, something sparked between them. Something that usually led to kisses, in his experience.

'You don't need to come out and view your handiwork again,' he said gruffly, setting her aside. He had no business to be thinking about kissing her, after the dreadful night she'd already been having. Hadn't she already suffered enough shocks? First to have had a lecher like Baxter climb in through her window, probably with evil intent, and then the horror of accidentally killing him.

But when he stepped outside, she followed closely behind him. All the way along the terrace to the stone parapet that separated it from the shrubbery. In which lay, as she'd warned him, what looked at first glance to be a shapeless bundle of clothes.

'You see?' she said, though when he turned to look at her, she'd closed her eyes. 'He cannot possibly still be alive, can he?'

But just as he was about to agree with her that nobody who was lying in that position could possibly still be alive, the shapeless bundle of clothing let out a groan.

Chapter Four

Rosalind gasped and opened her eyes. Looked up at her window and then down at the bushes. It wasn't all that far, now she came to think of it. Could he really have survived the fall? If he'd been the sort of boy who'd climbed trees, he would surely have learned how to fall from much higher than that, without breaking *very* many bones.

'It might not mean anything,' she heard Lord Caldicot mutter darkly, as he swung one leg over the parapet. 'Wind has to escape, whether a fellow is dead or alive.'

What? Did he mean Mr Baxter might be still be dead, even though he was making…those sorts of noises?

'And sometimes, it can sound very convincing…' He stopped talking as he bent over the body.

Then he straightened up, rather abruptly, and let out a curse. The third one she'd heard him utter. Though she ought not to be keeping count. Her behaviour this evening was bad enough to make *any* man curse, although, she couldn't really understand why he was so angry right now. Though, to be honest, he had not reacted to anything the way she might have expected since he'd caught her trying to flee from the house. He hadn't sounded the least bit shocked, for instance, when she'd admitted to accidentally killing a man. If anything, he'd seemed...*amused*. So what could he have learned, from that one swift inspection of Mr Baxter's body to make him look so cross? And say such an ugly word?

'What,' she therefore asked, 'is the matter?'

He turned to her, his expression grim. 'I am sorry to have to inform you,' he said, making her heart sink, 'that Baxter is not dead.'

'Well, but that is a good thing, isn't it?' He couldn't possibly really wish she'd killed the man. 'I mean, you couldn't possibly have wanted to have to preside over a murder trial, not during Susannah's debut, could you? You specifically said,' she reminded him, 'you didn't want her Season ruined by scandal. Surely nothing could be more scandalous than a girl's governess murdering a suitor, could it?'

Was she talking gibberish? He was certainly looking at her as though she'd taken leave of her senses.

'And also,' she added, 'how can you possibly be so certain he isn't dead? You scarcely looked at him.'

'I didn't need to look at him. He spoke.'

'He spoke? I didn't hear him.'

'No, well,' he said drily, 'I dare say your teeth are chattering so loudly with nerves that you couldn't hear him.'

'My teeth,' she objected, 'are not chattering.' Though she was trembling, she had to admit. Just a little.

'Then I fail to see why you did not hear him say turpentine!'

'Turpentine? Why on earth would anyone say the word turpentine, at such a moment?'

'Well, there is no accounting for the absurd things some men say, is there,' he said bitterly. Then he bent down over the body—well, Mr Baxter, that was. She couldn't refer to him as the body if he wasn't dead, could she?

When Lord Caldicot straightened up, he had something in his hand. Something that looked dark and sticky.

'This,' he said, giving her a strange look, 'is what you thought was blood, isn't it?'

Just as she was about to nod, he tossed it up in the air.

It showered down, like confetti.

'Rose petals,' he said with derision. 'The silly chump climbed up to your window with about a dozen of them stuffed down the front of his waistcoat.'

And the fall from the window had crushed them.

Not blood.

Not dead.

All of a sudden she began to do more than tremble just a little. Before she could do something foolish, like fall to the ground because her legs had given way, she groped her way to the parapet, sat down, and bent over, resting her head on her knees.

She heard a scuffling sound, then Lord Caldicot was beside her. 'You aren't going to faint, are you?' He sounded anxious. Far more anxious, she noted, than he had when she'd told him she'd killed Cecil Baxter. 'Aren't you glad you won't have to stand trial?'

She glared up at him. 'If that is your attempt at try-ing to defuse an awkward situation with humour,' she said, suddenly deciding that this had been his modus operandi from the moment she'd run into him on the front steps, 'then I have to tell you that it falls short of the mark. Besides, I distinctly recall telling you that I *never* faint! Only a…a pudding heart would faint in a situation like this!'

'And you are certainly not that,' he agreed, wiping his hands of the last remnants of crushed rose petals.

'Perhaps I am,' she said despondently. 'After all, I could not make myself look at him all that closely. If I had, I wouldn't have had to go through all this… this…'

'Drama?'

'Anxiety,' she corrected him, sitting up. 'Instead of

running around like a chicken with no head, throwing clothes into my bag and writing a note that was so hysterical I shouldn't think anyone would have been able to make head or tail of it, I would have just gone straight out and fetched a doctor. And, oh,' she cried, turning to him and clutching at his sleeve, 'that is what we ought to do now, isn't it? After all, he's been insensible for ages.'

'Probably from the moment of his birth,' he said, enigmatically.

'Oh. You mean he has never had any sense, I suppose. Very droll. However, that doesn't alter the fact that now we know he isn't dead, but badly injured, we ought to fetch a doctor to him.'

He sighed. 'Now that you have suggested it, I suppose that is what we should do, yes.'

'Of course we should!'

'I just said so, didn't I?'

'Yes, but you sighed first.' All of a sudden she realised her fingers were still clutching into the cloth of his coat sleeve. And that he hadn't made any attempt to remove them. What did that mean?

'Well, a man cannot help how he feels,' he said a touch defensively, 'can he? About men like Baxter, particularly. And how could you guess what I was thinking from the fact that I sighed?'

She had no idea. After all, she couldn't begin to guess why he hadn't immediately brushed her hand from his sleeve. It was such a very forward thing for her to do.

She'd better let go of him.

And she would, in a minute. It was just that, for the moment, she didn't think she could make herself. He was so solid. So unflappable. She would have thought that most men would have been furious to come home and find an employee fleeing the scene of what they'd thought was a murder. Instead, he'd been calm. And hardly shown any signs of being cross with her at all. Not even now that she was clinging to his sleeve like a drowning man clinging to a lifeline.

'It was the *way* you sighed.' She suddenly realised that had made her think he was reluctant to send for a doctor. 'All...regretful.'

'Perhaps I was thinking of the bill I shall have to pay on that cur's account,' he said, nodding his head in the direction of the shrubbery.

'As if you aren't rich enough to care nothing for such things!'

He turned his head sharply and gave her a look that she guessed he had employed in the past to make his subalterns quake in their boots. It didn't have the effect upon her that he was probably hoping for. Instead of making her nervous, it made her wish she hadn't said something so personal. Now he must think she was not only an idiot, but a rude, tactless one as well.

It was just as well she'd never been able to cherish

any hope he might think well of her, because he certainly wouldn't after this night's work.

She removed her hand from his sleeve under the cover of getting to her feet. 'We have delayed for too long already. I should have seen if there was anything I could do for him straight away instead of just trying to avoid looking...' She shivered.

'No,' he said, getting to his feet as well, so that he could glower down at her. Not many men could do that. They usually had to glower *up* at her, which tended to make them far crosser than they might have been with a shorter woman, she'd always suspected. 'You shouldn't have tried to do anything, not if you have no medical experience. You might have made things worse.'

'Oh! Do you really think so?'

'Absolutely. And since I have few medical skills either, *I* shall go and fetch the doctor. Which,' he said, giving her a look of resentment, 'was exactly what you hoped I'd do once you suggested going yourself, wasn't it?'

'I am flattered,' she retorted, 'that you think me capable of planning anything at all at a moment like this, when I still feel decidedly headless chicken-like.'

His expression softened. 'Then forgive me for thinking such an uncharitable thing. I have just grown so used to females trying to manipulate me since I've inherited the title that it has become hard to take anything any of you say at face value.' He rubbed his hand over his face in a way that revealed how weary he was.

'I promise you,' she said on a wave of compassion, because she understood exactly what he meant about manipulative females, after working for his family for the last five years, 'that I shall never say anything to you that is not the complete and utter truth.'

He looked at her for a moment. 'After the whiskers I have heard you telling Susannah, in order to get her to toe the line, you expect me to believe you?'

She flinched. Surely he could see that she'd had to make use of strategic ruses in order to improve Susannah's behaviour? And as for her telling whiskers—no! She'd *never* done that. She might have drawn the girl's attention to factors that would help her to understand why certain types of behaviour were preferable to others in terms that would mean something to her. Such as pointing out all the things about eloping she wouldn't like, when Susannah had been turning over plans for doing so.

Why couldn't he see that? For a while there, it had felt as if he'd understood her. Sympathised with her. That they'd come to a sort of understanding.

It had clearly all been a bag of moonshine, brought on by wishful thinking. Of course a man like Lord Caldicot would not consider her in that light.

Dropping him a perfunctory curtsy, she turned and strode along the terrace.

'Just where,' she heard him say, 'do you think you are going?'

'To my room, sir,' she said over her shoulder. 'As you bid me.'

She thought she heard him mutter yet more curse words. She wouldn't blame him. He must be heartily sick of her by now. And the mess she'd made for him to clear up.

But at least she hadn't killed Cecil Baxter.

It wasn't until she reached her room and shut the door behind her, then caught sight of the open balcony window, that her legs finally went out from under her, making her drop to the floor halfway to her bed.

She might have killed a man!

It was only by the merest chance that he'd fallen into the bushes, rather than on to the terrace. And only the greatest of good luck that she'd run out of the front door just as Lord Caldicot was returning from wherever he'd been. If she'd gone, leaving that incriminating note...

She broke out into a cold sweat. She'd almost thrown away this job along with any hope of ever gaining another one. When would she learn to...just stop and *think*, before lashing out? Hastily, she went over to the dressing table, picked up her running-away note and tore it into little shreds, then put the shreds in her washbasin, lit a taper from her bedside candle and put the taper to the shredded remains of her evening's folly.

Only when the flames had reduced the letter to a little pile of ashes did she go to her bed and begin to return the belongings she'd piled there into their proper places in the room.

When that was done, she sat down for a moment or two, her hands raised to the sides of her head. What was she to do now? She didn't think she could possibly get herself ready for bed, not until the doctor had been to tend to Mr Baxter. She wouldn't be able to get to sleep until she'd learned how badly she'd injured him.

She could only learn that by going downstairs and asking Lord Caldicot, but she couldn't do so once she'd donned her nightgown and cap. Imagine, walking into his study, in her patched and darned flannel nightgown with her knitted shawl over her shoulders and her hair all bundled up under her ancient nightcap! And the look of revulsion she'd surely see come over his face at her frightful appearance.

The very thought made her blush all over.

She leaped to her feet again, and tried to relieve her feelings by striding back and forth. There was plenty of room to do it. Thanks to Susannah's fear of heights and her consequent reluctance to have the room with a balcony overlooking a drop of some twenty feet,

Rosalind had by far the best room on this floor. She had not only a bed, wardrobe and washstand at one end, but also several chairs and tables at the other, with the balcony window between the two halves.

Though no amount of pacing could help to calm her nerves.

Eventually, after she felt as if she'd been pacing back and forth for about an hour, she heard the sound of men's voices floating in through her open balcony window.

He was back with the doctor!

She edged over to the open doors, hoping that she might be able to hear exactly what they were saying, without either of them being able to catch a glimpse of her.

But, frustratingly, the voices seemed to be getting further away. As though the men had gone inside.

They had done so, she discovered a few moments later, when she heard two heavy sets of feet coming up the stairs and heading along the corridor to her room.

After knocking on her door, Lord Caldicot came straight in, his face set in grave lines.

'Miss Hinchcliffe,' he said, giving her a piercing look. 'I have brought Dr Murgatroyd to see you.'

To see *her*? Why on earth had he done that?

Chapter Five

He shot her a warning glance, hoping to goodness that she was as intelligent as she usually appeared to be when dealing with Susannah's tantrums or Lady Birchwood's vapours. Hoping she'd understand that he was trying to conceal what had gone on in this house this evening.

Then he turned to the doctor, whom he'd prevented from barging in on her by remaining standing in the doorway, his hand on the latch.

'Miss Hinchliffe insisted she did not need a doctor, but as her employer, I have a duty to care for her. I hope, Miss Hinchliffe,' he said, turning to address her again, hoping that she'd understood that what he'd just said was as much for her benefit as the doctor's, 'that you will not be too angry with the good doctor. After all, he is only following my orders. And when I told him how agitated you became when you claimed to have seen an intruder in the grounds, he agreed to

come and check that you have recovered from the…
er…shock.'

'*Claimed* to see an intruder in the grounds?'

She looked so indignant he feared she was about
to give the game away by reminding him that Baxter
had intruded right into her room and that he'd seen
the fellow lying in the shrubbery. But then her eyes
darted to the doctor, who was trying to sidle past him,
and she swallowed back her objections.

Thank heavens she *was* as clever as he'd hoped!
She might not fully understand, yet, why he'd come
up here with the doctor in tow, but she was prepared
to play along until she found out.

So he stepped aside, allowing the pompous little
man who was Lady Birchwood's favourite physician
to oil his way into the room.

'Miss Hinchcliffe,' he said, in a voice so full of
syrup that it invariably set his teeth on edge whenever he reported back to him before depositing his
hefty bill on the study desk, 'Lord Caldicot and I have
made a thorough check of the garden and we can assure you that there is nobody there.'

He saw understanding spread over her face. In the
interval during which he'd been fetching the doctor,
Baxter must have recovered and taken to his heels.

He'd tell her later that when he'd reached the spot
where he'd left him lying, with the doctor in tow, but
no patient to tend to, he'd swiftly gone over in his

mind what he'd told Dr Murgatroyd. Realising that he hadn't specified exactly why he wanted him to come out at that time of night, he'd decided to provide him with an alternative patient, since the one he'd had in mind had done a runner.

The doctor looked over at the open windows and frowned.

'My dear girl,' he said to Miss Hinchcliffe, 'have you no idea how injurious the night air is to delicate constitutions?' He strode over to the window as fast as his little legs would allow and pulled the window shut. 'No wonder you have become prone to hysterical fancies, if you will breathe in the noxious miasma of the night air. It would not surprise me to learn that you are in the early stages of a feverish condition. Only look at those spots of colour in her cheeks, my lord,' he said to Michael. 'And the feverish glitter of her eyes!'

The spots of colour in her cheeks probably stemmed from temper at the patronising way the oily little man was speaking to her. And the glitter in her eyes warned him that she was within a hair's breadth of giving them both a piece of her mind.

'It is as I thought, then,' Michael said, shooting her a glance which he hoped denoted the sympathy he wished to convey. 'She is ill. Or,' he said, glancing at the doctor, who always made him feel a bit queasy, 'about to be.'

'Sit down, my dear,' said the doctor, indicating a chair next to a small table on which rested two volumes of *Sense and Sensibility*. The first and third, he noted absently. Did that mean she'd thrown the second volume at Baxter?

She went to the chair, with her lips pulled into a mutinous line, and sat down with clear resentment.

'I shall take your pulse,' said the doctor, reaching for and grabbing her hand. Because he was pulling out his pocket watch as he spoke, he didn't notice her clenching her other fist, then gradually uncurling her fingers, while her jaw worked, as though she was counting slowly to ten.

'Tumultuous,' said the doctor, snapping his watch shut, then patting her hand before releasing it. 'I think,' he said, looking at the books on the table at her side, 'that you may have been addling your wits through reading too much, rather than going to bed at a sensible hour and getting your rest. Women,' the doctor continued, turning to him, 'should not sit about, inactive, while their minds get all worked up over these sorts of silly romances,' he said. 'It can often lead to episodes of hysteria.'

If anything was likely to induce a fit of hysteria in this particular woman, he would warrant it was having an ignorant quack like this one coming up with such a demeaning prognosis. And far from being silly, the particular novel she'd been reading had come in jolly handy. Why, it had almost become a lethal weapon!

She was breathing heavily now and barely managing to keep herself sitting still.

'I shall,' said the doctor, turning away to the bed where he'd dropped his bag a moment before, 'mix up a soothing draught for her. It will help her to sleep. And from now on, I prescribe less reading and more exercise, to restore the balance of the humours.'

She was so livid now, that steam was practically coming out of her ears.

'Perhaps,' Michael couldn't resist saying, 'I should remove the offending items from her vicinity, in case she is tempted to make use of them again.' As he went to pick up the two volumes of *Sense and Sensibility*, he met her eye. Oh, how she would love to have got to them first and hit someone with one of them. Probably the doctor, who was busy mixing up some powder from a packet he'd taken out of his bag with some water that he'd poured from a jug he'd found on her nightstand. Or possibly him, now that he was teasing her by appearing to go along with what the doctor was saying.

'Now, drink this up like a good girl,' said the doctor, holding out the glass of cloudy liquid.

'Must I?' She gazed up at him with entreaty in her eyes.

'I am afraid,' Michael said, 'that you must. It will help you sleep, you know,' he added.

'Yes,' she said and sighed. 'I suppose I was finding it hard to…to be at ease…while you were out fetching the doctor.'

She took the glass, downed the contents in one go, shuddered and made a face.

What a trump she was!

After seeing the doctor off the premises, he ran back up the stairs and knocked on her bedroom door again.

She opened it so quickly she must have been standing just inside it, waiting for his return.

'I know, I know,' he said, holding up his hands in a gesture of surrender. 'But when I got to the spot where we'd left Baxter burbling on about turpentine and found he'd vanished, I had to think of some reason why I might have summoned the doctor with such urgency, in the middle of the night.'

'And a hysterical woman,' she said tartly, 'was the best you could come up with?'

'Well, I didn't know who else was in the house. And I couldn't very well say I was in desperate need of a quack at this hour of the night, since I'd gone to him myself and could have consulted him in his own rooms. Besides, I knew you'd catch on to what was afoot and play along.'

'You did, did you?'

'Well, I hoped, at any rate. You have always struck me as being of above average intelligence.'

'Huh,' she said. 'Pardon me for pointing it out, but a short while ago *you* were accusing *me* of telling whiskers!'

'So you will completely understand why I had to resort to doing the same. Sometimes, employing a ruse of that sort is the only way to scrape through a tight spot, isn't it?'

'Huh,' she said again, although she did look slightly less annoyed. 'Well, at least,' she said pragmatically, 'I looked the part, didn't I? After you took that vile little man away, I took a look at myself in the mirror. And I *do* look positively demented.'

'Well, who wouldn't after the things you went through? Most women would have indulged in a fit of the vapours long before that doctor shoved his oar in. And how you kept a straight face when he pointed out the dangers of *Sense and Sensibility*,' he said with admiration, 'I cannot imagine!'

'I was within an ames-ace of showing him exactly how dangerous books can be, I admit,' she said with feeling. 'Only I had just been scolding myself for acting before thinking and thought it would be better to count to ten. Or relieve my feelings by hitting something, *after* he'd gone away.'

'You did the right thing. If you had hit him—not that I would have blamed you, after all the provoking things he said—he would only have thought that it proved he was right. But anyway,' he added, glancing over his shoulder, 'we cannot stand about discussing the doctor's stupidity, or we will be here all night. And my ward and Lady Birchwood are likely to be returning fairly soon. The last thing I want is for them to discover me in your room.'

She blushed. 'Yes. And now you have mentioned it, might I remind you that you ought not to be in here?'

'I don't need a reminder. I know it is rather unorthodox. But I just needed to make sure that you were aware of the facts. Baxter has vanished. Which, in one way, I suppose, is a good thing. That is to say, it must mean that he cannot be that badly injured or he couldn't have got up and run off.'

'We don't know that he ran…'

'Whatever speed he went, the point is he made himself scarce the moment the coast was clear. Which means he's out there, on the loose, planning his next move. Which means we will need to start planning *our* next move.'

'Our…next move? What do you mean?'

'Just that now we know how unscrupulous Baxter can be—for what decent man would attempt to climb into an innocent girl's room, with flowers? We will need to be on the alert for further attempts to…win Susannah away from her home. And since it would not be proper for me to remain here, at this hour of the night, and anyway we are likely to get interrupted by the last persons we want to know anything about this night's work, then I suggest you attend me in my study in the morning after breakfast. And help me thrash out a plan.'

'Pardon me for being stupid, but why don't we want Susannah to know about Baxter trying to get in by the window to see her? Surely, forewarned is forearmed?'

'Isn't it obvious? If she knows the lengths to which he will go to thwart my wishes, I wouldn't put it past her to think of that as the epitome of romance. Or some such nonsense. Besides, we don't want her to know that you threw him out of the window, do we?'

'*Knocked* him out of the window,' she corrected him. 'By accident.'

'However he went out of the window, the point is that at the moment Susannah trusts you completely. Otherwise, why would she have insisted that you came to London? In spite of Lady Birchwood being equally insistent that she was the proper person to preside over her presentation.'

'Yes, well, Lady Susannah's aunts have been passing her from one to the other to suit their convenience ever since I have been working for the family,' she said. 'So, for the last few years, I have been the one person who has stuck with her through thick and thin.'

'There, you see? If she should find out that you dislike the man so much you caused him actual bodily harm, that trust is bound to get dented, if not destroyed completely. And I need her to trust you. At the moment you are the only person on my staff that has any success at keeping her in line. Unorthodox though your methods may be. Look,' he said, seeing her eyes take on a glassy sheen, 'I can see that whatever the doctor gave you is beginning to take effect. You are not thinking as clearly as you usually do.'

She frowned. 'You could be right. I do feel rather... lethargic.'

His conscience smote him. 'I apologise for foisting that nasty little man on you. And for allowing him to give you a dose of what I suspect is laudanum. But he regularly doses Lady Birchwood with it and she has never come to any harm from it.'

'No,' she said, making a dismissive gesture with her hand. 'I am already getting sleepy, but it won't do me any harm. Though I do wonder if she may have come to rely on it too much. I recall, when she was first widowed, that it really did help her. From what I could observe. Only...' She blinked, rather owlishly. 'That is to say...to be honest, without it, I wouldn't have been able to sleep at all, I shouldn't think. Before you came in I was...pacing,' she said with a rueful shake of her head. 'Back and forth. Getting nowhere.'

'Then let us bid each other goodnight and meet again in the morning to discuss tactics.'

'Tactics, yes,' she said, giving him a rather wan smile. 'In the morning.'

'I shall look forward to it,' he said. As he closed the door on his way out, he realised that he had spoken nothing but the truth. He *was* looking forward to meeting Miss Hinchcliffe in the morning and having what was bound to be a completely unorthodox conversation with her.

To think that when he'd left the army, he'd feared his life would become one long tedious round of duties. Well, so far, it had been. At least, a great deal of it. Having to spend so much time in London, dancing attendance on his ward, who was the most spoiled little madam it had ever been his misfortune to encounter. And having inane exchanges with fluttery debutantes.

But this evening, or at least, from the moment Miss Hinchcliffe had run into him on the front step, babbling tales of murder, mischief and library books, he hadn't felt the slightest bit bored. For the first time since he'd returned to England, he'd felt like…himself.

It was probably reprehensible of him. But then he'd never been a staid sort of chap, had he? Not like his pompous cousin, who'd never put a foot out of line. No, life in the army had suited Michael's character perfectly. He'd enjoyed being on the move, with no knowing what adventure each new day would bring.

A smile pulled at his lips as he laid his hand to the door latch of his own bedroom. For it sounded as though Miss Hinchcliffe, under that stern, unflappable front which was all she'd permitted him to see before tonight, was the kind of person around whom things *happened*.

And he, for one, couldn't wait to find out what might happen next.

Chapter Six

Rosalind woke with a start and sat bolt upright, her heart pounding.

The room was stuffy, probably because the sun was shining in through the window. The closed window.

She looked at the little clock which she kept on her bedside table, groaning when she saw that it was past eleven. No wonder the room was so uncomfortably hot. The sun must have been shining in for some time.

She flung back the covers, got out of bed and strode over to open the window. As she stepped over to the balcony, to breathe in some fresh air, the events of the previous night came flooding back to her.

Her stomach roiled. She might have killed a man! For a few dreadful hours, she'd believed she had. Only for Mr Baxter to make a remarkable recovery, before vanishing into the night, leaving Lord Caldicot to clear up the mess he'd made. Or she'd made.

But never mind that. Why hadn't someone come

and woken her up? It was well past the time she normally rose and broke her fast. Even on nights after balls, when Susannah slept past noon, she made sure she had the first part of the day to herself, before her charge began making demands on her.

It was only after she'd taken a wash in rather dusty water that had been standing there all night, since she didn't want to waste time ringing for hot water, and waiting for someone to fetch it, that she noticed a slip of paper lying by her bedroom door. Just as though someone had pushed it under the door while she slept.

She hurried over and picked it up.

When you awake, come to my study straight away.
M.

M.? Who was M.?

Him. He was *Michael*, Lord Caldicot.

But why had he signed it M? They were not on such terms that she might expect to address him by his first name.

Or perhaps, after last night, he thought they were.

But they weren't. Still… She took the note to her dressing table, took out her writing case and slipped the note inside, then slammed the drawer on her sentimental piece of foolishness, before scrambling into her clothes. He was her employer and the note reminded her that he'd clearly been waiting for her to keep the appointment they'd made the night before. Nothing more, no matter what significance she might wish it had, from the way he'd signed it by his given name rather than his title.

He must already think badly enough of her for all the trouble she'd caused. It was what had made her swallow that vile medicine with such meekness— the feeling that she deserved to be punished for her crimes. Or, if not quite a crime, since it appeared Mr Baxter hadn't died after all, then…her reprehensible behaviour. For it was only by the greatest stroke of luck he'd landed in the bushes, rather than on the terrace.

Oh, when would she ever become the person she'd tried to pretend to be since coming to work for Susannah's family? A calm, dependable, rational person who didn't go about throwing things at stray men and knocking them out of windows?

Once she'd taken a swift glance at her reflection in the mirror, to make sure she looked as much like the stern, dependable governess companion she was trying so hard to be, she ran down the stairs, and tapped at the door of Lord Caldicot's study.

'Come in,' she heard him call out.

She squared her shoulders and went in.

He looked up at her from behind a mountain of paperwork and grinned.

Yes, *grinned*.

'I was wondering when you were going to emerge,' he said, without the slightest sign of irritation. 'That stuff the doctor gave you must have been stronger than usual. Lady Birchwood quaffs gallons of it and it never makes her sleep so soundly that she doesn't even hear a person knocking on her bedroom door.'

'You knocked on my door?'

'No, of course not,' he said, looking surprised. 'I sent a maid up, to see if you were awake yet, after I'd had my breakfast. I don't make a habit of going into a female's bedroom, not during the hours of daylight. Um, I mean...'

She felt her cheeks heat as she thought of why he might enter a female's bedroom during the hours of darkness.

His own cheeks had darkened, too, she rather thought.

'That is, last night was different,' he said, in a rather defensive tone. 'I acted in an unorthodox manner, yes, but there was nobody else about. At least...' he shifted in his chair '...that would normally not be a sufficient excuse, but the maids must have been up in their attics. If Baxter falling out of the window and the arrival of the doctor and all that didn't alert them, then me running softly up the stairs and tapping on your door wasn't going to, was it?' His cheeks went darker still. 'Besides,' he said, rallying, 'surely you must know that the last thing I want is to sully your reputation.'

At that moment, fortunately, before the encounter could become any more embarrassing for either of them, her stomach emitted a most unladylike rumble. His eyes shot to that portion of her anatomy, meaning he had heard it. Right across the other side of the room. Oh, how much lower could she possibly sink in his estimation?

His brows drew down.

'Haven't you had your breakfast?'

'No. Your note said I was to come here the moment I woke, so...' She spread her hands, to demonstrate that here she was.

'Yes, because we have some serious matters to discuss and time is of the essence. But I didn't,' he said, giving her a look of exasperation, 'mean for you to appear so famished that you might faint away at any moment.'

'I never faint,' she retorted before she'd thought about how insubordinate she must sound. Oh, dear. It appeared that all that...arguing and bantering they'd done the night before had robbed her of the ability to speak to him with the deference due to his station. Or...no, it couldn't be that. It was more probable that, having thought she'd killed a man, and been in such a state, only to find him being so...solid, so calm, so...dependable that she'd come to look upon him in a different way to anyone else. And he hadn't helped by signing that letter with an M., as though they were on terms of intimacy, had he? But it wouldn't do. She bit her lip.

But he was grinning again. 'Yes, so you told me last night,' he said. 'How stupid of me to forget.'

'I don't think you did forget,' she was goaded into retorting by that grin. 'I think you said it to be provoking.'

'Hah!' He barked out a laugh. 'Nothing gets past you, does it, Miss Hinchcliffe?' He got to his feet, went to the bell pull by the chimney breast, and tugged on it. 'I will order some food, so that you may eat while we are talking. It will save time,' he said, going back to his desk and sitting down. 'And you'd better sit down. We might be here for some time.'

As she took a chair across the desk from him, Timms, the butler, came in answer to Lord Caldicot's summons.

'Miss Hinchcliffe is in need of some breakfast,' said Lord Caldicot, waving his hand at her.

Timms turned to her and raised one brow.

'Well, go on,' said Lord Caldicot in an impatient tone of voice. 'Tell him what you'd like.'

Rosalind hesitated, then decided that since she had the chance to order whatever she wanted, for once, then she was going to make the most of it. 'I would like two slices of toast, well done, with butter and marmalade on the side, two rashers of bacon, crispy, one poached egg, a spoonful of mushrooms, some fried potatoes, a pot of tea and an orange.' She might not have room for the orange, after the eggs and bacon, but she could certainly slip it into her pocket as a treat for later.

Timms's other eyebrow rose, but after giving Lord Caldicot a deferential bow, he made his stately way out of the room.

'Are you sure,' said Lord Caldicot, with all appearance of being serious, 'that will be enough?'

'It is a bit late to be asking that, isn't it? Timms has gone.'

'Well, I didn't want to embarrass you in front of the man. But you look to me as though you need to eat a great deal more than most women.'

'What do you mean by that?'

'Only that you are twice as tall as most of them,' he replied smoothly. 'Since I've been in London I've begun to feel like Gulliver among the Lilliputians. You cannot think how much I appreciate being able to speak to someone without getting a crick in my neck.'

'Oh.' That was the first time anyone had said that being tall was a good thing. She was far more used to being called a maypole, or a long Meg.

'What,' he enquired, 'did you think I meant?'

'Oh. Um...only that perhaps I eat too much.'

He looked her up and down. 'It looks to me as

though you don't eat anywhere near enough. You are very thin.'

'You are very rude,' she snapped back before she could help it. She couldn't help lacking feminine curves. And normally she was glad she didn't have any. So why was it that it stung her to the quick when *he* remarked upon it?

'You are in a bad skin this morning,' he replied, with a chuckle. 'I wonder—are you always like this before you have breakfast, or is it an unfortunate by-product of that medicine the quack forced on you last night?'

'I should like to blame the doctor,' she said. 'I mean, what kind of idiot thinks that reading books could make someone hysterical?'

'On the other hand, one could argue that you demonstrated just how dangerous books can be,' he said, with a twinkle in his eye.

She couldn't help letting out a huff of laughter as he reminded her just how dangerous *Sense and Sensibility* had proved, last night, to Mr Baxter. Which made her drop her guard with him, yet again. 'I fear,' she admitted, 'that my mood this morning has more to do with the fact that you somehow have a knack of making me blurt out what I'm really thinking. I usually manage to behave in a perfectly proper manner with everyone else.'

A strange sort of expression came over his face. A sort of…arrested look.

And then, as quickly as it had appeared, it vanished. He bent his head and moved a sheet of paper from one of the piles on the desk to another. He cleared his throat.

'Perhaps it is time we got down to the matter in hand.'

'Yes, indeed,' she said with some relief. So far, this interview had been most peculiar and most unsettling.

'Firstly,' he said, leaning back in his chair and looking at her more keenly, 'I want you to explain some of the things you told me last night, when you were also not guarding your tongue.'

'Which things?' She could barely remember any of the things she'd said last night, she'd been in such a pucker.

'You told me that your parents were both from good families *"to their own way of thinking"*. What does that mean?'

'Oh.' Well, that was easy to answer. 'My mother's people were rather proud of being connected to the aristocracy, although it was some way back, while my father's people were self-made. My mother's people therefore regarded my father's family as vulgar mushrooms, while my hardworking, dissenting father's family thought my mother's lot were idle parasites.'

'So…you father's family were wealthy, while your mother's family were merely well connected?'

'Exactly! Or so I've been told. I was too young when they died to be aware of the discord. It was later that I picked up bits and pieces, from what people let drop.'

'Might I enquire who this distant, aristocratic connection might be?'

'Oh, well, the Earl of Framlingham.'

'Is that so?' He studied her for a moment or two. 'If that is not so very far back in your lineage, you would have the right to be attending all the events to which Susannah is now being invited.'

She snorted her derision at that. 'Not Almack's! Don't forget, on my father's side I am tainted by the stench of trade.'

'Not Almack's, admittedly,' he agreed. 'But then the patronesses are notoriously picky about whom they admit.'

'Why are you even mentioning it?'

'Wouldn't you like to go to balls and picnics, and things?'

'I have been to several picnics and things with Susannah,' she said bitterly. 'Any event to which Lady Birchwood suddenly finds herself too fatigued to attend, during the day.'

'Yes, she claims she needs to recoup her strength for attending the events to which Susannah is invited in the evening. The events,' he added, with a twinkle in his eye, 'that she actually wishes to go to herself.'

'Precisely!'

'Well, you know,' he said slowly, looking as though he was about to say something outrageous, 'the doctor did recommend that you get more exercise.'

'Oh, no,' she said, with deep misgiving. 'What are you plotting?'

'Before I tell you, I wish to ascertain a few more facts.'

'So you *are* plotting something!'

'Well, it depends.'

'On what?'

'On what you meant, precisely, about those other victims you mentioned.'

'I never did!'

'Ah, but what was I to think when you said that *the other times* were nothing like last night, but that they made your family think you were not fit to live in a house with civilised people?'

'Do you,' she said with resentment, 'remember everything everyone tells you?'

'Not usually. But what you said last night must have been particularly fascinating. I found myself, later on, lying in bed imagining you leaving a trail of broken, bleeding men strewn across the countryside…'

'You didn't!'

'Coupled with the rather ominous-sounding way

you described the behaviour of predatory men, pouncing on defenceless females…'

'Oh. Yes.' She lowered her head. 'I suppose I did gabble on in a rather indiscreet fashion.'

'Come now,' he said, 'you had better make a full confession. You will feel better for it.'

'You don't really believe that, do you?'

He looked up at the ceiling, as though he was considering how to reply. 'Well,' he eventually said, 'that is what I've heard. But you are right. I am just eaten up with curiosity. You cannot dangle such fascinating titbits of information about your past and then refuse to elucidate me. It would be most unkind. After I was about to dispose of your latest victim, too!'

'Oh, were you?'

He nodded. 'Had it been necessary, you can be sure I would have hushed it up to the best of my ability.'

'Because you don't want any whiff of scandal marring Susannah's come-out.'

He gave her an enigmatic look. 'If you like. But never mind Susannah for now. Stop trying to distract me and give me a straight answer to my question. What, exactly, had made you flee to your grandfather, on several previous occasions? And, while we are at it, who precisely *is* your grandfather?'

She sighed. 'The grandfather who keeps on coming into my life to straighten it out,' she said, preferring to answering that question, than delving into the murky depths of her past disgraces, 'is General Smallwood.'

He sat up straight. 'General Smallwood? Not *the* General Smallwood? Scourge of the Spanish Sierra?'

'I haven't heard him referred to by that name,' she said. 'But he did spend a lot of time with Wellington in Spain, so he might well have scourged something Spanish. He certainly struck terror into his family, whenever he came back to England,' she added, with feeling. 'So much so that, against their judgement, one of his sisters took me into her home.'

'Wait a minute, I thought you said you were an orphan. And that both sides of the family cut off your parents for marrying against their wishes.'

'Yes. So that when my parents died, I ended up on the parish, as they say. In a shabby little orphanage in Leeds. Picking oakum and the like. Only, when Grandfather came home on furlough and learned that his daughter had died and that I was in that...place,' she said, unable to prevent herself from shuddering at the memory, 'he was furious.'

'With whom? I mean, surely he was the one who'd cast his own daughter out?'

'Yes, but you cannot expect a man of his temper to behave with any consistency. There is no knowing what will cause him to fly into the boughs and bark orders left, right and centre. Many of them contradictory to ones he's uttered before.'

'Yes, that sounds like the Scourge of the Sierras right enough,' he said with evident amusement. 'On campaign it made him rather an effective leader, strangely enough. He was so terrifying in one of his tempers that subordinates took great care not to provoke him. And, since they were far more scared of him than the notional enemy, his unit became renowned for bravery in action.'

'That doesn't surprise me,' she said, thinking of the few times she'd met him and the way his whole family quaked at the prospect of *seeing* him, never mind offending him. 'Anyway, I think what happened was that he took it into his head to decide that my father's family had no right to complain about the connection. He told me that they should have taken me in and brought me up. After all, they had so much money they'd bought up half of Derbyshire. He was so angry with *them* he forgot about not wishing to acknowledge me.'

'And how old were you when he snatched you from the orphanage and told you what he thought of your father's family?'

'About twelve, by then.'

'He must have scared you, shouting like that.'

'Well, that's the funny thing. He never did, because—'

'You,' he cried as though experiencing an epiphany, 'have a temper just like it!'

'No. At least, I *do* have a temper, but I don't think anyone can match Grandfather for irrationality. It is just that I was so glad to have been rescued from that orphanage that I didn't care how much he shouted. And he wasn't actually shouting at me, you see. Only about how annoying everyone else was.'

'The orphanage was very bad, was it?'

'It was...' She bit down on her lower lip. It was always hard to think about that place, let alone speak about it. Not that anyone else had ever asked her much about it. Because nobody else had been interested. Not in her, specifically, only what she represented.

'It was a shock, going to a place like that after living with loving parents,' she told him, unsure why she had started with that, when really it had very little bearing on what she'd meant to say.

She pulled herself together. 'But the worst thing was the hunger. I was always so hungry and there was never enough food to go round. And I soon learned that having manners was a positive hindrance to survival. Polite little girls always ended up at the back of the queue for what little food there was. Polite little girls tended to have whatever they did manage to get stolen from them.'

'So you abandoned what manners you had.'

'By the time Grandfather descended on the place, all guns blazing, I had, let us say, learned to survive.'

He leaned forward, as though he was about to ask

her something of great importance, when someone knocked on the door.

Timms, with her breakfast.

Naturally, he couldn't ask whatever it was while the butler was there, fussing over dishes and covers, and the teapot.

She could only hope that by the time Timms left, he would have forgotten whatever it was he'd wanted to ask her. Because he'd already dredged up too many memories which she'd thought safely buried.

And she didn't like the way she kept on confiding in him.

Why did she keep forgetting he was her employer? That he could turn her out of her position, and therefore her home, without a reference in the blink of an eye?

She had to stop treating him as though he was her friend, just because he'd been so surprisingly understanding about last night's incident with Mr Baxter.

And remember just how much she had to lose.

Chapter Seven

He saw her face shutter.

That was a pity. Because she'd been confiding in him in a manner that had moved him in a way he wasn't able to put into words. But it had felt...good. And he'd been hoping for more of the same.

But then, as she picked up her knife and fork, her face changed again. Expressing relish.

'You *were* hungry, weren't you?' he said, as she tucked in with gusto.

'Mmm,' she agreed, with a nod.

Was she really that hungry, though, or was she using the excuse of table manners to avoid speaking to him with her mouth full?

He wouldn't put it past her. She was a fascinating mixture of behaviour, was Miss Hinchcliffe, as he'd somehow always suspected she would be. Alternately frank, in a way that few people ever were, then re-treating behind a façade of prim and proper manners.

Although good manners didn't seem to apply to the rate at which she was consuming her meal. Just as if she feared that if she didn't clean her plate swiftly, someone else might come and snatch it away. A habit she'd fallen into at that orphanage?

Still, it meant that she wouldn't have the excuse of having her mouth too full to answer his questions, for all that long.

'So,' he said, leaning back in his chair with a smile. 'You learned how to survive in that orphanage. And the habits you'd learned, I presume,' he said, eyeing the way she was demolishing her bacon, 'went with you into your new life.'

She nodded again.

'But, for all his blustering about your condition, I presume General Smallwood didn't take you into his household?' He rarely returned to England, so far as Michael knew. He much preferred being in the thick of the action.

'No, he forced one of his sisters to admit me to her household, since she had children of a similar age to me and governesses, and what have you.'

'From the expression on your face, I gather it was not a happy experience. Unless there is something wrong with the mushrooms?'

'No, the mushrooms are delicious,' she said. And carried on eating.

'And your aunt's household?'

She paused. Then sighed. '*Not* delicious. But I didn't last there very long, anyway. And I suppose you want to know why they threw me out?'

'Did you, perchance, threaten to eat them out of house and home?'

She glared at him with a forkful of mushrooms halfway to her mouth.

'You are—' She snapped her mouth shut and blushed.

'You were saying?'

'Well, I very nearly did,' she admitted, 'but then I thought better of it.'

'You remembered, perchance, that I am not the most obnoxious man,' he said silkily, 'you've ever met?'

'Oh, no. Far from it,' she said with feeling.

'Yes, you said something to that effect last night,' he reminded her.

She lowered the fork to her plate. 'Yes, I did, didn't I?' She looked at the mushrooms, then, with a shrug, lifted them to her mouth and chewed for a moment or two.

He waited, sensing that she was thinking about how to respond. Which he found he didn't like. He much preferred it when she spoke without thinking. When she just said what she really meant.

'I will just tell you of the incident which pushed my great-aunt to expel me from her home, I think.'

'Very well.' If that was all she was willing to tell him, for now, he'd have to accept it.

'I was, as you have reminded me, always hungry. And there was an orchard on the property. So, naturally, when the apples ripened, I went off to pick some. Only…my cousin, an odious boy who had decided, from my first day under his parents' roof that it was his prime duty to remind me that I didn't belong with decent folk, followed me out there. I tried to avoid him by climbing a tree, but he was persistent. He had got halfway up the tree I'd chosen and I was certain that he would have pushed me out of it once he caught up to me, so I…well, I just kicked out at him. I only meant to dislodge his hand from the branch he was holding, but unfortunately, from his point of view, I caught him square in the mouth.'

'Ouch.'

'Indeed,' she said, spearing her egg with deliberation, so that the yolk flowed out across the plate. 'I found it hard to be sorry that he lost some teeth, or that he claimed I'd broken his nose. Because he'd so frequently held that very nose whenever I walked into a room, saying that he could smell the foul whiff of my origins. A phrase he must have picked up from his parents,' she said, slashing the unfortunate egg completely in half.

No wonder she hadn't been able to credit the fact that he might have attempted to hush up her part in what might have been an accidental death, just to spare her feelings. For it sounded as though nobody had taken her feelings into account for so long that she expected nothing but mistreatment.

'So where did they send you?'

'To school,' she said, in a voice that was rather more cheerful than when she'd been dwelling on the failings of her family. 'They paid for me to go to a place where girls of a similar station to mine learned how to earn a living when they grew old enough. Well, even my grandfather hadn't expected them to launch me into society, not with my father's family owning mills. That would have meant finding a dowry big enough to tempt some man into demeaning himself by taking me on,' she said with a slight shrug, which he supposed was meant to look nonchalant, but which, to his eyes, portrayed a good deal of hurt.

'There, I learned how to teach little children to read and write, and, when they found my intelligence was more than that of some of the other girls, and how much I loved books, how I might be able to teach older girls how to go on in society. How to play the piano and how deeply to curtsy to people of varying ranks and all that sort of nonsense,' she added, wrinkling her nose.

Well, that did it! He thought it was about time she had some fun to make up for the years of hardship she'd endured so bravely. 'Did they teach you how to dance?'

'Yes,' she said, looking bewildered, 'although I don't see what that has to do with anything.'

'That is because I haven't yet told you what I have in mind.'

He could see her working it out. He'd asked her if she knew how to dance and he'd asked her about her background, saying that she had almost as much right as Susannah to go about in society, and so…

'No,' she breathed, shaking her head. 'You cannot mean that you want me to attend balls?'

'That is exactly what I mean.'

'But…but…'

'Come now, you know that we are going to have to watch Susannah closely, now that we know to what lengths Baxter will go.'

'*We* are going to have to watch her?'

'Yes. Clearly Lady Birchwood is just not up to the task. Baxter must have got to know Susannah while she was supposed to be watching her. And he must have had unfettered access to her, or he would not have managed to worm his way so deeply into the girl's affections that she declares she loves him and throws herself on to the hearth rug when I refuse to give my permission for them to marry.'

'No,' she said, laying down her knife and fork, in a manner that signified the subject was closed.

'May I remind you,' he said, 'that it is entirely your fault that Mr Baxter is at large?'

'It is not!'

'If you had not insisted I go and fetch the doctor, he would not have had the chance to sneak off when I wasn't looking.'

'Fustian!'

'Or,' some imp of mischief prompted him to add, 'if you had done the job properly in the first place...'

'If I had done the job properly, as you put it,' she retorted, 'then Susannah would be so angry with me you would have had to dismiss me.'

'But not for committing murder?'

'I'm beginning to suspect you wouldn't have considered *that* cause for dismissal,' she retorted.

He let out a bark of laughter. 'You malign me. I cannot have a woman with a propensity to go about murdering people left in charge of an impressionable girl.'

'I haven't murdered anyone!'

'The way you spoke last night gave me the distinct impression you had left the countryside strewn with your hapless victims.'

'Well, last night my wits were disordered.'

'Or you would not have revealed what you did,' he agreed affably.

'Though I definitely remember telling you that I have never harmed anyone *deliberately*.'

He sighed, in mock regret. 'That is a pity, because

what I really need from you is to act as a sort of…
guard over Susannah. And I am sure that after last
night, Mr Baxter, for one, will definitely think twice
before attempting anything similar, if he sees you
hovering about the ballroom.' He leaned forward to
emphasise his point. 'I doubt he will dare go anywhere near her.'

She took in a sharp, offended breath. Opened her
mouth. Closed it. Took another breath as she tried to
marshal her arguments. And, true to form, it was not
long before she came up with a corker.

'If I am going to have to attend balls and things,
when, exactly, am I going to get any time off? I trail
around after her all day. I regard the evenings as my
own.'

'If you recall, I said *we* are going to have to keep
a close eye on her.'

'Ye…es…'

'Which obviously implies that I, too, will take my
share of guard duties. With about as much enthusiasm as you show for it, I must admit. Though I would
have thought you would have enjoyed getting dressed
up and going to balls.'

She snorted her disgust of such an assumption.
'What, so that I can watch feather-brained females
making fools of themselves over vile men?'

'Not all men are vile…' He had been about to say
that he was sure Susannah could meet someone per-

fectly acceptable, if only they could keep the worst sort of fortune hunters out of her orbit.

But she forestalled him by exclaiming, 'Well, I should like to meet one!'

'Are you not looking at one, right now? Or do you consider me vile, as well?'

She blushed. 'Oh, well, I mean, I thought it was clear that I didn't mean you. Although,' she added, her brows lowering, 'you are capable of pretty reprehensible behaviour, aren't you?'

'Me?' He tried to look the picture of innocence.

'Yes. Saying that you wished I had succeeded in doing away with Mr Baxter...'

'I never said that!'

She thought for a bit, as though swiftly reviewing all their conversations. 'Well, you definitely implied it.'

'It comes from spending so much time in the military, I dare say. I have grown so used to just putting a bullet into any enemy I come across that it chafes, yes, positively chafes me to have to rely on governesses to toss such fellows off balconies.'

'I did *not* toss *anyone* out of...oh,' she spluttered, 'you...you are outrageous!'

She regarded him for a moment or two, and then, just when he'd begun to give up on her, she burst out laughing. 'Oh, you have been roasting me!'

It amazed him how different she looked when she

laughed. Not only less guarded, but also far younger. He would wager that the things she'd endured thus far in her life were what had drawn her features into such disapproving, disappointed lines. Without them, she was, he saw with satisfaction, an attractive woman. Not pretty, precisely, but…handsome. No, not that, either. What showed in her face, he decided, was character. Intelligence, too, with those heavy frowns and the sarcastic twist to her lips she indulged in so often.

'So,' he said, shaking off the speculation about what it was about her that made him find her attractive, 'I have your agreement, then?'

'You have nothing of the sort!'

'Come, come, Miss Hinchcliffe, you know that we are the only two sensible people in this household. We are the only two capable of protecting her from herself.'

'But…' She looked positively pained.

'We can draw up a roster, if you like.'

'A roster?'

'Yes, a chart, detailing who will be on duty at any given time…'

'I know what a roster is! I am not, as you have already pointed out, an idiot.'

'Oh? It was just you did not seem to understand.'

'I don't. I mean, I don't understand why you would propose such a thing.'

'Well, because you are, as you pointed out with

such belligerence, entitled to time off. So we will have to divide up the days into watches, so that between us, we can keep Mr Baxter at bay.'

'Oh.' She looked nonplussed.

'Did you expect *me* to treat you shabbily, just because circumstances have obliged you to work for your living?'

She blushed. Again.

'I beg your pardon,' she said stiffly, 'for misjudging you, but it has been my experience so far that men of your class, or rather *people* of your class,' she corrected herself, when he frowned, 'do not consider the feelings of their servants to any extent.'

'Perhaps I am not doing so either,' he said. 'Perhaps I am just thinking that if I drive you too hard, you will either run off, screaming into the night, like so many other of Susannah's governesses, or collapse with exhaustion.'

She gave him a reproving look. If she'd worn spectacles, he reflected with amusement, it would have been over the top of them.

'Once again,' she said, 'I suspect you are roasting me. You know I am not so faint hearted that I would do either.'

'Well, I do hope not. Because you are going to have to start right away. Today.'

'You think Mr Baxter might attempt to contact Susannah, in a…clandestine manner, today? But…he must be pretty badly injured. I mean, he did not stir for such a long time that I believed him to be dead!'

'Yes, but then the minute we both left him unattended he got up and ran away.'

'Oh. You mean…he might have been shamming it?'

'He is the kind of man who is shamming it all the time, I dare say. It would have been second nature to him to lie still until he was sure the coast was clear.'

She frowned, thoughtfully. 'So…how are we to explain to Susannah that I will be suddenly going to balls and such from now on?'

'Oh, because the doctor recommended it, of course!'

'What?'

'Yes, don't you remember him saying that you ought to get more exercise and read less?'

'I remember him saying all sorts of stupid things,' she said darkly.

'Yes, but Susannah won't know they're stupid, will she?'

'I…but—'

'So,' he cut in ruthlessly, while she was still sputtering instead of coming up with a coherent objection, 'as soon as she emerges from her room, I will inform her that she is to take you shopping.'

'Shopping?'

'Yes. You do know what that is?'

'Of course I know what it is! I just don't see why I have to do any!'

'Oh? Your cupboards are stuffed full of ball gowns and the fripperies to go with them, are they?'

'No,' she said, looking dejected.

'There you are then. You need to kit yourself out and Susannah, I would warrant, will love having an excuse to go out spending my money, which will kill two birds with one stone.'

'You mean…while she is overseeing my shopping, I will be doing my part as a guard dog?'

'See? You're catching on. Then, when you come home, you will need to inform me how Susannah plans to spend the rest of the day, so that we can divide the guarding duties between us.'

'You want me to spy on her,' she said glumly.

'Protect her,' he corrected her firmly.

'For how long? The rest of the Season?'

'And beyond, if necessary. Like you, I have no intention of running off screaming into the night. Susannah may be a bit of a handful, but it is my duty to protect her. And I shall carry on doing so until I have seen her married to a man of honour.'

She smiled at him with approval, which gave him a warm glow inside.

He cleared his throat. 'In the meantime I shall think of a way to put a spoke in Baxter's wheel, permanently. I have already thought of several ways that I might be able to achieve that, without going to the lengths of doing him irreversible, physical damage.

Men like Baxter are usually motivated by greed. If I can find him and come to some sort of arrangement… a sort of stick-and-carrot approach…'

She nodded approvingly again. Then frowned.

'But it isn't just Mr Baxter, is it? London is probably heaving with men of his stamp, attempting to dupe rich young heiresses out of their fortunes.'

'Exactly. Which is why we will both be doing our utmost to protect her.'

She sighed. 'Very well. You have convinced me.'

'Capital!' He leaned back in his chair, smiling. Not only because he'd won her round regarding his plan to watch over Susannah, but also because it would mean he'd now have all sorts of reasons, valid reasons, for spending time with her.

Chapter Eight

When Rosalind told her, Susannah clapped her hands with glee.

'Shopping for you? Oh, famous!'

'You don't mind?' Rosalind had been unsure how her charge would react to the news that she was going to have to abandon whatever plans she might have made for the day and go shopping with her governess–companion instead. She'd braced herself for a bout of the sulks, so this display of pleasure was a very welcome surprise.

'Oh, no! I love shopping. And I have always thought that you could look much better if only you didn't dress in such dowdy clothes.'

Rosalind bit back the response that sprang to her lips. That she had never had the means to buy anything that was either in fashion, or of good quality. Or had even wanted to look…*better*. For better, in Susannah's estimation, probably meant attractive to men. And that was the last thing Rosalind wanted. She'd learned during her previous post as a governess that if a woman in her position dressed as though she wanted to attract male attention, then she would get it. And would then heartily wish she hadn't.

'And now that Lord Caldicot has said we can send the bills to him, you can have whatever you want! Oh, this is going to be such fun!'

It was at times like this that Rosalind so often experienced strong surges of affection for her young charge. For Lady Susannah was perfectly capable of thinking of others and not solely of herself. If only someone had nurtured that side of her when she'd been younger, rather than encouraging her to be so self-indulgent…

Although, not half an hour after they'd entered the first modiste's shop, which Susannah had insisted they should visit, Rosalind began to wonder whether Susannah was treating her more like a doll to dress up for her own amusement, than as a person with feelings.

'That blue crepe,' Susanah said, pointing to a bolt of pale material draped across the counter. 'That would look wonderful with an overdress of silver gauze.'

It probably would look charming on a girl of Susannah's age. But on Rosalind, who was not only older, but also taller and far thinner, she had a suspicion it would make her look like a streak of blue pump water.

But there was no point in complaining. What did she care what she looked like? This whole exercise was about keeping Susannah safe and occupied in a way that put her beyond the reach of men like Mr Baxter. And the one thing of which she was certain was that men like Mr Baxter did *not* spend their days in establishments like this one.

'Does Madame,' said the modiste, probably noticing the look of resignation on Rosalind's face, 'approve?'

'Oh, Miss Hinchcliffe has never had the chance to buy clothes like this before,' said Susannah blithely, 'so she can't possibly have much of an opinion.'

'It is very pretty material,' said Rosalind with complete honesty. For it was. She just wasn't convinced that it would do anything for her. Not that she wanted it to do anything for her. Apart from having a fleeting, and extremely silly, wish to find an outfit that would make Lord Caldicot see her...differently. As an attractive woman. 'Lady Susannah,' she said, pulling herself back from the brink of wistful longing with an effort, 'is being most kind in giving me her advice.'

Susannah beamed at her and carried on discussing such mysteries as spangles and shell scallops and Circassian sleeves with the modiste while Rosalind submitted to being measured and draped in a variety of materials.

'Now,' said Susannah, after declaring that she'd done as much as she could in that particular establishment, 'we should go on to a milliner. And then we must think about shoes. And gloves.'

'Must we?'

'Of course we must! Oh…' she peered at Rosalind's less than enthusiastic demeanour '…are you tired? Of course, at your age this must be terribly tiring, especially since you are not used to it.'

'Um…' Susannah probably thought she was being most considerate. For her, that was a huge step in the right direction. So Rosalind decided not to tell her that mentioning a lady's age was not at all polite. Or remind her that Susannah was only six years her junior.

'So let us go to Gunter's for tea and cake, before continuing with your wardrobe.'

Gunter's. The kind of place where anyone might *accidentally* meet with someone they were forbidden from meeting anywhere else.

Was that why Susannah had seemed so keen to come out, with only Rosalind for company? Did she think she was a fool?

'I think,' said Rosalind, 'I would prefer to carry on shopping until it is all done, then return to Kilburn House.'

'You don't want to drink tea at Gunter's? Honestly,

they do far better cakes and things than that cook Lady Birchwood engaged for the Season. And ices! Oh, you cannot imagine how delicious they can be on a hot day.'

'Well, perhaps, later on...' And anyway, when she came to think of it, what harm could Mr Baxter do in a tea shop? There would be plenty of other people about.

'Hurrah!' Susannah clapped her hands again.

She was, Rosalind reflected with deep suspicion, in a very good mood today, considering the fact that only yesterday she'd declared herself to be heartbroken.

'You haven't,' Rosalind therefore said, as they climbed into the carriage, so that they wouldn't have to have the tedium of walking all the way from Bruton Street to Conduit Street, 'told me anything about Almack's last night. Did you enjoy it?'

She had been a little surprised when Susannah had the barouche brought round for their shopping trip, since they could easily have walked such a short distance. But perhaps Susannah had done enough walking for one day, she reflected as she'd climbed in and sat beside her. Perhaps she preferred to conserve her strength for all the dancing she was bound to do that evening. And she was not about to complain about the fact that having a carriage also meant they had the protection of a driver and a footman. Plus, somewhere to deposit their parcels, rather than having to either carry them all home, or have them delivered later on.

Susannah pouted as she arranged her skirts more tidily once she'd sat down. 'It was terribly stuffy. So many rules, you cannot imagine. But I was a perfect paragon of good behaviour, you know. Throwing dust in everyone's eyes. Everyone will think that I've forgotten all about Cecil, I was so...gay and charming to all my partners!'

'You had plenty of dance partners, then?'

'Of course I did,' she replied with a look of astonishment that Rosalind could ask such a silly question. 'I am so wealthy, and well connected, that even the highest sticklers can find no fault with me.'

As long, Rosalind reflected darkly, as they didn't examine her too closely and learn how temperamental she could be.

'I suspect,' Susannah confided, with a mischievous grin, 'that my Aunt Birchwood believes that I was so flattered to be singled out by such a notoriously good catch as Lord Wapping that it put all thoughts of the lowly Cecil completely out of my head.'

'Lord Wapping?'

'Yes. Only a baron at the moment, but he's the nephew of the Duke of Yardley, who is about to expire at any moment, apparently, and the only male in that branch of the family. So that although he is not a duke now, it won't be long. And his wife will

of course therefore be a duchess. And Lady Birchwood,' she said scornfully, as the carriage pulled up
outside a shop whose windows were full of the most
terrifyingly flamboyant hats Rosalind had ever seen,
'thinks that it must be every girl's ambition to become a duchess.'

'But not yours?'

'Absolutely not! When I marry, it will be for love,'
she declared, as she climbed down out of the carriage.
'Not rank or wealth!'

As Rosalind followed her charge into the shop, she
felt a surge of admiration for Susannah. Many girls
of her class *did* only marry for position, or wealth,
and nobody thought any the worse of them for that.
Furthermore, nobody seemed to think it wrong that,
once such girls had done their duty by their husbands,
in presenting them with a legitimate heir, they would
then go on to take lovers.

At least, she mused, as Susannah launched into
an animated conversation with the milliner, the girl
meant to love and honour her husband, whoever he
might be, rather than use him as a stepping stone on
the way to some nebulous goal.

But then Susannah had the freedom to choose. Almost in the same way she could choose one of the
many hats the milliner started bringing out for her
inspection. Within certain limits, of course. Lord Cal-

dicot was not going to grant his permission for her to throw herself away on a man of Mr Baxter's character.

If his character genuinely was bad. Now she came to think of it, she had no real evidence upon which to base her distrust of the man. Apart from the mounting irritation that had grown over the weeks while Susannah kept on saying how wonderful he was.

Oh, and the way he'd crept into her room via the balcony—there was *that* to consider.

But then Lord Caldicot surely wouldn't have refused, point blank, to permit the man to pay his addresses to Susannah, simply because he wasn't wealthy, would he? He *must* have more reasons to refuse the match than the fact that he was a younger son with only a tiny income.

Then again, Mr Baxter *had* climbed in through the balcony window. No decent man would do that. Unless, perhaps, he was deeply in love and acting out of desperation...

Was there a clue, in that word he'd moaned? Turpentine? Might he be an artist? Struggling to make a living...

'If you don't like that turban,' said Susannah with a giggle, 'you don't have to scowl at it like that. Just tell me and we'll find something you do like.'

Turban? Oh. The milliner was holding out a bundle of blue wrappings, heavily interspersed with cordage and tassels. Which she was meant, she presumed, to balance on the top of her head.

'The colour,' said Rosalind, after due consideration, 'will definitely match the material that you are having made up into a ball gown for me.' And at least it wasn't covered in flowers like so many of the confections she'd glimpsed, with horror, in the window.

'Precisely!'

Susannah waved her hand and the milliner set the blue monstrosity on top of Rosalind's head.

Then brought her a mirror.

The sight that met her gaze put Rosalind in mind of a story she'd once read about a mythical creature called a gorgon, who had hair made out of snakes. Whose stare turned mortals into stone.

She was still trying to work out how to explain her dislike of the headgear, in terms that wouldn't sound ungrateful, when Susannah declared it was just the thing, the milliner was removing it, and placing it reverently into a box lined with tissue paper.

Perhaps, Rosalind reflected, watching the milliner putting the lid on the box, thus hiding the gorgon headdress from sight, she didn't have much taste. At least not in terms of what was fashionable, or what suited her. For Susannah always looked attractive, in whatever she wore, and she'd had free rein to choose her own clothing for some time now. Or at least, she corrected herself, the females who had been in charge of her before had stopped trying to talk her out of buying whatever took her fancy.

'And now,' said Susannah, having told the milliner to deliver the headdress to their house and to send the bill to Lord Caldicot, 'Gunter's!'

Rosalind, like most of the females who'd been nominally in charge of Susannah before, surrendered. Not only because she chose her battles with the strong-willed girl carefully, but also because she'd never been to Gunter's before and couldn't resist the chance to sample its famous delights.

When the barouche drew to a halt in Berkeley Square, Susannah surprised Rosalind by making no move to alight. Instead, she sent the footman, who'd been sitting up beside the driver, over to the shop to summon a waiter.

'Won't we be going inside?' she asked Susannah.

'Oh, no. Nobody goes *inside* on a lovely day like this,' said Susannah, with a giggle.

Rosalind supposed she meant nobody of the *ton*, since she could definitely see people going in and not coming out again.

'We just sit in our carriage, then, do we?'

'Yes, and in a minute, the waiter will bring us whatever we want. Do you want to try an ice? They do all sorts of flavours. Like parmesan and lavender.'

That sounded disgusting. 'I think I would prefer a cup of tea. And some cake.'

For what Susannah had said about the cook at Kilburn House had been no less than the truth. She didn't seem to have much skill at baking. There was nothing wrong with the savoury dishes she cooked. But it was sometimes hard to decide whether she'd produced small cakes that had failed to rise, or biscuits that were strangely spongey.

Once the waiter had dashed out, taken their order and dashed back to the shop again, Rosalind noticed that Susannah was looking round at the occupants of other open carriages, dotted about the square. As though she was searching for someone.

She very much doubted that Mr Baxter would have access to a carriage that he could park up in the square, even if he wasn't in bed nursing half a dozen broken bones, which was where he most likely was today.

So she decided not to remark on the fact that Susannah was clearly hoping she might see, if not him, then someone.

'I must admit,' Rosalind therefore said, 'that it is very pleasant, sitting here in the shade of the trees while a waiter fetches refreshments. Much better than going into a crowded room where we might have to rub shoulders with heaven alone knows who.'

'I know! I knew you'd enjoy it. Oh…' Susannah

sighed '...if only Mr Baxter might decide to take a walk in the square just now and happen to see me sitting here, then he could come over and we could chat, with perfect propriety. It is so silly,' she said petulantly, 'for Lord Caldicot to have taken against him. Without knowing the first thing about him.'

She sighed, pouted and leaned one elbow on the edge of the carriage, then her chin upon that hand, as she gazed wistfully about her.

Lord Caldicot *must* know something to Mr Baxter's detriment. He must! Or he would not have put his foot down so firmly. Or spoken so scathingly about him, when he'd been lying in a broken heap among the bushes.

Mustn't he?

Of course he must! He wouldn't act so unjustly, without any reason at all, not when Susannah was so clearly in love.

Would he?

Unless he had some sort of prejudice against men who had to work for a living, the way one side of her family had against her own father's people. If Mr Baxter was an artist...

At that moment, the waiter returned, with a tray held aloft, and began doling out dishes, plates and cups.

After one taste of her lavender ice, Susannah pulled

a face. 'This tastes like soap,' she cried. 'Oh, I have never been so...bamboozled!'

For some reason, that use of the word struck Rosalind with the force of a stone dropping into a lake. Had *she* been bamboozled? By Lord Caldicot?

Until this afternoon, she'd assumed Susannah was the one who'd been deceived, by Mr Baxter. But now she was starting to wonder if *she* was the one who'd been deceived, by Lord Caldicot.

After all, hadn't she accepted every word he'd said and approved of everything he'd done *without question*? Not just because he was her employer, either. She'd never had any trouble taking anything her former employers, or any of the aunts who'd drifted in and out of Susannah's life, had said with a hefty pinch of salt. No, it was, she suspected, because she had a *tendre* for him.

There. She'd admitted it. She'd behaved in just as silly a fashion as Susannah, allowing herself to be taken in by a man about whom she knew hardly anything at all. Apart from the fact that he was tall and manly. And rather curt in his ways with his female relatives. Oh, yes, and very nonchalant about discovering apparently dead bodies in the shrubbery.

Put like that, it wasn't much of a recommendation, was it?

'Oh, no,' breathed Susannah, as she set aside the ice she'd been longing to try and now denounced as completely unpalatable. 'The very last person I wanted to see.'

Rosalind followed the direction of her gaze, to see Lord Caldicot striding along the pavement. Her heart did a little bounce. Probably, she suddenly perceived, the kind of bounce that happened in Susannah's chest whenever she saw Mr Baxter.

He altered course when he saw them sitting in the carriage and came over.

'Out enjoying the lovely weather?'

'We have been shopping,' replied Susannah scornfully. 'As you might have gathered,' she added, indicating the boxes littering the floor of the barouche, 'if you had the slightest bit of intelligence.'

'Yes, but you are not shopping now,' he countered. Then his eye fell on the melting puddle in Susannah's dish. 'Never say you fell for the lure of the lavender ice?'

Susannah sucked in an indignant breath.

'Well, at least now you have learned it is completely inedible,' he finished cheerfully, before Susannah had a chance to tell him how unkind it was of him to taunt her. 'Waiter!' He snapped his fingers in the direction of the shop and, somehow, a waiter appeared as if by magic. 'Take this away and bring the ladies something more to their taste. What do you really like, Susannah?' he asked her.

She pouted and shifted in her seat, but finally admitted, 'Chocolate cake.'

'Then you shall have some.'

Susannah frowned at him with suspicion. 'Why are you being so affable today?'

'Well, perhaps I felt you deserved a reward. For being so kind to Miss Hinchcliffe. Taking her shopping is one thing, but treating her to tea and cake from Gunter's is going the second mile.'

I am here, Rosalind wanted to say, as they talked about her, rather than to her. But, of course, since she was merely an employee, she had to keep her mouth firmly closed.

'Oh.' Susannah was flushing. 'It is nothing, really. I… I wanted to come myself, you know,' she admitted.

'And did you,' he said, finally turning to Rosalind and speaking to her, 'wish to come to Gunter's and sample the ices?' He glanced down at her lap. 'I see you had too much sense to fall for the lavender ice, at least.'

An incoherent noise burbled from her lips. Typical! After she'd been resenting the fact that neither of them had been speaking to her, the moment he *did* address her, she lost the ability to reply. It was just… he was leaning on the railings, looking all…well… much more tempting than a dish of ice cream, anyway. And she'd just been thinking about how he made her heart flutter and how she oughtn't to trust him simply because of that.

'Miss Hinchcliffe has been a bit overwhelmed, I think,' put in Susannah, 'by all the money we've been spending on her. I keep trying to persuade her into satins and gauze, but she would much rather stick to her boring old kerseymere and calico.'

His eyes sharpened. 'You cannot possibly go into a ballroom in a gown made up of calico.'

'She was joking,' Rosalind replied on a surge of resentment. Did he really think her so foolish that she would attempt to do such a thing?

Probably. After all, he'd caught her trying to run off in the dead of night in the belief she'd killed a man with a copy of *Sense and Sensibility*.

Which was typical of her. She had a terrible tendency to act first, then regret what she'd done later. Over the last couple of years, while she'd been trying to persuade Susannah that it might be a good idea to try to control *her* temper, she'd thought she'd cured herself of that besetting fault as well. But had she?

'Ah, I can see the waiter coming with your chocolate cake,' said Lord Caldicot. 'So I shan't keep you ladies from your innocent pleasures any longer.' He tipped his hat and made to move away from the carriage.

'I wonder,' said Susannah as he strode off, 'where he is going. And how he is planning to spend his day.'

'I have no idea,' Rosalind replied, a little stung by the statement he'd made about their pleasures being innocent. Because it implied that his weren't.

Was there some lady, waiting for him in a discreet little...love-nest? Men of his rank kept such ladies, didn't they? In luxury.

Oh! How could she be sitting here thinking about a man with his mistress with anything but...disgust? How could she feel even a touch envious of whichever woman he might be spending an afternoon kissing and caressing? In return for financial gain? Had her wits gone wandering? Not to mention her morals!

'You look rather warm, Miss Hinchcliffe,' Susannah observed as she dug her fork into her slice of chocolate cake. 'Is the heat too much for you?'

'Um...yes. Yes, it is rather a warm day,' she said, flustered to have been caught out entertaining the most inappropriate thoughts. 'But I have a fan with me...' Lowering her head, she opened her reticule and avoided Susannah's perceptive gaze by becoming busy with locating, spreading and then employing her fan.

While Susannah enjoyed her cake, she mulled over the entire situation again, in the light of the revelation she'd just had. About the way Lord Caldicot made her feel. As if she might, just might, cast all her morals to the winds, for a chance to...to...

She snapped her fan shut. She already suspected

she might, just might, have made a mistake in believing Mr Baxter was evil and Lord Caldicot a paragon. She might well have been as mistaken as…as Susannah had been, taking the word of whoever it was who'd told her that she'd enjoy lavender ice cream. But then, how could any female make a sensible decision based on someone else's word, rather than on experience?

It was about time she started looking for some first-hand evidence regarding Mr Baxter, to observe him, if she had the chance, so that she could make up her own mind.

Because if Susannah really loved him, and he truly loved her, then what right had she, or anyone else, to keep them apart?

Chapter Nine

Michael shut the door on his study and went over to the table where Timms had thoughtfully set out a decanter of good brandy and some glasses. He felt as if he was going to need it, if he were to survive yet another evening as Susannah's escort.

To think that only two weeks ago, he'd frowned upon the amount of drink that men of the class he now inhabited consumed. Now, he could completely understand what drove them to do it. Since the night Miss Hinchcliffe had thrown Baxter off the balcony and they'd agreed to take turns guarding Susannah from any further approaches from undesirables of the same sort, he'd attended what felt like nineteen balls, twenty-four Venetian breakfasts and, worst of all, an entire evening during the course of which his ears had been assaulted by harpists, pianists and at least a brace of out-of-tune sopranos. One after the other. Relentlessly.

He poured himself a medicinal measure of brandy into the bottom of the glass. A finger to fortify himself against what lay in store for him that evening was one thing, but he needed to keep his wits about him.

It wasn't so much the watching of Susannah that was proving so difficult. The mere fact that he was in the ballroom, or drawing room, or wherever, was enough to deter the sort of men like Baxter, who looked upon green girls with large fortunes as pigeons for the plucking. While he was around, the kind of men who asked her to dance, or if they could fetch her glasses of lemonade or ratafia, were the kind who were her social equals and who seemed to genuinely find her appealing.

No, it was the matchmaking mothers who were making him feel as if he'd rather march over the Pyrenees, in the dead of winter, than stay in London during the Season. Because they kept on flinging their daughters in his path. Girls who were barely out of the schoolroom, for the most part, who didn't have a single opinion in their heads, or, if they did, took care not to let him suspect them of having any.

No, they all agreed with everything he said, looking up at him as though he was some sort of oracle.

He rather thought he was supposed to feel flattered by the way they gazed up at him and treated his every word as though he'd said something wonderful. Instead, it made him feel as though he was getting old.

He much preferred the way Miss Hinchcliffe told him exactly what she was thinking. When he could get her alone, that was.

In company she was as dull and decorous as any debutante. Well, apart from the occasional quirk of her lips, or slight lift to the eyebrows which was far more eloquent than any amount of so-called conversation he'd had with any of the so-called eligible girls he met.

He finally tossed back his drink in one go, moodily placing the empty glass back on the tray, when he heard the sound of female footsteps and feminine giggles descending the stairs. Because he was a man of duty and was determined to do his duty by Susannah, no matter what it cost him, he strode over to the study door and flung it open.

And came to a halt at the sight of not only Susannah and Lady Birchwood standing in the hall, fussing with cloaks, but also Miss Hinchcliffe, garbed from head to toe in a variety of shades of blue.

He'd never seen a more welcome sight.

'Miss Hinchcliffe! You are coming with us tonight?' What a stupid thing to say. Of course she must be, or she wouldn't be wearing a gown that revealed so much of her arms. And moulded her breasts, rather than disguising the fact that she had any, the way her workaday clothes did.

'Doesn't she look lovely?' gushed Susannah.

She certainly did. Now that she wasn't swathed from neck to ankle in something shapeless and unflattering, he could see that she had a splendid physique. Not all flabby and dimpled, like so many society ladies, but slender and toned. Though he might have guessed as much from the ease with which she'd knocked Baxter off the balcony, with only a book to use as ammunition.

'I look,' she said gloomily, 'like a scarecrow got up in the vicar's wife's cast-offs.'

'No, no, you don't,' said Susannah, in exasperation. 'Tell her, Lord Caldicot, that she looks fine as fivepence!'

'You look…' He sought for some appropriate words. But all of a sudden, all he could think was that if she had on a helmet and carried a spear in one hand and bore a shield over the other, she'd resemble the Greek goddess Athena. 'Formidable.'

'Thank you,' said Miss Hinchcliffe drily. 'Just what every woman wishes to hear.'

She looked so very much as if she was experiencing the same sort of feelings that he'd been suffering alone in his study just now that he took the cloak, which Timms was holding out to her, and went to place it round her shoulders himself, while Susannah's and Lady Birchwood's maids performed the same office for them. He might have nobody in whom to confide, but at least he could provide some support for a fellow sufferer.

'Isn't that the aim,' he reminded her, softly, in the hopes that the others wouldn't be able to overhear him, 'of this venture? Don't you want to be able to repel curs like Baxter with one withering glance?'

'You know, it's funny,' she replied, in a murmur to match his own, 'that the very first time I clapped eyes on my reflection, when wearing this turban, I was reminded of the myth of the Gorgon.'

Her response made him feel, for the first time since the night they'd concealed the fate of Baxter, as if he had a comrade in arms.

'Then you shall be the perfect chaperon,' he said. 'Which means that I will no longer have to endure many more evenings such as the one we are about to undergo.'

For a moment, he thought he could detect a look of panic in her eyes. Her breathing quickened. Was she going to beg him not to abandon her, on her first foray into society? He wanted to tell her that he had no intention of doing anything so shabby, no matter how tempting it might be.

But then she lifted her chin.

'You are making me feel so much better about going out this evening,' she replied, tartly. 'Should it be as tedious as you clearly expect it to be, I shall be able to alleviate my boredom by turning random young men to stone, with one glare.'

Oh, how he admired her pluck. She was clearly nervous, but she wasn't about to admit it, or betray it, to anyone. Instead, she was going to brazen it out, by making caustic comments such as that. Or self-deprecating ones about herself.

'Oh, how I wish,' he told her, 'you *did* have that power. Not that I particularly wish any of the young men any ill will, but there are one or two of the young ladies…who *giggle*,' he concluded on a shudder.

'How very irritating for you,' she replied with false sympathy.

Timms chose that moment to fling open the front door, through which he could see that the carriage stood waiting. And somehow, although only moments ago he'd thought he would seize upon any excuse to avoid going to Lady Templeton's ball tonight, now that he had the perfect one, in that Miss Hinchcliffe would be in attendance, he found himself taking her by the arm, and escorting her out of the house and into the carriage.

He liked Miss Hinchcliffe, he reflected as he took his seat beside her, facing his cousin's sister and his cousin's daughter. *She* didn't make him feel as if he was an elderly, wealthy, mark for marriage-minded schoolgirls. But like…well, himself. Or a version of himself, anyway. The one he really was deep down inside. Not the one he had to pretend to be now he was trying to behave like a marquess.

'Miss Templeton,' Lady Birchwood said to him, with a titter, as the carriage set off, 'will be *so* thrilled to see you tonight.'

'Why,' he replied, 'would that be?'

'Well, because of the particular interest you have shown her,' said Lady Birchwood archly.

'Have I?' No. He couldn't have done. He couldn't even recall what she looked like.

'Every time you have attended a ball,' put in Susannah, smoothing a tiny little wrinkle from her gloves, 'you have made sure to ask her to dance. Every single time.'

That was news to him.

'Everyone has noticed,' put in Lady Birchwood. 'Especially since you have not danced with any other young lady more than once.'

'Are we,' asked Susannah mischievously, 'to expect an announcement?'

'Because I happen to have danced with some chit, whose face I cannot even recall, more than once?' He shook his head. 'Don't talk such nonsense.' He was going to have to be more careful to mind who, exactly, he asked to dance if the fact that he'd inadvertently favoured one above all the others was causing comment.

'She's the *pretty* one,' said Susannah, looking a bit annoyed.

'Wealthy, too, don't forget, dear,' added Lady Birchwood. 'We don't blame you for preferring her to some of the others, if that is what has put you in a pelter.'

'That Lady Susan Pettifer, for example,' said Susannah, with a moue of distaste.

Ah, now, at least he could recall exactly who Lady Susan Pettifer was. 'I don't believe that saying her name is cause for you to pull that face, young lady,' he snapped. 'She, at least, has the virtue of being able to hold a rational conversation.' It was the one thing that made her stand out from the crowd. That, and the fact that she was clearly a little older than most of the others.

'Rational?' Susannah shook her head in mock pity. 'That girl has a tongue like a rapier. She enjoys nothing more than cutting everyone around her down to size!'

Well, he knew *that*. He hadn't said he *liked* her, had he? Only that he remembered who she was.

'It doesn't do to speak ill of another lady,' said Lady Birchwood, shooting Susannah a look of reproof.

'Even though,' Susannah argued, 'it's true?'

'Not if that lady may well become your guardian's wife,' said Lady Birchwood, giving him an arch look.

Susannah pouted, but fell silent. And thankfully before anyone thought of any more fatuous comments to make, they drew up outside Lord Templeton's London house.

He got out first, so was able to perform the service of helping all three ladies alight.

But the moment they'd gone to the ladies' cloakroom, to put off their shawls and put on their dancing shoes, he made a beeline for the card room.

Because, now that Miss Hinchcliffe was here, he could rely on her to look after Susannah's best interests. Besides, the only way to make sure he didn't raise false hopes in any female breast would be to keep well away from the lot of 'em.

Which suited him perfectly.

Chapter Ten

Rosalind watched him go with a sinking heart, for he'd led her to believe he'd be there to support her.

'See what you've done with all your teasing, Susannah?' Lady Birchwood said waspishly. 'You have made His Lordship run away to hide in the card room, just when I had such high hopes of seeing him come up to scratch.'

Run away? Was that what he'd done?

No! Whatever else he might be, he was no coward.

'I don't see why that has anything to do with me,' Susannah retorted. 'Besides, you spend most of the time, when we go anywhere, in the card room yourself!'

'That,' said Lady Birchwood loftily, 'is different. *I* will be going to the card room to catch up with my dearest friends. *I* am not hiding from anyone, or anything!'

And to the card room she went, leaving Rosalind and Susannah standing side by side at the edge of a room that seemed, to Rosalind, to be teeming with well-dressed, bejewelled, confident people. The cream, in fact, of society.

'I cannot believe,' said Susannah indignantly, 'that she just scolded me for making His Lordship uncomfortable, when *she* was the one who brought up the topic of him raising expectations in Miss Templeton's breast! But, oh, it is *just* like her! Like *all* my aunts, in fact. They...they start conversations and then, when I join in, they *rebuke* me. For agreeing with them! Oh, they make me so angry sometimes I could—'

'I shouldn't think,' Rosalind interjected, soothingly, 'you made His Lordship uncomfortable at all. He probably just enjoys playing cards.'

Susannah gave a derisive little laugh. 'Not he. Whenever he's been at a ball with us before, he's always gone straight over to the group of prettiest, most eligible girls, and systematically danced his way through them all.'

It was stupid to feel sad to hear that. She ought to feel pleased that she'd distracted Susannah before she'd descended into a fully-fledged tantrum. And of *course* Lord Caldicot would be looking for a wife. He had a duty to produce heirs to ensure continuance of his line. He might have *said* that he was only going to balls, et cetera, to keep a close watch on Susannah, since he clearly couldn't trust Lady Birchwood, who was much more concerned with her own enjoyment than keeping Susannah safe. But if that were the whole truth, he wouldn't need to ask so many girls to dance, would he? He could just stroll round the edge of the room, glowering at importunate suitors.

There! She'd made the same mistake again. Believing what he said, *completely*. Without question.

And yet…

'So, he doesn't appear to prefer any one of them,' she said, with a small flicker of hope, 'above any of the others?'

'Not *one*, no,' Susannah mused. 'I would say that at the moment there are three front runners. Miss Templeton, who you saw standing with her parents in the receiving line…'

The stunningly pretty, dainty girl who'd given Lord Caldicot a positively languishing look as he'd bowed over her hand.

'And Lady Susan, who I mentioned in the coach.'

The one with a spiteful tongue. Surely, he would not be seriously considering marrying someone like that?

'And then there's Miss Eastwick. Not as pretty as Miss Templeton, but her father is as influential as Lady Susan's and she is nowhere near as nasty.'

'Oh,' said Rosalind faintly, that brief glimmer of hope flickering and dying.

'But never mind *him*,' said Susannah, linking her

arm through Rosalind's. 'Let's go and find you a seat with the other chaperons.'

As they made their way across the room, she couldn't help noticing that Susannah was looking round at the other guests as though she was searching for one particular person. By the time they reached a group of chairs, stationed so that the occupants would have a good view of the dance floor, Susannah was looking rather woebegone.

'Miss Hinchcliffe,' she said, as Rosalind took a seat right at the end of the row, 'do you think I may have been mistaken? About Cecil? He has not made any attempt to see me since Lord Caldicot forbade the match. And surely, if he really loved me, he would not just…run away with his tail between his legs?'

What an opportunity! Now that Susannah had begun to express doubts about Mr Baxter, Lord Caldicot would, no doubt, expect her to deal the death blow to Susannah's infatuation. By implying he was a coward, or unworthy in some other way.

The trouble was, Rosalind knew *exactly* why Mr Baxter had not been to any balls or tried to see Susannah since that night. And it had nothing to do with how he felt about Susannah. It was because she, Rosalind, had injured him. Possibly seriously.

She glanced up at Susannah's unhappy face and discovered that she knew just how the poor girl must feel. Because she, too, was wondering if the man she admired so much was worthy of her total devotion. And, in her case, *knowing* that he was looking elsewhere, rather than merely suspecting it, might be the case.

'Perhaps,' said Rosalind, 'something has happened…not connected in any way with Lord Caldicot and what he said, or anything to do with his feelings for you…to prevent him from attending balls, or trying to contact you.'

'You mean, he may be unwell?'

Rosalind flinched. Mr Baxter was certainly very unwell. She could easily imagine him lying on a bed of pain, somewhere, as he recovered from his injuries.

But before Susannah could notice her uneasiness and she had to give an explanation for it, a group of young men came over, practically jostling each other out of the way as they vied for Susannah's attention.

It was exactly what Susannah needed. As the girl looked from one eager face to the other, all the misery and doubt she'd been expressing slid from her shoulders as though it was as insubstantial as a gossamer scarf.

'I will dance first,' she said, holding out her hand to a serious-looking dark-eyed man, in what looked like a naval uniform and whose face was disfigured by a couple of livid scars, 'with you, Lieutenant Minter.'

His jaw dropped. But after only a brief moment of looking as though he couldn't believe his luck, he seized her hand and tucked it possessively into the crook of his arm.

'And before the rest of you even ask,' Susannah added, 'Lieutenant Minter will be my partner for the supper dance, too.'

Susannah had mentioned this Lieutenant Minter once or twice when telling Rosalind about the balls and parties she'd gone to before Rosalind had been expected to attend as well.

And for a moment, Rosalind felt rather proud of Susannah, for what looked like an act of kindness. For thinking that since she couldn't dance with the man she really wanted to, she might as well spend her evening cheering up that disfigured veteran of the war with France instead.

But only for a moment. Because, as he led her on to the dance floor, she caught an expression on the girl's face that looked suspiciously like defiance.

Defiance? Oh, dear. What game was Susannah playing now? Was she trying to rebuff one of her other suitors, who were all watching her taking her place in the set, with varying degrees of disappointment? Or did she have something else in mind?

She watched the couple dancing keenly, in case she could detect something, anything that might give her a clue as to Susannah's motives in favouring him above the others. And began to wonder if it was simply that Susannah needed someone like Lieutenant Minter to gaze at her as though she was a goddess, far beyond the reach of a mere mortal man. Because that was what he was doing. Rosalind didn't know how he managed to avoid bumping into the other dancers, so reluctant was he to tear his gaze from Susannah's face for even a moment.

Rosalind sighed. It must be balm to Susannah's wounded pride, to have someone adore her so blatantly. None of the other men who danced with her, after that set finished, had anywhere near the intensity. They charmed, they flirted, they showed off their physical stamina and dexterity with all the leaping and hopping that most of the country dances demanded. But not one of the others gazed at Susannah with such a potent mixture of adoration and despair. As though she was a prize beyond his reach.

When it came time to cease dancing, and go in to supper, Rosalind also discovered that Lieutenant Minter was a very correct sort of young man. Because, rather than bearing Susannah into the supper room and taking advantage of the chance to snatch a few moments with her away from prying eyes, he brought her over to where Rosalind was sitting and held out his arm to offer his escort for her, too. And when they reached the supper room, once he'd found them a good seat, he fetched her a plate of delicacies, as well as serving Susannah, even though she worried that half of it was going to end up on the floor, so often did he glance over to where they were sitting, as if to make sure Susannah didn't disappear.

He had barely taken his own seat at their table when Lady Birchwood appeared, lured from the card room by the promise of refreshment, no doubt. Naturally, he stood up, as it was the polite thing to do. But then, to Rosalind's surprise, instead of greeting him, or acknowledging him in any way, Lady Birchwood waved him away with an impatient gesture of her fan. And took his chair. She had a smile on her face all the while, but Rosalind could tell from the glitter in her eyes that she was, for some reason, furious.

Susannah was smiling, too. But she was smiling in a way that put Rosalind in mind of a cat that has just caught a mouse in its paws.

The only person who looked as though he was not trying to pretend to feel something he didn't was Lieutenant Minter. He had taken his dismissal with a sort of grim resignation, as though it was exactly what he'd been dreading all along. Then he slouched out of the room in dejection.

Lady Birchwood shot Rosalind a look of barely repressed annoyance, although the smile returned almost at once, because, she suspected, a couple of Susannah's previously rejected suitors came over to set up a flirtatious conversation.

* * *

For the rest of the evening, Susannah danced every dance, with a fixed, yet to Rosalind's eyes, rather strained smile on her lips.

At long last, both Lady Birchwood and Lord Caldicot emerged from the card room, signifying it was time to return to Kilburn House. As they climbed into the coach Lady Birchwood finally let her smile drop. But when she glared at Susannah the girl returned a smile that was not only genuine, but also full of the same sort of defiance she'd displayed when accepting that dance with Lieutenant Minter.

Lady Birchwood sucked in an outraged breath.

Lord Caldicot, looking from one to the other, took in a breath of his own as though about to ask a question, then appeared to think better of it. In the end, the four of them conducted the entire journey home in a tense, simmering sort of silence.

When they reached Kilburn House, Lady Birchwood tottered, as though with extreme fatigue, to the foot of the stairs and took hold of the newel post.

'That girl,' she said to nobody in particular, 'will be the death of me.'

The girl in question flounced past her and ran up the stairs, presumably, by the sound of a door slamming, going straight into her bedroom.

'Miss Hinchcliffe,' said Lord Caldicot, 'would you mind attending me in my study before you retire?'

'Not at all,' she replied with alacrity. Apart from anything else, if she didn't, everyone would expect her to follow Susannah upstairs, and *'deal with'* her mood. So, she turned to follow Lord Caldicot as Timms went over to lend Lady Birchwood his arm to help her up the stairs to her own room.

'What,' said Lord Caldicot, the moment they reached the sanctuary of his study, 'has provoked the latest skirmish between my ward and her aunt?'

'You did.'

'I? I did nothing!'

'No, instead of dancing your way through all the prettiest debutantes, as is apparently your custom,' she said, allowing bitterness and disappointment to rule her tongue, 'you ran away and hid in the card room, just when Lady Birchwood had high hopes of you *"coming up to scratch"*. She said it was Susannah's fault for *"teasing"* you and Susannah said that was unfair since she'd started it.'

'And that,' he said with incredulity, 'kept them going all night?'

'Well, no, I think the quarrel might have languished had Susannah not flaunted Lieutenant Minter in Lady Birchwood's face.' Which, she was pretty sure by now, from Lady Birchwood's reaction to finding the young man sitting down to supper with them, was what Susannah had done. 'And I'm sorry,' she added, 'if Lieutenant Minter is another fortune hunter, from whom I should be protecting Susannah. And I don't know why,' she said, flinging decorum to the four winds by going over to the sofa and, without asking his permission, dropping heavily down on to it, 'you thought I could be of any use. I *liked* Lieutenant Minter,' she said defiantly. 'He seemed perfectly respectable to me. But what,' she said, tartly, 'do I know?'

She leaned her head back on the cushions and closed her eyes in a mixture of despair and exhaustion.

'At least *you* did not desert your post, no matter how hard you found your duties,' said Lord Caldicot, making her open her eyes and look to him with a slight lessening of the inadequacy she was feeling. 'From what I've been able to gather, this past couple of weeks, Lady Birchwood seems to think she has done enough by depositing Susannah among a group of equally silly girls and leaving them to their own devices while she goes off and enjoys herself. Which may well be how Baxter managed to get so close to Susannah.'

'Oh, dear.'

'Quite,' he said with feeling. 'Furthermore, it is only Lady Birchwood who considers the Lieutenant ineligible, not I. Well, not *completely* ineligible. He is, as I am sure you have gathered, a half-pay officer in the navy. With the war at sea faltering, it means he has few prospects of further promotion, or prize money. You know that promotion in the navy comes through merit, rather than purchase?'

She nodded.

'But worse than that, in her eyes, is the fact that he does not come from some old, or aristocratic, family, but merely from gentry stock.'

'But…that does not bother you?'

'Not, perhaps, as much as it should,' he mused, 'since my own mother was merely a doctor's daughter. And the thing is, not only is his service record exemplary, but, try as I might, I have not been able to find anything to his detriment, regarding his character or behaviour, since he's been on the town. Which is more than can be said for most men of his age.'

He held out a glass of brandy to her, which he must have poured while she was leaning back with her eyes closed.

'So, I need not,' she asked, as she accepted the glass, 'forbid Susannah from dancing with him?'

'Not on my account.' He swirled his own drink around, looking into his glass rather than starting to drink it. 'But if she really doesn't care for him, it might not be kind of her to encourage him too much. For if I'm not mistaken, he likes her rather too well. I would not approve of her carelessly breaking young men's hearts for sport.'

'No,' she said with conviction. 'Nor would I.'

'I suppose,' he said, 'that I need not ask you if *you* enjoyed your evening?'

'Enjoyed it?' She shuddered. 'Though I suppose,' she added morosely, 'at least I didn't have to dance, on top of everything else.'

'You don't like dancing? What an unusual young woman you are.'

She eyed him with some resentment. 'I have only really danced while having lessons, at school, which wasn't so bad. But I certainly don't think I would enjoy the kind of dancing I watched tonight. It was… relentless. All that skipping and hopping, and smiling at people over your shoulder to make your current partner jealous. I don't have the stamina for it,' she admitted. 'Nor the dexterity. And as for this turban…' She put her hand up to touch it, briefly. 'It wouldn't have stayed in place for five minutes. Perhaps that is why,' she mused, 'they make chaperons wear such ridiculous headgear. To remind them of their place, should they be tempted to join in the fun which belongs by rights only to the young.'

'You *didn't* enjoy the ball,' he said, with a chuckle, 'did you?' His face sobered. 'Look, if you really don't want to continue acting as Susannah's chaperon… and really, it was rather unfair of me to ask it of you.

I mean, I employed you to be her teacher, originally, didn't I, not her chaperon?'

'Oh,' she said, a wave of gratitude washing over her. How *kind* he was. How *considerate*.

'And it wasn't just the dancing,' he added, 'was it? Something else has upset you.'

'What makes you say that?'

'You said, *on top of everything else,*' he reminded her. 'So, what is it? What is troubling you?'

That, she sighed, was what made her like him so much. The way he noticed her. The way nobody else did, or ever had done. And was interested enough to ask her what troubled her, when nobody else cared.

It tempted her to confide in him. Though not, naturally, about how it hurt to think of him marrying one of those eligible girls. Or about wondering if he had a mistress in keeping, who he visited in the afternoons while innocents like she and Susannah went shopping and ate ices.

'I feel guilty,' she blurted out, while still in the throes of that heady mix of gratitude and yearning to be able to share *some* of her feelings with him.

'About what?'

'Not being honest with Susannah,' she admitted. Only then she remembered that he was the one who'd started her on this course, when he'd told her Susannah must never find out she'd caused Mr Baxter to fall from the balcony.

'Even though,' he said with a perplexed frown, 'it is in her best interests?'

'I know, I know,' she said, shaking her head over the brandy glass she still held in her hands, of which she hadn't taken one sip. 'Deep down, I do know it is best for her. It is just that the poor girl is under the illusion that Mr Baxter has just walked away without making even a single attempt to defy you. Which makes her fear he might be a coward. Or that he doesn't love her enough to fight for her.'

'So?'

'Well, it isn't true, is it? He did try to fight for her. He climbed in through my window...'

'The act of a rogue. You'd never catch a man like Lieutenant Minter climbing in through a girl's window. He'd stand outside, clinging to the railings, and just gaze at her as she went out, if he'd been forbidden from speaking to her.'

'Yes, but she doesn't know that. And even now, she thinks he is avoiding her, when really, he must be lying in a bed somewhere, nursing his injuries. Injuries that I caused...'

'Well-deserved injuries. If a chap tries to sneak in, what can he expect but a spirited rebuff?'

'Yes, but...oh, you are not even trying to understand!'

'I do understand,' he said more gently. 'You have a delicate conscience. It is to your credit that you are so sympathetic to the girl, but you are only doing what you need to, to protect her.'

Was she though? What if Mr Baxter was no worse than, say, Lieutenant Minter? What if Lord Caldicot's objections to that young man were no more substantial than Lady Birchwood's to the impoverished naval officer?

And how could she possibly find out?

Chapter Eleven

Rosalind didn't think she'd be able to get a wink of sleep, she had so many conflicting thoughts swirling round in her head at the same time.

But it seemed as though staying out so late at night had tired her out. For when the maid, Constance, came in to open her curtains she sat bolt upright, her heart pounding, with a bewildering sense of having only just laid her head upon the pillow.

When she looked at the clock, it informed her that it was almost midday.

'What?' she said in a hoarse voice that had her reaching for the glass of water at her bedside. 'Why have I been allowed to sleep in so late?' She flung aside the covers. 'I should have been about my duties hours ago.'

'Oh, it was His Lordship's orders,' replied Constance. 'He said as how you wasn't used to keeping late hours and we was to let you sleep as long as you needed.'

She was just starting to feel grateful for his consideration, when it dawned on her that she hadn't actually been allowed to sleep as long as she needed, or Constance wouldn't be in here drawing curtains and generally bustling about.

'So, why are you here? Not that I'm not grateful…'

'Coz Lady Birchwood wants to have a word with you,' she said, with a grimace.

Ah. She was about to be told off for allowing Susannah to dance twice with poor Lieutenant Minter, she suspected.

She was proved correct when Lady Birchwood launched into a long, involved account of why the Lieutenant was not a suitable person for Susannah to encourage.

Rosalind listened with her head bowed, her hands clasped at her waist. She made no excuses for not having tried to stop Susannah from dancing with whomever she'd wanted, the night before. For one thing, it sounded as though that was what the girl had been doing ever since the start of the Season, if Lady Birchwood was spending so much time in the card room with her own friends.

Once again, it made her understand just why Susannah lost her temper so often, when what little guidance she received from the people who were supposed to have her welfare at heart was so inconsistent. What was more, nobody had given Rosalind a list of those who might be welcomed and those who were not. The only person she'd known for certain ought to be prevented from getting anywhere near Susannah was Mr Baxter. And he hadn't put in an appearance.

Eventually Lady Birchwood ran out of complaints and said, 'Well? What have you to say for yourself?'

'I shall,' said Rosalind meekly, 'have a word with Susannah about Lieutenant Minter.' She'd intended to, anyway. Because she was pretty sure that although the Lieutenant looked upon Susannah with stars in his eyes, Susannah had encouraged him mostly because she'd known it would annoy Lady Birchwood. Which wasn't fair on the poor man.

'And perhaps,' Rosalind suggested, 'you could furnish me with a list of who is, and who is not, an acceptable partner, so that I do not make the same mistake again.'

'How tiresome,' sighed Lady Birchwood, closing her eyes for a moment or two as though the notion of picking up a pen and finding a sheet of paper had already exhausted her. 'But I suppose I shall have to do something of the sort, since you don't come from the kind of background where you would instinctively *know* a good catch from an ineligible partner.'

And nor do you, Rosalind silently seethed as Lady

Birchwood waved a languid hand in dismissal. *Or I wouldn't have had Mr Baxter climbing in through my bedroom window.*

Rosalind set about finding Susannah at once and eventually found her in the drawing room, sitting at the piano, shuffling through some sheet music in a distracted manner.

'How lovely to see you practising your piano pieces,' said Rosalind bracingly, hoping that leading with a compliment would put Susannah in a receptive mood.

Susannah, however, shot her a suspicious look. 'I haven't even begun yet.'

'No, but you were about to. Or at least, you were thinking about it, without me having to remind you, which is most commendable. In fact,' she added, shutting the door softly behind her, 'I am, on the whole, extremely pleased with your progress. *And* your behaviour…'

'But?' Susannah sat up a little straighter and lifted her chin.

'Well, it isn't my opinion, really. It is Lady Birchwood. She is very cross with me for allowing you to dance, twice, with Lieutenant Minter last night.'

'Good!'

'You wanted her to be cross with me?'

'What? Oh, no! I didn't mean for you,' Susannah

said, with contrition, 'to get into trouble. I just wanted to annoy her.'

'I thought as much. And, though I sympathise with you, because, really, the way she spoke to you after the conversation in the coach, which, as you pointed out, *she* started…' She paused as she realised her sentence had become as muddled as the various sheets of music, which, as far as she could see, were all from different sonatas.

With a rueful shake of her head, she started again.

'That is, from observing Lieutenant Minter last night, I gained the impression that he rather…um… worships you. He looked at you as though…'

Susannah began to look confused as well. 'What are you trying to say?'

'Well, do you think…um…it is *kind* to use the poor young man to score points off your aunt, when he is so susceptible to being hurt?'

Susannah pouted. 'I won't hurt *him*,' she scoffed. 'I couldn't possibly. I mean, he is a hero of all sorts of battles at sea.'

'Oh, no doubt he is terrifically brave in *that* respect. But in matters of the heart, he may be, well, I mean, I don't suppose he has had the chance to mix with many pretty girls, with all the years he spent at sea. And he does appear to have fallen for you rather hard.'

Susannah plucked a random sheet of music from

the pile on top of the piano and set it on the music stand.

'I don't want to be unkind,' she eventually admitted. Then sighed. 'I suppose I had better not encourage him to think he has any hope of me returning his affections, hadn't I?'

'I think that would be the kindest thing to do,' said Rosalind, with relief. 'If you don't think you can love him…'

'Well, how can I possibly? My heart belongs to Cecil!' She faltered. Blushed. 'That is, it *did*. But now I am starting to wonder if…if…much as I hate to say it, Lord Caldicot might have been right to say he is unworthy. I mean, if he really loved me, wouldn't he have…have walked through fire, just to catch a glimpse of me?'

Not if he was nursing half a dozen broken bones, no. Not that Rosalind could say that out loud.

'As I said last night, there could be any number of reasons why you have not seen him, which have nothing to do with anything Lord Caldicot has said or done,' she said. 'That is, gentlemen do go out of town, occasionally don't they, to attend race meetings, or…'

'Race meetings!' Susannah's eyes flashed dangerously. 'Are you suggesting that he would go off to a race meeting when things are at such a difficult stage in our relationship?'

'Well, no, I was just trying to think of some reason,

of something that might have taken him out of town.'
Which didn't involve admitting the truth. 'I mean,
Lord Caldicot has to go off, at a moment's notice
to attend to sudden pressing business on his estate,
occasionally, doesn't he?'

'Cecil doesn't have an estate.'

'No? Does he—I beg your pardon, but I know so
little about him, really.' And while Susannah was
looking at him a bit more clearly, this could be the
perfect time to find out more. To find out if he might
be a struggling artist, for example, without having to
mention the fact that she'd heard him muttering the
word *turpentine*. 'Does he…work for a living?'

'Work?' Susannah looked shocked. 'Of course not!
He is a gentleman.'

But even a gentleman might, discreetly, paint por-
traits though, mightn't he? To help eke out his slender
fortune. Or even because he loved art.

'Although,' Susannah added, with a frown, 'he did
mention something about having expectations, when
he asked me to marry him. So I suppose he might
have had to go and deal with some sort of business
connected with that. Though why,' she said, standing up suddenly, scattering sheet music in all direc-
tions, 'he couldn't have at least *written* to me, to let
me know…'

She paced across the room. 'Although I dare say
Lord Caldicot would have prevented me from receiv-

ing any such letter.' She stilled. Turned. 'Has he, do you think…?'

'I am sorry, but to the best of my knowledge Mr Baxter has not made any attempt to get a letter to you.'

Susannah's face tightened. 'How he could have left me to worry about him…with things at such a pass…' She turned and paced back to the piano.

Rosalind supposed she ought to be pleased that Susannah had progressed from pining for Mr Baxter to becoming annoyed with him for disappearing, but watching those sheets of music scatter all over the carpet somehow made her think of him tumbling out of the window and landing in an untidy heap in the bushes. And all she could feel was guilt.

'If only,' said Susannah, striking one fist into the palm of her other hand, 'I could find out where he is and what he's doing!' She went very still. Turned to look at Rosalind. 'Miss Hinchcliffe,' she said.

Oh, no. She'd come up with another of her notions. Rosalind could foresee the girl using her pin money to hire someone to track Mr Baxter down. Which would mean it would all come out.

Luckily, before Susannah could get as far as telling her what idea it was that had struck her just then, someone knocked at the door.

'Beg pardon, miss,' said Constance, poking her head round the door. 'But Mr Timms said as how

I was to let you know that you have some callers. And…er… Lady Birchwood hasn't come out of her room yet, so I was to check that Miss Hinchcliffe can be present to lend propriety to the proceedings.'

Susannah groaned. 'I don't want to see anybody.'

'Well, some of the gentlemen are very good looking,' said Constance, rather cheekily.

'Oh?' Susannah looked a little less bored.

'I expect it is some of the gentlemen with whom you danced last night,' said Rosalind. 'Don't they usually visit the next morning, with posies and such like?'

'Yes,' said Susannah pensively. And then looked thoughtful. 'Yes, they do.' She dashed over to the mirror, patted at her curls, tweaked the lace at her neckline, then took her seat at the piano. 'You may show them up,' said Susannah. 'For as you can see, Miss Hinchcliffe is already here, supervising me at my *piano practice*,' she said, giving Constance a meaningful look.

'Susannah,' Rosalind said as soon as Constance left the room.

'Not now,' Susannah snapped, spreading her fingers over the keys. 'I must start playing a few notes, at once, since Constance will be telling them I'm practising, so they must hear me as they come up the stairs, mustn't they?'

There was no faulting that logic. But Susannah's

decision not to confide in her did not bode well for whatever it was that had come into her head before.

She couldn't shake off that sense of foreboding over the next hour or so, even though, on the surface, Susannah behaved like a young lady who didn't have a care in the world, and who was simply enjoying the attentions of all the gentlemen who came to pay their respects and deliver their posies.

She behaved with such propriety that all Rosalind had to do was to sit in a corner, watching them come and go.

Which only deepened Rosalind's unease.

Eventually, Lieutenant Minter came in. He clenched his jaw when he saw Susannah talking with animation to two other gentlemen, one of whom was Lord Wapping. And then, like a man resigned to his fate, he came to sit next to Rosalind and spent the half-hour of his visit struggling to make polite conversation with her. Which was more than any of the others had done, though his clumsy attempt to make small talk, along with his complete inability to stake any sort of claim on Susannah's attention, confirmed her suspicions that he was not very experienced with ladies. Only when it was time for him to leave did he approach the piano stool where Susannah was holding court and bow over her hand.

She pouted up at him. 'Oh, are you leaving already?

How vexing! When I particularly wished to speak with you!'

'Well, I, well, you know,' he stammered. 'Half an hour is considered…'

'I tell you what you should do,' Susannah supplied, when it was clear that poor Lieutenant Minter was out of his depth. 'You should call and take me for a drive in the park later on.'

'Oh, I say,' cried several of the other men there. 'How unfair! When we asked you ourselves and you refused!'

'Ah, but you have all had plenty of time to talk to me and he has had none. You quite cut him out. Isn't that the correct expression,' she said, looking up at him and fluttering her eyelashes shamelessly, 'Lieu-tenant?'

'Ah, yes,' he breathed, gazing at her as though all his birthdays had come at once.

What on earth, Rosalind fumed, was Susannah playing at? Singling the Lieutenant out, again, when she'd promised she was not going to hurt him?

'He doesn't,' put in Lord Wapping, with disdain, 'even have his own carriage.'

'I can soon hire one,' the Lieutenant retorted.

His look of determination was so ferocious that for the first time Rosalind could see exactly how he'd had such a successful career in the navy. He would never consider any obstacle too great to overcome. He would always, to judge by the set of that jaw, come up with some stratagem to surmount it.

'There, that's settled,' said Susannah.

Making Rosalind's heart sink. As if injuring Mr Baxter, physically, was not bad enough, now it looked as though yet another young man was about to become a casualty of Susannah's Season.

Where was it all going to end?

Chapter Twelve

'It's no use looking at me like that,' Susannah protested as she stalked out of the drawing room once the last caller had left the house.

'But you promised,' Rosalind said as Susannah went into her room.

'If I am to persuade Lieutenant Minter that he has no hope,' Susannah said, tugging on the bell rope to summon her maid, 'then shouldn't I give him just one treat, first?'

'He isn't a dog, Susannah! You cannot talk of tossing him treats!'

'Well, not a treat, then,' Susannah replied as she went to her armoire and opened the door. 'I should have said, a proper explanation.' She pulled out a pale green spencer and began rummaging among her dresses, for, Rosalind presumed, the carriage dress that went with it.

'For I *do* want to explain things properly,' she said,

abandoning her search through the dresses to pull out
a hatbox, open it and take out a creation covered with
a profusion of flowers and feathers. 'And for that, I
need privacy. Which a girl can only get when out driving with a gentleman in something like a phaeton. I
know you advised me that sitting at a piano would be
conducive to a little privacy,' she said, discarding the
feathered headdress and pulling down another hatbox
from the top shelf, which meant she didn't see Rosalind flinch with a pang of guilt.

For she had, indeed, told the headstrong girl, when
she'd declared she couldn't see the point of learning
to play any musical instrument, that playing the piano
would be a useful tool in the art of flirting with men.
She'd reminded her that a potential suitor would be
able to draw close enough to her to whisper things
nobody else could overhear, on the pretext of turning
the pages of music, for example. But she'd only said
that because she couldn't think of any other way to get
her to practise, not because she approved of flirting.

'But a piano,' said Susannah, taking out a bonnet with a pale green ribbon round the crown and
smiling, since it was an exact match for the spencer,
'must always remain in a room, containing all sorts
of people, so that any of them might overhear things
I wouldn't wish them to know.'

'That's all very well, but…'

'Besides,' Susannah added with a mischievous grin,

'I don't want it to look as though I am obeying Aunt Birchwood's stricture straight away, do I? How tame would that appear? As though I have no backbone!'

'Nobody who knows you at all,' Rosalind observed, 'could possibly accuse you of not having any backbone.'

Fortunately, Susannah was in a sunny mood and chose to be amused by that comment, rather than annoyed.

'Now, since there will be no room for you in the phaeton,' Susannah continued, as Pauline came in, 'why don't you take the afternoon off?'

Rosalind could certainly do with a lie down in a darkened room, recouping her strength for the evening ahead. And, since there was nothing further she could say in front of the maid, she drifted out of Susannah's room and into her own, which was just next door.

On the table, she spied a sheet of paper, covered with Lady Birchwood's distinctively spidery handwriting. The list, she sighed, of the men that Lady Birchwood considered ineligible and whom she must therefore discourage.

She picked it up, sank to her reading chair and glanced through the almost illegible list of ineligibles with a sigh. It looked as though she was going to have to acquire the skills of something like a tight-rope walker, to be able to maintain the delicate balance between annoying neither Susannah, nor Lady Birchwood, and all while fending off hordes of importunate men clamouring for permission to dance.

She was definitely going to need some time to herself, both to decipher this list of names and commit it to memory, and to recruit some stamina for the ordeal that clearly lay ahead of her.

But then she changed her mind. It was as she was standing on the front step, watching the Lieutenant hand Susannah into a rather shabby little curricle while the groom he must also have hired from somewhere to lend propriety to the proceedings held the heads of a pair of dispirited-looking hacks, that it struck her that she'd never had the chance to just go out on her own since they'd come to London. Every single outing here had been in the company of Susannah, either as a chaperon, or as a puppet for her to dress up.

A delicious breeze was making the branches of the trees that grew in the square bob about almost as though they were dancing. The sun was shining. And she really did need to return the three volumes of *Sense and Sensibility* to the circulating library at some time. On reflection, she would much rather do so without having to explain to a third party just how volume two had ended up looking so battered.

It didn't take her long to choose a hat to go with *her* outfit. She had only the one for day wear, a serviceable straw bonnet which shaded her eyes, framed her face and covered her hair into the bargain. Having tied it securely under her chin, she picked up her books, informed the footman who was loitering in the hall where she was going and set off in the direction of Bond Street.

She had only walked for a few minutes, when she gave a huge sigh. She'd made the right decision to get outside for a walk, she decided, as she felt a huge great weight of care roll from her shoulders. She rarely had a moment to herself. She was always at someone's beck and call. So, to be outside, walking along, and at her own pace at that, felt like an immense treat, even if it wasn't to admire the bluebells in the woods that surrounded Caldicot Dane, or to pop into the village post office to collect letters from friends she'd made at school, who still corresponded with her.

Once she'd exchanged her books, if the librarian would permit her to take any more out, after returning the last set in such a state, she could...well, what could she do in London? She could stroll in a park, she supposed, though it wouldn't have the same soothing effect as the woodlands of Caldicot Dane. Or go to Gunter's for tea and cake, though she wouldn't know anyone to chat to, or just wander along the street looking into shop windows at all the fripperies she couldn't afford.

Oh, yes, that would be grand, wouldn't it? Knowing her luck, someone would mistake her for a woman of loose morals if she went strolling through a park and she wouldn't be able to find a table if she went to Gunter's.

Still, once she had a new book to read, she could travel into the realm of imagination, as she delved into the adventure of the heroine. Much better. And much safer.

The encounter with the clearly irritated and dreadfully patronising man to whom she had to return her books went about as badly as she'd expected. For one awful moment she even feared he was going to refuse her permission to take out any more. But she'd paid her subscription, or at least, Lord Caldicot had done so on her behalf, and was still, according to the rules, entitled to borrow six more books.

Having survived that encounter, Rosalind made her way to the reading room to browse the shelves. She could make her choice from the catalogue, of course, but it was so pleasant to wander along the shelves of books, dreaming of the endless possibilities for entertainment or enlightenment hidden within the covers.

What would it be like to have her own library, stacked from floor to ceiling with books she had chosen herself, rather than relying on the taste of the man who'd purchased them? So lost was she in daydreams of her own, personal, perfect library, while contemplating the pleasures and possibilities she had to look forward to from the one she was actually in, that before long she didn't notice anyone else was in the room.

That impression was shattered when, just after she'd pulled a book, intriguingly entitled *The Miser and his Family*, from the shelf, someone addressed her directly.

'Miss Hinchcliffe, if I am not mistaken?'

She looked up, startled to be addressed by name by what sounded to her ears like a total stranger. And saw a man whose face was a mass of greenish bruises and whose arm was supported by a sling, making her what she could only assume was an ironic bow.

'Mr Baxter?' Her stomach turned over with guilt to see him looking so bruised and battered.

Oh, dear. What could he possibly want?

Well, obviously, he must be furious with her for reducing him to this state.

Which thought made her cling a bit more tightly to the book she'd just selected, though she really hoped she wouldn't need to use it.

He followed the movement of her hand with a wry smile.

'My dear lady,' he said, in an oily voice, 'you have no need of a shield. Indeed, you never had any need to attempt to defend yourself from me. I mean you no harm. I never have. And I am only sorry that I startled you so badly last time I attempted to get you alone.'

What? Was he saying that he'd climbed in through *her* window, on *purpose*? That he hadn't mistaken his way to Susannah's room at all?

'I can see I have surprised you,' he said, looking terrifically pleased with himself. 'But don't you think we *ought* to be allies?'

'Allies?'

'Yes,' he said, shifting a bit closer and lowering his voice. Since Rosalind was already standing with her back to a bookshelf, she had nowhere to go. Which meant she'd have to listen to whatever he wanted to say. Unless she thwacked him with the book she was holding and made good her escape.

Only…hadn't she decided that acting before thinking things through was generally a mistake? And that, moreover, she ought to find out if he really loved Susannah and try to discover what sort of man he was. For her own peace of mind. And what better chance was she ever likely to have?

Nevertheless, she was glad she had a hefty tome to hand. Just in case.

Mr Baxter took a quick look round the room, as if to make sure nobody could overhear what he was about to say. Which didn't bode well. But she'd decided to hear him out. She owed him that much, after injuring him so badly, didn't she? And Susannah, too. If they really loved each other...

'That night,' he hissed. Yes, hissed, in a manner that put Rosalind in mind of a snake. 'I had come to put a proposition to you. The family's opposition to the match is extremely stupid, don't you think? For it is based on foolish things like status. They don't really have Susannah's best interests at heart, do they? They take no account of how painful it is to be young and in love.' He then did something with his face that put her in mind of a spaniel. All sort of woeful and pleading.

'And look,' he continued, 'I know it cannot be easy for you, working for a girl of Susannah's temperament. Very few have stayed with her as long as you. Which means, I suspect, that you have no alternative. Or at least, that your options are limited.'

Surely a man who was in love would not speak in such a way about the object of his affections?

'Furthermore, once Susannah marries you will be out of even the job you have, is that not so? New husbands do have a tendency to dispose of women in your position as soon as they can. Especially if, as you have, they have gained a reputation for being a bit of a dragon. Out the door in a flash! And then you will have to go through the sordid process of seeking new employment.'

That was, of course, depressingly true. She'd been

aware of it from the very start of Susannah's Season. Coming to London at all was only, to be honest, a sort of reprieve, because she really ought to have started looking for a new post the moment Susannah's family decided she had no further use for a governess. In fact, what she ought to have done with this unexpected afternoon off was to have gone back to the agency she'd signed on with before, to let them know she might soon be in need of a new position and to keep her name in mind should anything suitable turn up.

'But I think,' he continued, 'no, I *know* I can be of help there.'

'You know of some other family in want of a governess?'

He grinned. 'Better than that. If we put our heads together, I can make sure you will never have to work again.'

'How,' she said in disbelief, 'do you think you could accomplish anything of the sort?'

'Well, it would be a kind of quid pro quo kind of deal.'

'Deal?' She felt her hackles rise.

'Yes, shall I spell it out?'

'I think you had better,' she replied in mystification.

'It is simple, really. You have it in your power to either grant or deny me access to your charge. Once I regain my looks and can go about in public again, you need only ease my way into her orbit and I shall soon get my ring on her finger. And then…'

'And then what?'

'Well, once I get my hands on the prize, I shall be sure to share the loot with you. Set you up in a neat little cottage, with an annuity. No other suitor, may I add, would make you anything like so generous an offer.'

'I am sure you are right,' she said, stunned by the way his mind worked. For it would not occur to any man who genuinely cared for Susannah to think of her as a commodity he could do a deal over. 'But how can you speak of loving Susannah, in one breath, then speak of her in terms of a prize, in the next?'

His eyes narrowed, as though sensing, finally, that she wasn't as interested in his deal as he'd assumed she'd be.

'I think,' she said, 'that the only thing you love, or are capable of loving, is money.'

'That isn't true,' he retorted. 'I love Susannah with all my heart. And if my words are not those of a poet, it is only that I am a forthright sort of chap.'

'So forthright that you climbed in through a window of the house when you *knew* she was out,' she said, suddenly wondering why that hadn't occurred to her before, 'to attempt to strike a deal with the one person you know could really stand in your way.' Because Susannah listened to her advice. Because

Susannah had learned that Rosalind wasn't put off by her moods. That, on the contrary, she understood and sympathised with what brought them about in the first place.

'It is all very well for you to be so high and mighty,' snarled Mr Baxter. 'You don't know what it is like to have to do without the necessities of life!'

'Fustian!' She'd wager he'd never spent time in an orphanage, fighting over the meagre rations available. 'Hardly high and mighty—what woman would choose to work for a living if she didn't have to?'

'But I am offering you the chance to retire! If you help me win Susannah's hand, I can make sure you can live in comfort and idleness for the rest of your life!'

She didn't want to live in idleness for the rest of her life, not if it meant betraying Susannah! The girl might be, on the surface, a bit selfish and thought-less, but deep down she wasn't malicious, not in the way she sensed Mr Baxter was malicious.

Hadn't she agreed to stop fostering false hope in Lieutenant Minter's heart and seemed genuinely re-luctant to hurt him? And, when he'd come to call in that shabby, hired curricle, even though wealthier men had offered to take her out in their smart phaetons, she hadn't shown any sign of disappointment or dis-dain, had she?

What was more, there had already been too many

people who had professed affection for her, then shown it didn't run all that deep. One aunt after another had come to Caldicot Dane, showering Susannah with kisses and treats, only to walk away the moment she became what they called 'difficult'.

Oh, Rosalind knew only too well what it felt like to have family members tell her she was 'unmanageable'. Which was why she'd ended up having to work as a governess, instead of having a debut ball and hopes of marriage. Even when Susannah had deliberately provoked Rosalind, as though attempting to drive her away, she'd felt it was important to show her that at least one person didn't think she was as bad as so many kept telling her she was. That Rosalind, for one, wasn't even tempted to leave. That she didn't think Susannah was 'unbearable' in the slightest.

And she wasn't. Yes, she had a temper. Yes, she could be a bit wilful, but she most definitely deserved better than Mr Baxter.

Well, any woman did! *No* woman deserved a husband of the sort Mr Baxter would prove to be. A man who looked upon his bride in the light of a sudden windfall that would solve all his financial difficulties.

'I am sorry,' she said firmly, though it was a matter of form to say so. She was not the slightest bit sorry about what she was about to say. 'But I cannot help you.'

'You could if you wanted to!'

'Yes, but I don't want to.'

'Why not? I have offered you everything you want, in exchange for just a few moments of looking the other way…'

'Apart from any other consideration,' she said, 'I don't trust you. You may *say* that you would set me up for life, but from what I know of you…'

'You think I would go back on my word?'

She said nothing. Only gave him her sternest, coldest look.

She saw it have its effect. The spaniel look disappeared. And in its place came something rather ugly.

'You will be sorry you made an enemy of me this day,' he said. Rather dramatically.

'I don't think so,' she said dismissively and shoved at him, hard, in the stomach, with the book she'd been clutching.

And then, when he reeled back, winded, she stalked out of the room with her nose in the air, trying hard not to imagine the look of loathing he must be hurling at her back.

Chapter Thirteen

Michael drew off his gloves as he began to climb the front steps of the house he still thought of as belonging to his cousin, the Marquess of Caldicot, feeling the by now familiar weight of it all bearing down on him the nearer he got to the front door.

It was all he could do to keep mounting the steps, steadily, as though it was the most natural thing in the world, when what he'd much rather do was go back to the set of rooms he'd hired last time he'd been in London. Just off Half Moon Street. They'd been a bit shabby and a bit cramped, but he could just toss his gloves on to a table when he went into his front door and know he could find them still there when he wanted to go out again.

The man who'd served him there had looked after his clothes and whatnot, but not to the extent of taking them from him at the door and stowing them away somewhere he couldn't lay his hands on them at a moment's notice. And it was just the one man. Not a butler, half a dozen footmen, and a valet, not to mention the coach driver, grooms and what have you loitering about in the mews.

And that was before he got to the legions of female staff his cousin, Lady Birchwood, and her niece seemed to think were an absolute necessity. And here was one of them now. Marching along the pavement with a militant glint in her eye and her fists clenched.

Although the sight of *her* did not depress him. On the contrary. Of all the people he'd become responsible for, since stepping into his pompous cousin's shoes, she alone was always able to bring a smile to his face.

'Good morning, Miss Hinchcliffe,' he said as she began stomping her way up the front steps.

'Is it?' She shook her head.

It hadn't felt all that good before he'd seen her, but now he noticed that the sun was shining, there was a pleasant breeze stirring the air, and that all the trees sported leaves that reminded him of brightly dressed ladies in a ballroom fluttering their fans.

'Hmm, technically,' he said, drawing his watch from his waistcoat pocket, 'it is afternoon, I agree.'

'Hmmph,' she said crossly.

'Dare I ask where you have been, or what has happened to put you out of sorts?'

'As to where I have been…well, I went to Hook-ham's library.'

'And yet you have no books in your hand. I take it that they took umbrage at the state of the books you were returning and refused to let you borrow another one?'

She looked down at her hands, in a bewildered manner. 'I came out of the library without any books? Oh. That is the outside of enough! *That man…*'

He felt as if his ears pricked up, if such a thing could be said of a human being. 'Which man?'

She gave him a look heavily laced with revulsion. 'Need you ask?'

'I think,' he said, taking her by the elbow, 'that we had better take this discussion off the front steps and into my study.'

'I couldn't agree more,' she said.

His feet no longer dragged at the prospect of getting inside this house. Not with Miss Hinchcliffe on his arm. Not when he knew he was about to have a conversation that would neither bore nor irritate him.

'So,' he said, once he'd gone through the ritual of surrendering his gloves, hat and coat to Timms, listening abstractedly to the messages the butler wanted to give him and then explaining why he was not going to do anything about any of them until he'd attended to Miss Hinchcliffe, in his study, 'what did *that man* do? Surely, not all that much, in the hallowed pre-cincts of Hookham's?'

'You would be surprised at the audacity he is ca-pable of demonstrating,' she said darkly, before fling-ing herself down on the chair before his desk, her feet, rather shockingly, straight out in front of her rather than neatly tucked to one side. 'He accosted me in the reading room and made me a proposition that so…so angered me that I hit him with the near-est book to hand.'

He supposed he ought to go and sit behind his desk and make this like a formal interview. His cousin would certainly have done so, had he ever had a woman like Miss Hinchcliffe on her own in here. So naturally, he wandered over to the table under the window, where there were several promising-looking decanters and a matching pair of cut-glass tumblers set out on a tray.

'He accosted you? In the reading room? I would not have thought that possible. Was there nobody else there to intercede?'

He poured two drinks. Well, there were two glasses and two of them in here, and she certainly looked as though she could do with a drink.

'Oh, well, he was so…sneaky about it, that anyone watching us would probably have thought we were having an assignation,' she said, with a curl to her lip.

'So he didn't *physically* attack you.' He handed her the drink.

'Oh, no. I beg your pardon. Was that what you thought? No, he is far too…cunning for that,' she mused, taking the drink from him in an absent-minded way, as though she scarcely noticed she was doing so. 'No, it was, as usual, *I* who resorted to violence.'

'Well, with all those weapons to hand,' he couldn't resist teasing her, 'I am not surprised you made use of one of them.'

She took a swig of the brandy, then coughed. Reached into her reticule for a handkerchief and wiped her streaming eyes. 'One of the most annoying things about it was that I'd just decided to listen to him *calmly.*'

He shook his head in mock reproof as he propped himself against the front edge of the desk. 'Habits, once formed, are very hard to break, aren't they?'

She gave him a baleful look. 'Hitting a man twice with a book hardly constitutes a habit. Especially when the first time was an accident.'

'No doubt he fully deserved it.'

'Well, of course he did!'

'And would you care to tell me what it was he did, if he didn't physically assault you, that rendered him worthy of such treatment again today?'

She glanced down at the glass as if considering taking another sip. Grimaced, as though thinking better of it, and raised her head. 'Well, for one thing, he confessed that the reason he climbed in through my window was not, as we had supposed, to try to persuade Susannah to elope with him.'

'No?' He found that hard to credit.

'No.' She twisted her mouth as though tasting something unpleasant. 'He said that he wanted to speak to me, alone, in order to persuade me to take part in a…what he called a *deal*. To get Susannah to the altar.'

'Then all those flowers he had stuffed down his waistcoat were not a romantic gesture aimed at my ward?' No. If he'd had no intention of seeing Susannah that night, it meant he'd brought them for *her*. For Miss Hinchcliffe.

He didn't like the thought of that. He didn't like it at all. It was bad enough the fellow sneaking around after his ward, but to imagine him trying to…to *woo* Miss Hinchcliffe made him want to go straight round to wherever he was lurking, grab him by the neck and shake him until his teeth rattled.

'It was an attempt to butter me up, I dare say,' she said with revulsion. Completely refusing to regard the way that man had bought her all those flowers, and climbed up to her window, as romantic. Which most women probably would.

But she, to his approval, was frowning. 'Why mention those flowers, when I have just told you that he was going to attempt to…to *pay* me to let him get at Susannah?'

Yes. Why had he taken such exception to the thought of that man bringing her flowers?

Why had the whole day seemed brighter just because he'd caught a glimpse of her, come to that?

He pushed aside those stray thoughts, as the irrelevancies that they were.

'Well,' he answered her, 'I always did wonder why on earth he'd stuffed all those roses down the front of his waistcoat. And it seems even more peculiar now, if he was about to offer you money.' He gave a short, mirthless laugh. 'And what was he going to say he would pay you with? The man has so many debts I am surprised he is still at liberty.'

'Oh, he was going to use Susannah's money, naturally,' she said tartly, 'once he'd got his greedy hands on it.'

'Ah.' He shook his head. 'How very predictable of him.'

'Really? You knew he was the sort of man who would stoop to…sneaky, underhanded means to try to get his hands on Susannah's money?'

'Oh, yes. Which is one of the reasons I refused him permission to attempt to fix his interest with her in the first place. And told her in no uncertain terms that I would never allow them to marry.'

'Not because he is a…struggling artist?'

'Artist? Whatever makes you think he's an artist?'

'Well, I cannot think of any other reason why the first word he said when he began to recover should be turpentine.'

'Turpentine,' he said wryly, 'I have recently discovered, is the name of a horse which plodded home last even though it was firm favourite. I should imagine Baxter lost a great deal of money on it if it was preying on his mind to that extent.'

'And *he* said your objections were all based on, well, I suppose you'd call it snobbery! And after what Lady Birchwood said about him only being a younger son with no prospects and then how angry she became over the way Susannah favoured Lieutenant Minter, for a moment there, I almost believed him.'

Almost. But he was glad to see she was too intelligent to be taken in by a plausible rogue for very long.

'But it is because,' she said, 'he is addicted to gambling, then, isn't it?'

Not altogether, no, but he wasn't about to go into the other, more unsavoury aspects of the man's character he'd learned from asking around.

'Lady Birchwood,' he said, 'may dislike the notion of a union with Lieutenant Minter, but I would never forbid the match to such a man, if Susannah really felt something for him. I might try to warn *him* what *he* was getting into…'

'Susannah isn't as bad as you are making her sound,' she said with indignation. 'She may be spoiled and selfish, but she doesn't have a malicious nature. She would never set out to hurt someone deliberately, for fun, the way I've heard many society misses do. And when I pointed out that she ought not to toy with the Lieutenant, if she really couldn't see herself falling in love with him, she said she was going to stop encouraging him. Which she'd only been doing to annoy Lady Birchwood, you know. She had no idea the man was truly smitten.'

'Yet I saw her, not an hour ago, sitting up beside him in a curricle, going round Hyde Park, chattering away like a magpie, while he was gazing at her with such adoration I was surprised the horses didn't stray on to the verge.'

'Oh, dear. She said she was going to tell him that she couldn't return his feelings during this drive.'

'Perhaps,' he suggested, seeing her distress, 'she hadn't quite got round to it yet when I saw them.'

She sighed. 'Or perhaps she was enjoying herself too much to remember that she was supposed to be letting him down gently.'

'Were you,' he couldn't resist asking, 'tempted by Mr Baxter's offer? At all?'

She snorted with indignation. 'Absolutely not! Apart from anything else—' She stopped short, looking rather guilty.

'Please continue. You cannot leave me in suspense.' And he was pretty certain that he'd find whatever it was she'd hesitated to tell him vastly entertaining.

'Well,' she said grudgingly, 'it occurred to me that even if I had gone along with his plan, there was no guarantee that he would actually part with the unspecified sum of money he offered me. He is the sort of man who would say anything to get what he wanted. And then go back on his word without suffering a qualm.'

He couldn't help it. He burst out laughing. 'You are priceless, Miss Hinchcliffe!'

She drew herself up in her chair and attempted to look down her nose at him. 'If you are suggesting that, had he offered me a cast-iron contract, signed and witnessed by lawyers, I might have gone into partnership with him, you are very much mistaken. And it was only *after* I'd turned him down,' she added triumphantly, 'that I thought of how unlikely it was he would share any of the prize winnings, as he called them, with anyone, let alone me.'

'I beg your pardon,' he said, with a grin. 'But it is rather difficult to take you all that seriously when you are sprawled in that chair with a glass of brandy in your hand. In the middle of the afternoon.'

She glanced down at the glass in her hand as though only just noticing it.

'Well, you were the one who gave it to me,' she pointed out.

'Guilty as charged. But in my defence, you did look as though you needed some sort of…er…medicinal comfort. And also…'

'Now *you* must continue, if you please. It is not gentlemanly to leave a person in suspense, after dangling the hint of a confession in their ears.'

'Touché!' He flung up one hand in the gesture of a fencer, acknowledging a hit. 'It seems to me,' he added, 'that we bring out the worst in each other.'

Her face fell. She bent down to place the almost untouched glass on the floor, then sat up straight, tucking her limbs away neatly.

He could have kicked himself for blundering so badly.

'I didn't mean that the way it must have sounded,' he said.

She raised one eyebrow in a most quelling manner.

'No. I mean,' he said, feeling his cheeks heat, 'that just lately, whenever we get together, it feels as though I can be, well, *me*. The me I was before I became the Marquess of Caldicot, that is.' He ran his hand round the back of his neck. 'Before I had to conform to what society expects of me.'

She tilted her head to one side, as though considering his words. 'I see,' she said, giving a small nod, 'in part. Although I fail to see why you should behave in any other manner than you always have done, merely because you have inherited a title.'

'Oh, don't you?' He pushed himself off the desk and paced to the window. Leaned against the frame and glared out on to the view of the back terrace, beyond which lay the ornamental lawn and the path leading to the mews.

He heard her sigh. 'No, that isn't completely true. Not true at all. I know exactly why you put on...manners, like a suit of armour, whenever you are in the company of certain people.'

He whirled round, startled by the accuracy of her description.

'I do it myself,' she admitted, ruefully. 'Well, in my position, I have to. I mean, nobody would hire a governess unless they believed she was the epitome of discipline and etiquette, would they?'

It was why he'd hired her, in the first place, he recalled. Because with that nose, and those brows, she looked so stern. Like the kind of person who could bring some discipline into the life of his wayward, spoiled ward.

'And aren't you?'

'I am afraid not,' she said with a wistful smile. 'As well you know,' she added, glancing down at the half-empty tumbler at her feet.

'Let's make a bargain,' he said, turning to face her fully. 'Oh, not the kind that Baxter attempted to make,' he added quickly when he saw a suspicious look cross her face. 'I mean, let us promise each other to always just be…ourselves, when we are alone together. No pretence. No manners—'

'You mean you want me to be rude to you?'

'Well, yes, if I deserve it. Actually,' he said, a smile tugging at his lips, 'you already are, aren't you? Perhaps that is why I like you so much.'

Her cheeks went pink. 'Well,' she said, 'I don't think I can do otherwise, anyway. For some reason, as you said before, you do bring out the worst in me. Whenever we are alone, since the night I thought I'd killed Mr Baxter, I don't manage to behave with the slightest bit of propriety at all!'

All of a sudden a vision sprang to his mind of Miss Hinchcliffe behaving with the sort of impropriety which he was certain she'd never imagined. And everything in him strained towards her.

But that would not do. If he were to yield to the impulse to haul her out of the chair and kiss her, she'd slap his face. And he'd destroy all the camaraderie which, so far, they'd enjoyed during the course of their unorthodox friendship.

Besides, she was in his employ. Living under his roof. Only a seedy sort of cove would take advantage of a woman under his protection in that fashion. What was more, Susannah needed her. Not one of his predecessor's haughty sisters had stood by her, the way this plucky governess had. Not one of them had won her trust, to the extent that she'd begged to have her stay on rather than demand her dismissal, the way she apparently had with so many others.

'You know,' she said, with a slightly lopsided smile, 'I find that this is a bargain I am only too happy to shake on.' She stood up and held out her hand.

Bargain? Oh, yes, she'd promised to always be herself with him.

He extended his hand, too, and she shook it in a brisk, no-nonsense way. Which was just typical of her. And was, in part, why he liked her so much.

But already, only moments after suggesting the deal, he was regretting he'd suggested it. Because how the devil could he tell her that, out of all the women he'd met since coming to town on the pretext of searching for a wife, she was the first, nay the *only* one, he'd wanted to sweep into his arms and kiss senseless?

Chapter Fourteen

Rosalind knew she shouldn't feel insulted by the way Lord Caldicot suddenly started to attend balls whether she was going or not. He was looking for a suitable bride, wasn't he? But she couldn't help worrying that he no longer trusted her to keep Susannah safe. Did he know about Lady Birchwood's list? Was he watching to make sure she didn't allow any of the men on it to dance with Susannah?

Or hadn't he believed her when she said she'd turned down Mr Baxter's offer of money? When she'd told him about it, he *had* asked her if she was tempted and had then appeared satisfied by her denial. But if he believed it, then why was he…*watching* her? With that strange, irritated look in his eyes?

Not that he looked at her that way if he thought she might notice. But she caught it several times when she looked up suddenly, before he could rearrange his features into a calmer, less perturbed pattern.

But then didn't she do much the same? Follow him round the ballroom, or drawing room, or supper room, with her own eyes? Although in her case, it was yearning, and hurt that she had to try to keep from showing in her expression.

Oh, if only she wasn't merely a governess. If only she could hope he might ask her to dance, the way he asked so many younger, prettier, *eligible* females to dance. Or if only she didn't have to sit on the sidelines, watching while he selected his bride, if that was what he was doing. He certainly never looked as if he was really enjoying himself with any of his dance partners. She never saw him grin at any of them the way he did at her when they were chatting. Come to think of it, she never saw him chatting with any of them, either before, or during the dance. If she could discern any emotion at all, she would say it was boredom.

'Miss Hinchcliffe,' said a deep, hoarse voice at her ear, startling her out of her brown study.

She looked up, to see Lieutenant Minter hovering at her side. She felt an immediate pang of sympathy for a fellow sufferer of unrequited longing. His case must be very much worse than hers, though, because Susannah kept on giving him cause to hope, even though she'd said she'd explained that he must not. Whereas Rosalind knew there was *no* hope for her, unless one morning Lord Caldicot woke up and decided that she was the only woman for him.

Which would only happen if he suffered some sort of seizure during the night that rendered him both stupid and half-blind.

'Yes,' she said, in as friendly a tone as she could, considering how low she felt, 'Lieutenant?'

'May I have your permission to take Susannah out on to the terrace for some air? She appears to be… rather out of sorts tonight and I thought a stroll in the moonlight might…' He petered out, his cheeks flushing.

'That won't make her change her mind about you, you know,' she couldn't help warning him.

To do Susannah justice, when she'd returned from that curricle ride, she'd told Rosalind that she *had* told the Lieutenant that she'd only singled him out for attention in a spirit of rebellion, merely because her aunt had forbidden her to have anything to do with him. And had apologised for treating him so shabbily. 'But do you know what,' Susannah had said, looking a bit perplexed, 'instead of taking umbrage and walking away, he said that my honesty and penitence made him admire me even more!'

'Even if I may never win her heart,' the poor besotted young man was now saying to Rosalind, 'I can at least be there for her, when she needs…a friend.'

Oh, yes! That was just how she felt about Lord Caldicot. That she would rather suffer hurt while watching him look for a suitable bride than risk offending him by pointing out that none of the girls he danced with were likely to make him happy, not if they all made him look so bored.

'And,' Lieutenant Minter continued, 'since a friend is all I can hope to be, or would ever be permitted to be by her family, I would like to ask if you would accompany us outside as well. So that she may be easy that I have no intention of trying to declare love to her, or anything she wouldn't like.'

She had half a mind to tell him that the more faithful he was, the less Susannah respected him. That the girl seemed to have started regarding him in the light of a sort of devoted hound.

No, perhaps that was being unfair. Susannah had said that at least the Lieutenant listened to her, rather than trying to impress her with a lot of idle boasting, the way so many other young men did. That she felt comfortable with him. That she could be herself, rather than having to remember all the rules there were about how girls were supposed to behave around eligible men. Which, she'd said, her hands clasped to her bosom, was very hard to do when her heart already belonged to Cecil Baxter.

Rosalind sighed. 'I shall go and fetch my shawl,' she said. 'But I warn you, Susannah won't like having me spoiling your tête-à-tête.'

'That is a risk,' he said with a grin, 'that I am pre-pared to take.'

She went to fetch her shawl and was just making for the terrace doors when Lord Caldicot came bearing down on her.

'Where,' he demanded, 'do you think you are going?'

'Outside,' she replied, wondering what was making him so cross with her all the time. 'To chaperon Susannah and Lieutenant Minter,' she added, before he had the chance to remind her that she had no business going outside for a stroll for her own enjoyment, in case that was what he suspected her of doing.

He gave a brisk nod. 'It *is* stuffy in the ballroom. A breath of fresh air is just what I need, too.' And then he moved so that he was in step with her and crooked his arm for her to take.

'I am perfectly capable of keeping an eye on them,' she said, stung by what appeared to be yet more evidence that he no longer trusted her capabilities.

'I don't doubt it,' he said. 'Nevertheless, I wish to go outside. As I said, I need some air that doesn't stink of stale perfume and hypocrisy.'

Well, that was a bit of a surprise.

'You don't…that is,' she amended, as she laid her hand on his sleeve, 'you are not enjoying this ball?'

He snorted by way of response as he pushed open the terrace door. 'I don't enjoy balls at all. Any of them. At least…' he mused as they turned to the right and began to stroll along the paved area running the entire length of Birkbeck House, 'I haven't enjoyed one since I've become the Marquess of Caldicot.'

Strange…he pronounced his title as though it was something unpleasant.

'Um… Would you mind me asking why that is?'

They walked a few steps before he said anything. 'There they are,' he said, pointing to a couple partially concealed by a gigantic urn, apparently deep in conversation.

She supposed she had to accept that for some reason Lord Caldicot didn't want to tell her why he didn't enjoy balls, since he'd changed the subject so emphatically. But at least she had reason to hope that perhaps he wasn't looking so cross all the time because of anything she'd done. That he was just…cross.

'We had better not go too much further,' she said, feeling far less unhappy than she had for some time, now that she knew it wasn't entirely her fault he was looking so glum lately. 'We don't want them to think that we are attempting to eavesdrop on their conversation.'

'Don't we?' He gave her an indecipherable look. Of course, that might have just been because it was rather dark out here, in spite of the light spilling out from the ballroom windows and the addition of strategically placed torches along the terrace.

'In my opinion,' he said, 'that girl needs to know that we aren't going to let her get away with whatever scheme she's trying to entrap that poor defenceless young man into.'

She examined the way the couple were standing, and the gestures Susannah was making, and agreed that it did look as though she might be trying to persuade the Lieutenant to take part in some sort of scheme. For he had his arms folded across his chest and, though his face was in shadow, she could tell, from the angle of his head, that he was probably frowning.

'Nevertheless,' she said firmly, 'we are not going to approach one step closer.' To add weight to what she'd said, she removed her hand from his sleeve and turned as though to look out over the gardens.

'Why not, you infuriating creature?'

For some reason, the informality of the way he addressed her made any last, lingering worries that he was cross with her, or disappointed in her, take flight. 'Because,' she explained, 'if we don't allow her the illusion of privacy, then she is the kind of enterprising girl who will begin to devise ways of ensuring she really gets it. And then we wouldn't have a clue where she is or what she's up to.'

'Hmm,' he said thoughtfully, turning to stand next to her, but facing the house rather than the darkened gardens. 'That, I suspect, is how she became close enough to Baxter to receive a marriage proposal. Because when I asked Lady Birchwood about how she allowed her to associate with undesirables, she…well, after bursting into tears and having the vapours, and uttering a series of implausible excuses about what a good family he comes from,' he said with disgust, 'admitted that she'd had no idea Susannah had even been introduced to the rogue.'

Rosalind spread her hands wide, as though to say, *Exactly.*

He said nothing. Only folded his arms across his chest and heaved a sigh.

It was strange, but as they stood there, side by side, one facing the garden, and the other the house, she could almost imagine a kind of…well, not precisely a romantic atmosphere. She would have to be the kind of girl who believed in fairy tales to even begin to think that just because they were standing next to each other, in the darkness, with music playing in the background and the scent of roses and rosemary drifting lazily in the air, that *he* would be thinking anything romantic.

She also rather thought that she'd have to be able to see some stars, to create such an illusion. Or even a sliver of moon. But she could see neither, since clouds completely blanketed the sky. The best she could hope to claim, could *ever* hope to claim existed between them, was a sort of companionship.

Not even true friendship, since their stations in life were so very far apart.

'What the devil,' he said, shattering the stillness in which she'd been basking, 'can you possibly be looking at so intently out there?' He turned to peer into the shadows cloaking what by day would probably be a very well-maintained area of grass and shrubbery, to judge from the hints of fragrance she could detect whenever the breeze blew.

'Um…' She glanced up at him. At the perplexed frown knitting his brows. At the aggressive slant of his shoulders. And remembered her promise to be honest with him. 'I wasn't *looking* at anything. I was just thinking…wondering…well,' she said, taking the plunge, 'worrying, actually, whether you'd stopped trusting me, since I told you about you-know-who offering me money to make it easier for him to get to you-know-who,' she finished saying, jerking her head in Susannah's direction.

'Whatever gave you that idea?'

'Well, because you have suddenly started attending balls, even on evenings when it has not been your turn. Even though I am there. As though…'

'It is most emphatically not because I don't trust you. Far from it!'

'Oh?'

He shuffled his feet. Looked down at them as though he couldn't fathom what they might be doing.

Then gave a half-shrug. 'Well, you know, I am supposed to be finding myself a wife, am I not?'

Yes. That was just what she'd been telling herself, earlier.

'And this is the sort of event where one is supposed to be able to find one.' He raised his head and glared at the glittering wall of windows, through which he must be able to see the other guests dancing to the music she could hear.

'Oh.' Her heart sank. It ought not to have done. She ought to have been relieved to hear that he hadn't stopped trusting her. That he didn't feel obliged to check up on her.

Yet hearing that the change in his routine was all because he was trying harder to find a wife...

'Yes, I see,' she said. She was such an idiot. To think that not five minutes ago, she'd been pitying Lieutenant Minter for having some hope and congratulating herself for being sensible enough to know she had none. When all the time it looked as though, deep down, there must have been a tiny ember, stubbornly refusing to go out, because hearing him remind her that he was looking for a bride had felt as though he'd doused it with a bucket of icy water.

'Everyone keeps telling me,' he said gloomily, 'that it is one of the most important of my duties, now that I am a marquess. To marry and start filling the nursery. And having some woman, some properly reared girl, who would know how to do it, to act as hostess for all the…political meetings I am supposed to be hosting. To run all the properties for which I'm now responsible.' He kicked moodily at something by his foot.

'You don't sound,' she said, her foolish heart picking up speed, 'as though it is something you really want to do…'

'That is putting it mildly,' he said, turning his back on the house to gaze out across the darkened gardens with her. 'But the fact is,' he said, gripping the balustrade, which had the effect of making his shoulders hunch, 'that without a partner who…has been brought up to live at that kind of level, I…' He swallowed. 'I don't think I will be able to do it.'

'Do what?'

'Be a marquess,' he said through gritted teeth.

'But you *are* a marquess,' she pointed out.

'Only because my cousin didn't manage to marry again and beget his own heir after Susannah's mother died. Which is why all his sisters keep saying I need to stop hesitating and come up to scratch. Not to let some distant relation, who is even less worthy than I, take over if something should happen to me…'

She gazed up at him in astonishment.

'*Less* worthy? Oh, that means…' She felt herself swelling with rage. 'Who has dared to tell you that you are not worthy?'

He glanced down at her, his lips quirking in amusement. 'I don't think I should tell you. By the sound of it, you might go charging round there with a hefty book in your hand and give 'em what for.'

'I hit *one* man with a book and you seem to think I do nothing but go round whacking people!'

'Two books.'

'Nevertheless, that does not change the fact that whoever told you that you aren't worthy to hold your title needs a sharp set-down!'

'It wasn't only one of 'em,' he said, his brief flash of humour fading. 'The whole family thinks it.'

'But…*why*?'

He ran his fingers through his hair. 'Well, probably because they know me much better than you. They knew me when I was a wild boy, rampaging all over the estates I'm now responsible for protecting from youths like I was. And don't forget, rather than coming home and knuckling down when I inherited the title, I stayed with my regiment, rampaging all over the Continent *enjoying myself.*'

'And how, exactly,' she asked, looking rather puzzled, 'did you *enjoy yourself* while fighting for your country?'

'Well, to start with, I used some of the money I'd inherited to buy a promotion.'

'Because…you thought you could do a better job than your superiors?'

'Yes, by God! Although that's not saying much

when you think of the shambles that was John Moore's retreat to Corunna.'

'It sounds to *me* as though your heart was set on defeating Napoleon. An enemy of our country. As though you regarded abandoning your regiment as a dereliction of duty. As though duty to your country, and your comrades, trumped duty to your family,' she said, burning with indignation that he should have had to contend with that sort of criticism. 'Besides, even though you didn't come home, you made arrangements for your ward, Susannah, and all your properties to be taken care of in your absence. I mean, I haven't heard that they've all gone to rack and ruin, or anything like.'

'No, well, I have good, experienced men overseeing everything. The credit for which can be laid firmly at my deceased cousin's door. He left things in such good heart that I didn't feel as though, even if I did come back, I would make any difference. So what would have been the point? Then again, nobody ever dreamed I'd inherit anything, least of all me. So I didn't have any training in land management. Or wielding influence in political circles.'

'But you were in charge of men when you were in the army, weren't you? In the midst of war. Surely that was at times harder than running estates that are prosperous and thriving?'

'I told you. I have no training…'

'On the contrary, you have had plenty of training. You have experience in leading men. Which is what, by the sound of it, you still need to do with the ones put in place by your late cousin. You don't need to do their jobs for them.'

'Indeed, I couldn't if I wanted to.'

'Oh, stop harping on what you cannot do and think about what you can! If you want to make a difference, as you put it, I don't see any reason why you shouldn't. You have every right to make changes from the way your predecessor decreed things should be done. To have things done *your* way. I am certain you could inspire your employees to bring your vision of how things should be to fruition if you can lead men into battle.

'As for politics, well, if you have no ambition for yourself to rise through the ranks of any particular party and reach a position of power within government, then that leaves you free to vote according to your conscience on matters which really mean something to you. I wouldn't be a bit surprised if you didn't hold some very decided opinions when it comes to military matters and would enjoy weighing in behind, for instance, Lord Wellington.'

He turned so that he was facing her. 'In all the years since I've inherited, nobody has ever spoken to me with such...*sense*. All I've heard is that I cannot fill my cousin's shoes with any degree of success un-

less I change my ways. Settle down. Marry some...'
He waved to the ballroom windows in a dismissive
manner.

'Yes, and that's another thing,' she said. 'How old
was Susannah when her mother died? Two? Three?
And how old was she when her father died? Ten! In
all that time, why do you suppose he never bothered
to remarry, if it is so important to maintain the illus-
trious title of Caldicot? Why? Because he already had
an heir. You! And if he didn't think it was imperative
to father a son of his own, then *he* must have felt you
were worthy to step into his shoes, mustn't he? What
is more, if he was content to have you succeed him,
then he should have jolly well made sure you had the
training you feel you need!'

'Miss Hinchcliffe,' he said, taking hold of her shoulders and gazing into her eyes as though she was something...extraordinary. 'In a few short, pithy sentences,
you have just blown all the arguments that have been
flung at me about the extent of my failings and as to
what my future plans should be to smithereens. Do
you know,' he said, with a slow shake of his head. 'I
could kiss you?'

He could...what?

Kiss?

Her?

Could he hear her heart pounding above the noise
of the orchestra?

Could he feel her trembling?

Could he tell that she was hardly able to breathe for anticipation?

It would certainly explain the sudden change that came over his face.

Because of course he hadn't meant that he really wanted to kiss her. It had been a figure of speech. She'd just helped him to deal with a massive burden of self-doubt with which he'd been grappling ever since, by the sound of it, he'd unexpectedly inherited his lofty title.

And in that rush of relief, he'd said something he hadn't really meant.

How…mortifying that he must be able to tell that she'd taken him literally. Thank goodness it was so dark out here that he couldn't see the flush of shame that made her face feel as if it was on fire.

She took a hasty step back, before she could complete her humiliation by flinging herself on to his chest, or saying something like, *Go on, then, kiss me!* She moved so suddenly that his hands dropped from her shoulders.

He took a step back, too.

Then they just stood there. She, looking at the stone flags beneath her feet, and he, she rather thought, anywhere but at her.

She didn't know how long they might have stood there, neither of them knowing how to deal with their

mutual embarrassment, had not Susannah and Lieutenant Minter come sauntering over, arm in arm.

'Oh, Miss Hinchcliffe,' said the Lieutenant, 'there
you are. We could not see you for a moment...'

'Lurking behind the planter,' put in Susannah mischievously.

'We were not lurking,' said Lord Caldicot, irritably, 'behind anything.'

For the first time Rosalind noticed that they were,
indeed, standing in the lee of another of those large
urns containing trailing plants, which would have
partially concealed them from the younger couple.

Oh...no! She glanced up at Lord Caldicot. Could
he possibly suspect that she'd had an ulterior motive
for choosing to stand just here, other than it being a
matter of chance? Could he think she'd deliberately...
enticed him there, in an attempt to force some sort of
intimacy that might result in a kiss?

'I... I...' she said, wondering how to explain herself
without coming across as a complete zany.

'No need to counter Susannah's ridiculous remark,
Miss Hinchcliffe,' Lord Caldicot said sternly. 'Just
because she chooses to lurk behind planters does not
mean that every other person who has come out here
to take the air would do the same.'

Rosalind glanced swiftly along the length of the
terrace, at the other couples who were outside. A few
of them were strolling along. But the ones who'd cho-

sen to stop had all done so in the shelter of one of the urns. As though they were deliberately seeking whatever slim chance of privacy they could find.

Her heart sank further.

'And as for you, Susannah,' Lord Caldicot continued, 'can you not see you have put the poor woman to the blush?'

Susannah sighed. 'I beg your pardon, Miss Hinchcliffe. I was just teasing,' she said, coming up to her and putting one slender arm round her waist.

'Lieutenant,' said Susannah, over her shoulder. 'Why don't you cheer Miss Hinchcliffe up by asking her to dance? It sounds as if the current set is winding down, so there will be plenty of time to join the next. And I'm sure it must be very dull for her to have to trail about after me all evening and never having any fun herself.'

On the one hand, that sounded as though Susannah was making a very kind offer to make up for embarrassing Rosalind.

On the other hand, it could mean she wanted to make sure Rosalind was occupied, which would enable her to embark on some scheme or other.

'That,' said Lord Caldicot, before she could say something that would both express her thanks at what sounded like a kind offer, while making some solid excuse for why she could not possibly accept, 'sounds like a capital idea. Although...' he added, turning to

Lieutenant Minter, 'I am sure that this young fellow would far rather dance with you, Susannah.'

'B-But,' stammered the young man. 'I thought that her family, that is to say you, disapproved of me.'

Lord Caldicot shrugged. '*I* have never had any objection to you, Lieutenant. And if you have any trouble from your aunt about this,' he said to Susannah, 'you may tell her that I engineered the situation with such fiendish cunning that you found yourself unable to wriggle out of dancing with him.'

'Oh.' Susannah stared at him wide-eyed. 'But… what about Miss Hinchcliffe?'

'Don't you worry about Miss Hinchcliffe. I shall take care of her myself.'

'You mean,' said Susannah, in surprise, '*you* are going to ask her to dance?'

No. That was not what he'd meant. Rosalind was sure of it. He was going to come up with some stratagem that would mean she'd be able to keep an eye on Susannah, and foil whatever scheme she'd been plotting.

'Of course,' said Lord Caldicot, 'I shall ask her to dance.'

He was? Oh! Her heart soared.

'Because I have no intention,' said Lord Caldicot to Susannah, drily, 'of permitting you to outdo me when it comes to scandalising your aunt.'

Her heart sank.

Of course. He was going to take her out on to the dance floor to divert Lady Birchwood's attention from Susannah's misdemeanour. And also shield her from censure. Because of course Rosalind could hardly forbid Susannah from dancing with Lieutenant Minter when Lord Caldicot had engineered it.

'And nothing, I am certain,' said Lord Caldicot, a slow smile spreading across his face, 'would scandalise her more than seeing me escort your lowly governess on to the dance floor in the face of all the ladies she considers more worthy.'

Which also made total sense. He was so sick of hearing how unworthy he was, and of being badgered into selecting a bride who would somehow make up for all his supposed defects, that she couldn't blame him for rebelling. With the most inappropriate woman in the ballroom.

'Lord Caldicot,' said Susannah, giving him an impish grin, 'if you carry on like this, I might one day be able to quite like you.'

He chuckled. Which made him look all the more appealing. And, oh, what did it matter why, precisely, he'd decided to dance with her tonight? That it wasn't really, truly romantic. The fact was that he had done so.

It was a dream come true. A legitimate opportunity to be closer to him. Even if only for half an hour.

And no matter how it had come about, or what his motives might be, she was going to seize her moment, with both hands.

Chapter Fifteen

Miss Hinchcliffe didn't look totally happy about the way he'd arranged things. In fact, he'd go so far as to say she had an air of grim determination about her as she laid her hand on his sleeve and began walking back to the ballroom.

Thank goodness he hadn't forgotten himself so much as to yield to that wild impulse to lean in and kiss her just now, then. Just imagine how she'd have reacted to *that*!

She didn't have any books to hand with which to... *whack* him, though. Would she, he wondered, have used her fists to express her outrage?

She would have had every right to do so. As her employer, he ought to behave with more...decorum. Only, whenever he got anywhere near her, decorum seemed to fly out of the window. Made him revert to the way he'd behaved before he became a marquess.

Made him feel like *himself.*

Although there was more to it than that, wasn't there? More than just…a feeling that he needn't pretend to be something he was not. She made him… He felt a frown furrow his brows as they reached the door to the ballroom.

She made him behave like a jealous lover, that's what she'd done tonight. When he'd thought she'd been about to go outside with that idiot boy, after he'd been leaning in and murmuring in her ear, he'd been so incensed that he'd stormed over and accosted her before she could get outside to take part in any sort of assignation.

Assignation? With the lovelorn Lieutenant? How could he have suspected any such thing? The boy only had eyes for his irritating ward, Susannah.

And as for Miss Hinchcliffe… He gave her a swift appraisal out of the corner of his eye, as she walked beside him, the picture of propriety. She would have been astonished had he told her what he'd thought. Astonished to think any man would take that sort of notice of her.

She genuinely had no idea how appealing she was. No idea that she stood out like a rose amid a field of cabbages, whenever she sat down on the bench with the other ladies performing the duties of chaperon. For though Susannah had crowned her with the dreaded dowager's turban, she'd also gowned her in materials and colours which served as a reminder to everyone how very young she truly was.

And the other dowagers resented her for it. He could tell from the way they eyed her askance and began gossiping among themselves in a way that excluded her. Every time he'd seen her sitting there, on that bench, with the older women who made such a point of snubbing her, he'd wished she could have a chance to get out on the dance floor and enjoy herself, instead of just watching the other young ladies.

The dowagers began elbowing each other and muttering to one another as he led Miss Hinchcliffe past them and on to the dance floor. It made him wonder if he'd done the right thing by compelling her to dance with him. She was going to pay for it later, by the looks of it. Society was full of the kind of women who delighted in tearing the weaker among them to shreds.

Not that anyone could describe Miss Hinchcliffe as weak. She'd survive whatever women such as those could throw at her. He was certain.

For one thing, she could claim, with total honesty, that had any other man ever invited her to dance, she would have refused. She took her duties to Susannah too seriously to do anything as selfish as enjoy herself.

Unlike Lady Birchwood, who never did more than pay lip service to duty, before going off to gossip with her cronies, or play them for pin money in the card room. It had become increasingly clear to him, as the weeks went by, that the reason Lady Birchwood had been so keen to preside over Susannah's debut had less to do with any real fondness for her niece than because she'd wanted someone else to fund her own time in London. He didn't think her widow's jointure had left her uncomfortably off, financially, but she was certainly making the most of having the right to hang off his coat tails.

Whereas Miss Hinchcliffe played everything by the book. She'd only yielded to the opportunity to dance because he was her employer. And hadn't invited her so much as given her an order to do so.

He was jolly glad of the distraction created by walking on to the floor to join another two couples and making up a full set, because had Miss Hinchcliffe had the leisure to look at him too closely he was pretty certain she'd be able to tell that he was weltering in a slew of conflicting emotions.

For one thing, he'd lied to her, after promising that they'd always tell each other the truth.

But somehow, he just hadn't been able to admit that the reason he was attending far more balls than he needed to was entirely down to the fact that when she went out in the evenings, he…*fretted*. That was the word. He'd sit alone in his study, considering all the events to which he'd been invited, rejecting one after the other, knowing he would not enjoy any of them if she weren't there.

London wasn't so bad during the daytime. He could box at Gentleman Jackson's, fence at Angelo's, ride out on horseback, or drive his new team out as far as Richmond, if he wished. He could even enjoy the company of a woman, to judge from the lures that had been cast his way. The trouble was, none of the women who'd offered had tempted him for more than a moment or two. Either they laughed too often, or they couldn't respond with a swift put-down when he said something stupid. Or their eyebrows weren't full enough, or their noses were too small...

And when evening fell...

His eyes turned to her. The source of so much of his present turmoil. She was looking a little unsure of herself, he noted, now they'd formed an eightsome.

'I hope,' he said, thrusting his own dilemma aside as he bowed over her hand, 'that you have plenty of pins fastening your headgear on securely.'

Her hand flew, briefly, to her turban. Then she pursed her lips and shot him a look of annoyance. 'Thank you so much,' she said, as she swept him the requisite curtsy which heralded the opening figures of the dance, 'for giving me something *else* to worry about.'

He couldn't help chuckling at her quip. Oh, but it felt good to be with her, here, like this, even if he had been obliged to press her into dancing with him, under cover of…well, just under cover. She'd have been insulted, he would wager, if he admitted that he was here partly because he worried that the dowagers were being cruel to her. Or that Lady Birchwood was placing too much responsibility on her young shoulders, when it clearly needed at least two people to keep Susannah out of mischief.

No, that wasn't it, really, was it?

Was he lying to himself, now, as well as her?

The truth was that when she went out, he missed her. Simply missed her. He always wished he could be present at any event she attended, so that, even if he didn't get a chance to have any meaningful sort of discussion with her, he could at least *see* her. Even if, before tonight, he hadn't been able to come up with any scheme that would have broken down all her scruples and persuaded her to dance with him.

But far from looking as though she was currently suffering from the slightest twinge of guilty conscience at being his partner, she was clearly enjoying herself as she twirled round, retreated and clapped in time to the beat. She was still managing to hang on to her dignity, somehow, though, when so many other ladies he'd partnered could often resemble sad romps when performing a dance this energetic.

What a pity he hadn't timed it so that it was a waltz that had been starting up when they returned to the ballroom, he reflected, as he took her by both wrists to swing her round for the expected number of bars. For then he'd have had a legitimate excuse for keeping her in a hold for the entire dance, not just for the fleeting moments this particular country dance permitted.

For once he felt as if the musicians came to a halt all too soon, meaning all the couples in the set had to bow or curtsy to each other before leaving the floor.

Out of the corner of his eye he noticed the Lieutenant leading Susannah in the direction of the refreshment room. So he took the opportunity to stay close to Miss Hinchliffe by following suit.

'I am sure,' he said as he guided her into following the younger couple, 'you could do with a glass of lemonade after all that relentless hopping and twirling.' He paraphrased her earlier remarks about country dancing.

She looked up at him, her eyes sparkling. 'How thoughtful of you. I am quite sure your motives have nothing whatsoever to do with the fact that you do not wish to let Susannah and her partner out of your sight.'

'How could you suspect me of such a thing?' he asked with a grin.

She smiled back. But her smile dimmed as she caught sight of a wave of disapproving looks from the occupants of the various chaperons' benches.

'I fear,' he said, his conscience smarting, 'from the

expressions on their faces, that you are going to pay for enjoying yourself this evening.'

'Much I care for anything they might say,' she retorted. 'And what can they do, other than talk?'

'You really are not angry with me for exposing you to possible censure?'

'Oh, no! Far from it. I have not enjoyed myself so much in an age. Besides, I can produce the defence that you compelled both Susannah and myself to do as you bid us. We are not responsible for your eccentricities, are we? It is for us to obey,' she said, lowering her head in a display of false meekness. And then ruining the effect by darting a look up at him that had a good deal of mirth in it.

'Nevertheless,' he said, 'Lady Birchwood will no doubt have the vapours when she hears what you both did. When, eventually,' he added drily, 'she emerges from the card room.'

'You need not worry,' she said in a reassuring tone. 'Her maid is an expert with the vinaigrette.'

'Yes, but her maid is not here.'

'Ah, but Her Ladyship won't indulge in the vapours while you are about, will she? She is bound to wait until she is safely home. With the trusty Throgmorton on hand to tend to her.'

He laughed. He couldn't help it. She had just summed up Lady Birchwood to a nicety. The woman knew that he would take no notice of her if she tried to play off her tricks. So she would, indeed, wait until she had a more responsive audience.

'But,' he added, 'don't let her bully you, will you? If she tries to do so, just refer her back to me.'

'But of course I will,' she replied, widening her eyes. 'Because it is, after all, entirely your fault!'

Chapter Sixteen

Rosalind floated through the next few days in cloud of something she'd never felt before in her life, but rather suspected was joy.

He'd danced with her.

Oh, only to annoy as many people as possible and to make a point about something or other, but that did not alter the fact that he'd done it. He'd taken her out on to the dance floor. And appeared to have enjoyed the experience. Why, she'd made him laugh out loud, when no other lady, from what she'd seen, managed to do anything but bore him. He'd given *no* sign that he was merely being kind to the poor, plain spinster governess, which was what some of the onlookers, those who had marriageable daughters, with ambitions to latch on to his title and wealth, chose to say about him.

The ones with nothing to lose said nothing bad about *him*, either. No, they chose to find fault with her instead. Saying that she was pushing, or brassy, and really quite ridiculous to think she could possibly interest a man of Lord Caldicot's calibre. Not to her face, since none of them ever deigned to actually talk to her, but loudly enough so that she would be sure to overhear.

And as for Lady Birchwood…oh, she'd been like a pot about to come to the boil all the way home from the ball. It had not been until they reached Kilburn House, as Rosalind had forewarned Lord Caldicot, that she gave vent to her feelings.

'Have you,' she'd said to him, the moment they set foot in the hall, 'no sense of decorum? Or are you just ignorant of the kind of talk your behaviour tonight will have caused?'

'My behaviour?' Lord Caldicot had raised one eyebrow, then turned to hand his hat and gloves to Timms. 'I have been a model of propriety all evening.'

Susannah had made a noise that could have passed for a sneeze, but which was more likely to have been a stifled giggle.

'Not only,' Lady Birchwood had complained, 'did you cause speculation by partnering a mere governess in a set of dances, but worse, far worse, you permitted your ward to dance with a man who is completely ineligible in every way!'

'If you are speaking of Lieutenant Minter,' he'd said coldly, 'I have to inform you that I see no reason at all why Susannah should not dance with him. And further, it is a little late to make objections *after* the event.'

'Well, I couldn't say anything before, could I?'

'No,' he'd replied with a sarcastic smile. 'Because you were in the card room.'

Lady Birchwood had opened and closed her mouth a few times, but found nothing to say. Because the way he'd spoken had made it clear that he knew that if she really cared, she wouldn't be spending so much time in the card room, leaving the care of her niece in the hands of a paid employee.

His masterful set down had only silenced Lady Birchwood temporarily, though. The very next morning, she'd summoned Rosalind and Susannah to her room and, from the comfort of her bed and still crowned with her nightcap, let forth a stream of complaints. 'You both knew,' she said, 'that I frowned upon any association with Lieutenant Minter.'

'Yes,' Susannah had protested, 'but Lord Caldicot practically ordered me to dance with him.'

This retort had provoked a stream of reminiscences about times when Susannah had absolutely no qualms about disobeying orders from various members of her family.

'Yes, but,' Susannah had pointed out, 'Miss Hinchcliffe couldn't very well disobey him, could she?'

Lady Birchwood had flung herself back into the mound of pillows against which she'd been reclining, her mouth opening and closing again as words failed her. But, Rosalind suspected, clearly more furious about the whole episode than ever.

After a couple of days, during which Lady Birchwood had either made excuses for not coming to the dining table, or sitting there sighing and making use of her handkerchief to signify how upset she still was with them, Lord Caldicot took Rosalind aside and asked her how she was coping with the latest fit of the sulks.

Rosalind had shrugged. 'She will get over it, I am sure. And in the meantime, I can deal with her.'

'And Susannah?'

'Ah. Well, she *is* worrying me, rather.'

'I thought she seemed to be behaving rather better than usual.'

'Yes. Which is what is troubling me. Usually, if she is being docile, it means she is trying to lull me into a false sense of security, while she is hatching some scheme, only...'

'Only?'

'Well, I cannot put my finger on it, exactly. But if it weren't Susannah we were discussing, but some other, less spirited girl, I would describe her as...moping.'

'Or as though she's lost a shilling and found a farthing.'

'Yes! That's exactly it. And I very much fear…'

'What?'

'Well, I am wondering if she is pining for Mr Baxter.'

Lord Caldicot frowned. 'What, *still*?'

'You cannot expect her to give up on him just because he's playing least in sight, can you? A girl as stubborn as her? You know that she never gives up once she's got the bit between her teeth over some matter or other.'

Lord Caldicot sighed. 'Surely, by now, with all the other suitors clamouring for her attention and all the parties she attends…'

'No. A woman in love does not just forget the object of her affection if you dangle a shiny bauble in her face, you know. Once her heart is given, it remains true.'

She, for example, was never going to forget Lord Caldicot. The first man who had ever made her think about kisses in the moonlight. Though nothing could come of it, she'd never forget these precious, wonderful times when they spoke together as though they were almost equals. And especially not the evening when she'd danced with him, while every other female in the ballroom looked on with envy. Or at least, that was what it had felt like. It was what had enabled her to deal with the spiteful comments afterwards.

'Even though the fellow is not worth her devotion?'

'Well, they do say that love is blind, do they not?'

'It must be, in this case,' he snorted with derision. 'Either that, or the girl is an idiot.'

'I wonder…' she said.

'What do you wonder?'

'Well, if some of his allure isn't down to the fact that she cannot have him. That she has been forbidden to see him. I wonder if, had you allowed her to continue to see him, she might have seen through his smooth charm, to the snake he is inside.'

'May I remind you that it was not *I* who threw him out of a window? And put the fear of God into him?'

'You have freely admitted that you wished you had, though,' she retorted. 'But anyway,' she went on, having decided not to remind him that she hadn't *thrown* him out of the window and he jolly well knew it, 'as it is, she keeps on asking me where he can possibly be and why he hasn't made any attempt to see her. And does that mean he doesn't love her the way he said he did. Which makes me feel so…*guilty.*'

'Guilty? Why should you feel guilty? You have done that girl a true service in running off that bounder.'

'That's as may be. The fact is that I don't like seeing

her so upset and not being able to tell her the truth. Which is that it's all my fault.'

'Oh, no, it isn't. If you hadn't broken a couple of his bones, I'd have come up with some way to see him off. In fact...' He pondered for a while. 'It wouldn't surprise me if he wasn't the sort of snivelling cur who would have been willing to have been bought off. If he'd seen that he had a real hold over Susannah and thought he could entice her into an elopement...'

'Yes. You are right. We have only done what we had to, to protect the poor girl. But... I just don't like seeing her so unhappy.'

'He would have made her unhappy no matter what steps we had taken, you know. Just think how much more she would have suffered had the affair continued to the point of marriage. She would soon have learned that he only cared about her money. And that, legally, she would have had little chance of escape. Or, supposing he had persuaded her to elope and she had to live with the disgrace. She enjoys being the belle of the ball too much to cope successfully with the way society would shun a girl who went that far astray.'

'Yes, you are right, of course. I must just keep reminding myself that I am doing what is best for her...'

'And I tell you what else. Any fellow who truly cared for her would try to win me round, by reforming his ways, or by showing his loyalty to her, even though his case was hopeless.'

'Like Lieutenant Minter?'

'Just like that. You wouldn't catch him climbing in through a girl's window, or steering clear of her whenever her disapproving guardian is about, would you? Or trying to strike a deal with her chaperon?'

Yes, it was a great pity Susannah didn't appreciate Minter's worth. Or find Lady Birchwood's aversion to him as tantalising as she'd found Lord Caldicot's aversion to Mr Baxter.

The thing was, though, now she'd spoken to Mr Baxter herself she could picture him putting on what she'd thought of as that spaniel face and doing his utmost to tug at Susannah's tender heartstrings. Whereas Lieutenant Minter, if put in a similar position, would square his shoulders, grit his teeth and generally behave like a gallant officer of His Majesty's navy.

She felt calmer about Susannah after that talk with Lord Caldicot. And, well, just happy for having that tête-à-tête with him. Even though they had not discussed anything personal between them, for of course there never could be anything of that nature between them, she basked in the feeling that he did trust her after all. Trusted her in a way he didn't seem to trust many other people. Certainly not females.

She was just congratulating herself for knowing that he, at least, approved of the way she was dealing with Susannah, and the whole Cecil Baxter episode, when Lady Birchwood summoned her to her room.

And ruined it all.

Chapter Seventeen

Michael had been spending a perfectly pleasant hour or so shooting wafers at Manton's gun range when he experienced one of those feelings he'd sometimes had just before walking into an enemy ambush. A sort of…not foreboding exactly, but as though he'd forgotten something. Or that there was something he should have noticed, taking place just out of the corner of his eye.

He looked round the gallery, but at this hour in the morning there were few other patrons. So it wasn't a literal ambush he had to worry about.

Probably.

He raised his arm to take another shot, but knew he would not take any more pleasure in practising his skill with that strange feeling nagging at him. Since it had saved his life, and that of his men, on several occasions, he'd learned to pay heed to it. And though he wasn't on reconnaissance on some barren gulley in the Pyrenees, he thought it was probably as important to pay attention in the refined atmosphere of London.

In the same way as he'd known he had to halt and take cover, when on active service, he knew he needed to lay down his pistol and return to base. That was where trouble was brewing. Now he came to think of it, there had been a distinct atmosphere at the breakfast table that morning. Though he couldn't pinpoint exactly what it was that was now making him feel he needed to return as soon as he could, he was going to trust his instincts. The worst that would happen, after all, was that he'd arrive to find absolutely nothing amiss. He'd feel like a bit of an idiot, and no harm done.

It didn't take long to walk there from Davis Street, and, as he rounded the corner into Grosvenor Square, it was to see the front door of Kilburn House open and Miss Hinchcliffe come striding out.

His lips were just starting to lift in a smile at the mere sight of her when he noted the case she was holding in one hand. A case he recognised, though this time there was no length of petticoat trailing from it. This time, it appeared she had taken her time to pack carefully.

Though why she should have taken it into her head to pack a case and leave, now, he couldn't imagine. She had no reason to leave, surely?

What was more, he was not going to permit her

to do so. The very idea was…*abhorrent*. It was bad enough wondering where she would go and what would become of her when Susannah married and he'd no longer have any legitimate excuse to summon her to his study for a chat. But that day, he'd always thought, would be weeks away. Possibly months. He'd told himself he wouldn't need to worry about it until Susannah started to show a preference for one of her suitors. He certainly wasn't ready to face it today!

He strode out with even more urgency, reaching the foot of the front steps at the same time as she did.

'What,' he growled, leaning down and snatching the case from her gloved hand, 'is the meaning of this?'

She looked at him for a moment or two, her eyes welling up with an emotion that found an echo in his own heart, before replying.

'I should have thought,' she said, in a flat voice that didn't sound like her at all, 'it was obvious.'

'You are leaving me? I mean, leaving my employ? Is this such a bad post? I thought you were happy here.'

Her lower lip trembled. One tear spilled and ran down her cheek before she swiped it away, in a gesture that spoke to him of…defeat.

'I *have* been happy here,' she said, as a tear spilled from her other eye and ran down her other cheek.

'So why the devil are you running away?'

'I am not running away,' she protested.

He looked at the neatly tied bonnet, the coat buttons which were all fastened correctly, and realised that she had taken time over her appearance before walking out of the front door this time. As though she'd thought it all through and decided she'd had enough.

His heart plunged. The thought of enduring the rest of the Season without Miss Hinchcliffe around to make balls bearable by exchanging glances every now and then, or at musicales when someone failed to hit the right note…

The thought of enduring the rest of his life, in fact, without her…

'I won't allow it,' he said, taking her by the elbow.

'There is nothing you can do,' she said despondently. 'Lady Birchwood has made up her mind…'

'Lady Birchwood? What has she to do with this?'

Miss Hinchcliffe frowned up him, as though bewildered by the question. 'Why, it is she who has told me to leave. And…'

So she hadn't just decided to abandon him. That was, he hastily corrected himself, her duties as companion to his ward. She definitely didn't look as though she *wanted* to leave, either.

Good.

'Lady Birchwood has done what?' He'd expected her to be annoyed over the dance they'd all enjoyed at Birkbeck House. But he'd never dreamed the woman would go this far. For one thing, she had no right. 'How dare she? *I* am the one who hired you, who pays your wages. She has no right to turn you off!'

He tightened his grip on Miss Hinchcliffe's elbow, turned her round and marched her back up the steps once more. Timms opened the door to admit him so swiftly that Michael suspected he must have been standing on a chair, keeping an eye on proceedings through the fanlight.

'Lord Caldicot,' Miss Hinchcliffe protested, weakly, 'there is nothing you can do…'

'We'll soon see about that. Timms! Where might I find Lady Birchwood?'

'She is in the drawing room, having tea, My Lord.'

'Is she now?' He handed Miss Hinchcliffe's case to Timms. 'Have that taken back to Miss Hinchcliffe's room.'

'No!' Miss Hinchcliffe reached over and snatched it from the older man's hands. 'I will hang on to that, thank you. It is by no means certain that you will be able to persuade her to reinstate me.'

'She cannot reinstate you,' he argued, urging her up the stairs, 'since you have not been turned off. Not officially. Only *I* have the authority to do so.'

He thrust open the door to the drawing room and strode in, Miss Hinchcliffe's elbow still held firmly in his grip. Because, he found, he simply could not let go of her. No more than he could tamely let her go on Lady Birchwood's say-so.

She was, to his great annoyance, sitting on a sofa, calmly sipping tea and making inroads into a plate full of biscuits. Or scones. One could never be completely sure.

'What,' he growled, 'do you think you are about, my lady?'

She paused, a biscuit, yes, he'd give it the benefit of the doubt, halfway to her mouth, which hung open.

'I might well,' she said, rallying and adopting a forbidding air, 'ask you the same question. How dare you come in here incorrectly dressed?'

He was, he realised, still wearing his coat and hat. He'd been so angry and so determined to have things out with Lady Birchwood that he hadn't paused to take them off.

'And bringing,' Lady Birchwood continued, her nose wrinkling with disdain, 'that creature in with you?'

That creature?

'I have brought *Miss Hinchcliffe* in here,' he said, feeling as if he was hanging on to his temper by the merest thread, 'because I found her on the front steps, in some distress, telling me that you had so far forgotten yourself that you had taken it upon yourself to dismiss her. Without as much as consulting me!' To relieve his feelings, as much as to prevent the staff from overhearing the discussion, he kicked the door shut behind him.

'I suppose that is precisely the sort of behaviour I should have expected,' said Lady Birchwood with disdain, setting down her cup in its saucer, 'from a woman of her sort. Running off telling tales...'

'I only came across her by chance.' And thank heavens he'd listened to that prickle of premonition. If he'd shrugged it off and carried on testing out the new pistols he'd been thinking of purchasing, Miss Hinchcliffe would be heaven knew where by now. 'And the only thing she has told me is that you have had the audacity to dismiss her, without consulting me on the matter.'

'Surely the hiring and firing of female staff is in my remit, as your hostess in this house...'

'Yet I distinctly recall having to engage a companion for my ward, *myself*, because of your complete inability to choose one who had the nerve to remain in that post for more than a sennight.'

'That was years ago. And anyway...'

'You have no reason to dismiss Miss Hinchcliffe! She has not only been the only female with the backbone to stomach the kind of tantrums to which my ward has been allowed to indulge, but she has made positive progress. Before her advent, Susannah had no accomplishments, no manners. Now she not only manages to behave as prettily as any other well-born female when in company, but she can actually pick out a tune or two on a piano when occasion calls for it.'

At his side, he felt Miss Hinchcliffe attempting to tug her arm out of his hold. He supposed, if he deposited her on a chair and then took up a position by the door he'd kicked shut, she would not be able to escape.

So that was what he did. He led her to the sofa opposite Lady Birchwood's, made her sit on it, then went to the door to guard it.

'Nevertheless,' said Lady Birchwood, as Miss Hinchcliffe set her battered little case down at her feet, as though in readiness to snatch it up and run off with it at a moment's notice, 'I felt it my duty to remove this person from the house, with or without your consent. When I learned something…to her detriment.'

'What do you mean?' He leaned against the door and folded his arms across his chest, noting that Miss Hinchcliffe had bowed her head and that her cheeks were turning red.

'I have it on the best authority,' Lady Birchwood continued, darting Miss Hinchcliffe a disparaging glance, 'that she is prone to acts of violence.'

Good grief. Had someone seen her toss Baxter out of the window? No, they couldn't have. In fact, the only person who might have been able to tell Lady Birchwood anything about the events of that night was Baxter himself.

And he'd threatened Miss Hinchcliffe, hadn't he, when she'd refused to help him in his scheme to get his hands on Susannah's wealth? This was, by the sound of it, his notion of revenge.

'Someone has told you some fantastic tale,' he said witheringly, though his heart was beating rather fast, 'which they cannot possibly corroborate, and on that pretext you have taken it upon yourself to dismiss her?'

Someone, probably Baxter—yes, his money was on Baxter being behind this—must have handed her the excuse she'd been looking for ever since he'd danced with Miss Hinchcliffe at Birkbeck House. No, before that. She'd resented the way Susannah had insisted that the only way she would agree to having Lady Birchwood preside over her Season was if Miss Hinchcliffe stayed on and came to London with them. Lady Birchwood had argued in vain that Susannah no longer needed a governess. When Susannah made up her mind, nobody stood much chance of changing it.

And what he'd sensed over the breakfast table this morning, he perceived, had been the aroma of malevolent triumph, oozing from a woman who thought she was about to exact her revenge.

'On the contrary,' said Lady Birchwood, her own colour rising as her eyes flashed with anger, 'there are *several* persons who can corroborate the *tale*, as you deem to call it. You really should have looked into her references more closely.' She gave an arch little laugh. 'I mean to say, no person who spoke of a former employee in such glowing terms could possibly have wanted her to leave, could they?'

Her voice was rising to a squeal of such high pitch that it was a wonder she didn't set all the dogs in the neighbourhood to barking. 'And if you,' she said, jabbing one pudgy finger in his direction, 'had more experience in the hiring of governesses, or indeed, any at all, you would have smelled a rat at the time!'

That brought him up short. This wasn't about Miss Hinchcliffe ejecting Baxter from her bedroom window. She was referring to something that had happened before she'd ever come to work for him.

He turned to Miss Hinchcliffe slowly. She was hanging her head, biting down on her lower lip, her whole posture depicting a sort of defeated misery.

'Miss Hinchcliffe,' he said, his heart beating so fast now it was making him feel a bit sick, *'did* you gain employment with us by using false references?' If it was so, then she'd betrayed him. From the outset. And all the camaraderie that had sprung up between them, all the…affection he'd begun to feel for her, was all based on lies.

Chapter Eighteen

Rosalind couldn't bear the way he was looking at her. As though she'd betrayed him.

'Miss Hinchcliffe,' he said, in a rather cold voice, '*did* you gain employment with us by using false references?'

It was the way he put the emphasis on the word *did* that gave her the tiniest grain of hope. As though he didn't want to believe ill of her. As though he was hoping she could deny it. And so she lifted her head.

'No. Absolutely not.'

Lady Birchwood made a most undignified noise. If Susannah had made it, Rosalind would have accused her of snorting.

'Precisely what,' Lord Caldicot said coldly to Lady Birchwood, 'did you mean by that?'

'I have already told you,' she said, darting Rosalind a glance loaded with malevolence, 'that several persons can vouch for that creature,' she said, jabbing at her with the hand that was still clutching the thing that was masquerading as a biscuit, with the result that crumbs sprayed everywhere, 'who was dismissed from her last post for committing an act of violence!'

'You spoke,' he said in that same, cold, clipped tone, 'to these people, did you?'

'Well, no, not exactly. That is,' Lady Birchwood continued when he raised one brow, 'I heard it from someone who has told me that there were several people who can corroborate the story.'

'So, in effect, you dismissed Miss Hinchcliffe on the basis of a rumour, repeated by one person, without checking with these other so-called witnesses.'

Oh. She could have hugged him. Because that was exactly what it had been like. Lady Birchwood had simply seized on the first excuse she could find to send her packing.

'May I ask who this person was?' said Lord Caldicot, his eyes turning cold and hard. 'Who related this absurd tale?'

'A most respectable person,' retorted Lady Birchwood. 'Who had it on the best authority...'

'Just as I thought,' he said drily. 'You listened to unsubstantiated gossip.'

'How dare you?' Lady Birchwood's jowls quivered with indignation. 'I did no such thing. I challenged Miss Hinchcliffe to give an account of herself and,' she concluded with triumph, 'she refused!'

He turned to regard her, solemnly. 'Is that true? Did you refuse to explain how such a rumour may have come about?'

Rosalind lowered her head and picked at a seam in her left glove with her right hand. Her bare right hand. Somewhere between the street, and this drawing room, she appeared to have lost her right glove.

'Miss Hinchcliffe,' he said. 'I am waiting for you to tell me what happened.'

Oh, how she wished she could tell him. But she'd made a promise. With a feeling of resignation, she lifted her head to look at him, probably for the last time. And this was not how she wanted to remember him, standing there, looking down at her so severely. She wanted to remember him laughing with her, talking to her as though their minds and thoughts matched. As though he respected her opinions and shared them. The man who'd asked her to dance and then looked as though he was thoroughly enjoying himself while he did so.

Had that version of him gone for ever?

'I cannot speak about it,' she said bleakly.

'Why not?'

To her relief, his voice was not harsh. He was not looking at her as though she'd committed some crime. He just looked…curious.

'Is it,' he persevered, gently, 'because you made a promise not to do so?'

'Yes! But how could you have known?'

He hadn't known. She could tell from the look of relief that wiped the lines of strain from his face. He'd *hoped* that it was something of the sort, that was what he'd done. He'd *hoped* she had a good reason for refusing to defend herself from Lady Birchwood's accusation and that was the only reason he had been able to come up with.

And it was the correct one.

'Miss Hinchcliffe,' he said, 'it is clear to me that nobody would have given you the kind of reference Lady Dorrington did had she dismissed you for committing some random act of violence. Besides, during the years you have been in my employ, you have proved yourself worthy of every encomium written in it.'

A little sob escaped her throat at this evidence of his faith in her. Because he knew very well that she did sometimes act before she'd thought things through. That she had caused Mr Baxter to fall out of a window and, more to the point, had hit him again when he'd accosted her in Hookham's library.

He could easily have believed whatever tale someone had told Lady Birchwood. Instead, he had brought her back into the house and given her a chance to defend herself.

'However,' he said, rather more sternly, 'for the sake of Lady Birchwood's nerves, I think it is time you put whatever promise you made aside, and tell us both, in confidence, what grounds your enemies have for spreading malicious gossip about you. Because it must be some enemy, must it not? Someone who wishes you ill and wants to see you humiliated?'

Oh. Yes, why hadn't she thought of that? As soon as he'd put the emphasis on the word *enemy*, her mind had flown back to Mr Baxter's threat that she'd be sorry she'd made an enemy of him.

But Lord Caldicot had recalled it at once. And seen this whole episode for what it was. The attempt of a thwarted villain to exact his revenge.

'Pish!' Lady Birchwood threw the remnants of her biscuit back on to the plate. Which was probably the best place for it. 'A person of her sort doesn't make enemies. It is someone who is a true friend to our family who is warning us to beware of her, that is what this is!'

'Or someone who wishes to remove her, because she is doing such a sterling job of both guarding and advising Susannah. Have you forgotten,' he said, 'that you despaired of Susannah ever gaining any accomplishments before her Season? And how swiftly Miss Hinchcliffe persuaded her to practise at her piano? No other governess, nor any of her female relatives, was able to make her do anything she'd decided she didn't want to do, were they? In fact, I'd go so far as to say that nobody was able to as much as keep her in line, until I hired the redoubtable Miss Hinchcliffe.'

That was not a wise thing to say, to judge by the high colour which suddenly mottled Lady Birchwood's cheeks. It was a reminder that she'd failed to have any positive influence over her own niece whatsoever. That Susannah hadn't even wanted to go through her debut with only Lady Birchwood on whom to rely.

'Now, Miss Hinchcliffe,' he said in a rather more stern tone that he'd adopted during this interview so far, 'I really must insist that you tell us exactly why you left your former employ and how it came to be that you gave someone grounds for accusing you of acting in a reprehensible manner.'

She could refuse.

She could keep her promise to never speak of that day and just walk away, her conscience clear, knowing that he still had faith in her. That he'd perceived that this was the work of Mr Baxter, somehow.

Only, it would mean never seeing him again.

And she'd already spent most of this morning in an agony, believing that was exactly what was going to happen. She hadn't known how she would bear it. The pain of watching him cast his eye over prospective brides was as nothing compared to the prospect of never seeing him again. If there was a chance to prevent that happening, would it be so wrong to take it?

'I… I…'

'Look at her,' said Lady Birchwood scornfully. 'Struggling to come up with some story to excuse her behaviour!'

That did it. Before Rosalind could wrestle her conscience into submission, her temper flared, incinerating everything in its path, the way it so often did.

'I am not struggling to come up with a story,' she said indignantly, 'but with my conscience. It is not an easy thing to break my word, but now I come to think of it, somebody must have spoken out of turn, or you could not possibly have heard anything about my last day at Dorrington Hall. And we *both* promised. Both Lady Dorrington and I promised never to mention what her vile nephew had attempted to do to me…'

'Are you speaking, perchance,' put in Lord Caldicot, 'of Peregrine Fullerton?'

'Yes,' she said with loathing.

'Ah, yes,' he mused. 'I had forgotten the connection. Now it all begins to make sense.'

'What do you mean?' said Lady Birchwood querulously. 'What makes sense?'

'Only that Peregrine Fullerton has a reputation for being a…shall I say a rather unsavoury young man. Tell me,' he said to Rosalind, 'or rather, tell Lady Birchwood what he did, just to make things clear, although I have to say I have a pretty good idea.'

'It was my first post as a governess, you understand,' she said to Lord Caldicot, even though he'd urged her to explain to Lady Birchwood. But she no longer cared what Lady Birchwood thought of her. She didn't need to explain anything to her. She'd made an enemy of the woman the night she'd not only danced with Lord Caldicot, but aided and abetted Susannah to flout her authority by dancing with Lieutenant Minter.

No...actually...now Lord Caldicot had explained about the tension between the two of them, she could see that Lady Birchwood hadn't approved of her from the very moment she'd taken up the post as Susannah's governess. And that when they'd started making plans for Susannah's come out and Susannah had made her opinion of Lady Birchwood's dependability plain, in her typically heedless fashion, that disapproval had deepened into a dislike she'd been able to almost feel. And nothing she said or did was likely to change that.

But she did so want Lord Caldicot to hear it all. Even though he'd already reassured her that he had faith in her, she needed to...to confirm it. Oh, it was all so muddled in her head. Only one thing was clear. Whatever the outcome of this interview, she wanted to be able to look back on it, knowing she'd held nothing back from him.

'The family had young children, so were just beginning to need a governess rather than the education their nursery maids could provide. And I got the job through family influence, straight out of school. And I was…so *young*. So green.' She shook her head at how naive she'd been. She'd thought, because she was plain and bony, that no man would ever look at her in *that* way. And so she'd misunderstood the looks Peregrine had given her when he'd come to stay with his aunt and uncle. Had thought that he'd been mocking her.

'Which meant I hadn't taken sufficient care to stay safe. When he…erm…tried to take me in his arms, I was completely taken aback. And I acted on instinct. I…er…' She darted Lord Caldicot a look to see how he was taking it. To her surprise, she caught a look of what looked suspiciously like unholy glee before he swiftly straightened his face. Because he knew, or could guess, what was coming, the wretch!

'I punched him.'

'Where?'

'On the stairs. It wasn't even the back stairs, that was what shocked me so much…'

'No, I mean where, on his anatomy?'

'I don't see,' Lady Birchwood objected, 'what difference that makes.'

'I dare say it made a great deal of difference to *him*,' said Lord Caldicot. 'May I hope that it was somewhere particularly painful?'

'It was on the nose.'

'Oh,' he said, looking rather disappointed.

'But I rather think I broke it, because there was an awful lot of blood.'

'That's much better,' said Lord Caldicot with a nod of approval. 'And may we also deduce, since you were on the stairs at the time of the, er, altercation, that he fell down them?'

'Really!' Lady Birchwood was positively vibrating with disapproval. But Rosalind no longer cared. Because she could tell that Lord Caldicot was not in the least bit cross with her. That, on the contrary, he seemed to be enjoying hearing the story.

'Well, yes, he did tumble down an entire flight of stairs,' she said.

'Serve him right!' Lord Caldicot was actually grinning as he pictured the scene. 'Did he break anything else,' he enquired hopefully, 'on the way down?'

'No. He had a soft landing, you see. On the butler, who was hurrying up from the hall, to render, as he informed me later, what assistance he could.'

'That's a pity,' said Lord Caldicot, with a rueful shake of his head.

'Yes. For the butler's collarbone was broken. Peregrine was not what you would call a…a slender man.'

At that Lord Caldicot went off into a peal of laughter.

Which only served to inflame Lady Birchwood's sense of outrage even higher. 'This is no laughing matter! The fact is that after that…that outrageous display of…violence,' she said, shooting Rosalind a look of loathing, 'Lady Dorrington clearly had no alternative but to dismiss that creature, or heaven alone knows what kind of influence she would have had on her impressionable young offspring!'

'Actually,' Rosalind pointed out, 'Lady Dorrington did not dismiss me at all. It was I who *wanted* to leave. I found the whole thing very…'

'Yes, you must have done,' said Lord Caldicot, coming over to her sofa, sitting down next to her and taking her gloved hand in his.

Which sent Rosalind into a complete tizzy. For although it was wonderful of him to display this kind of concern, it was only going to make Lady Birchwood even crosser.

'Everyone was, actually,' she said, keeping her gaze fixed on her hand, which he was now patting, as though to soothe her, 'very kind to me. A couple of the housemaids said they were glad to see him get his come-uppance. And when I left, they gave me all sorts of presents. Even the housekeeper packed me the most sumptuous hamper you could imagine, for my journey.'

'And the poor old butler?'

'Oh, he said it was a small price to pay. Particularly since Lord Dorrington gave him, so I understand, a huge amount of money, before sending him off to recover from his injury at Hastings, with a nurse in attendance and all expenses paid.'

'I am glad to hear it.'

'And when I sought another post, I deliberately looked for somewhere that there were no stray men lurking about the place. So, you see, no matter how much of a handful people keep telling me Susannah is, at least I have been...*safe* with her. From that sort of attention. Because she always stayed at Caldicot Dane and whichever of her aunts came to preside over the household, they never bothered bringing any of their husbands with them. Or encouraged unattached young men to visit. They were all, I suppose, looking out for her reputation, but I have to say it suited me very well.'

Lord Caldicot cleared his throat, hastily let go of her hand and stood up. Oh! Had he taken her statement as a hint he ought not to be holding her hand?

'And,' he said, once he'd removed to a suitably decorous distance from the sofa, 'the reference?'

'Well, you see, Lady Dorrington was terribly worried that if my grandfather ever got wind of the incident, he'd hunt Peregrine down and horsewhip him. I reassured her that she need not worry about Grandfather, because I never wished to have to speak to anyone about the whole sordid incident. And that prompted her to admit she'd feared I might demand some form of...compensation, or an inducement for keeping quiet, and she then became rather gushingly grateful that I didn't. So when she wrote that reference, she *may* have been in the sort of mood to, um, *exaggerate* my worth…'

'There! You see?' Lord Caldicot turned to Lady Birchwood. 'Miss Hinchcliffe did *not* leave that post under a cloud. If anything, the disgrace belonged to the family that had hired her and then failed to protect her from a man who is known to be a menace to females. No wonder they wanted to hush it all up.'

Lady Birchwood glowered at him. And then at her. Then harrumphed.

'I had no idea that Mr Fullerton was a menace to females,' she said, looking a little disconcerted. 'One can meet him anywhere!'

'That's as may be,' said Lord Caldicot, 'but chaps talk about him in the clubs. He's the kind of man that other men make sure to keep far away from their own daughters and sisters.'

'People should know about him, then,' objected Lady Birchwood. 'It makes no sense to keep that sort of information from ladies!'

'In general,' he said, 'the aim of most men is to make sure that their female relatives are shielded from any sort of unpleasantness. It is one of the reasons I decided I had to return to England once I heard Susannah was to make her come out. For the first time in her life, she really was in need of masculine protection. For the first time, there was something practical, as her guardian, I could do. Because there are many men of his ilk on the prowl for innocent females. Particularly females in possession of large fortunes. I wonder...' He gazed down at Rosalind for a moment or two.

'Lady Birchwood,' he said, turning to her as if he'd come to a decision. 'Rather than dismissing Miss Hinchcliffe, do you not think it would be better to use her experience to teach Susannah how to defend herself from predatory males?'

Lady Birchwood gaped at him. 'The very idea!'

'What?' said Lord Caldicot, smoothly. 'Do you think that females should remain helpless and unable to defend themselves when men of that ilk attempt to force their unwanted attentions on them? What if it had been Susannah, innocently walking down a flight of stairs, when some rake tried to push her into a corner and take liberties? Would you denounce *her* for punching said fellow on the nose? Or even pushing him down the stairs?'

'Well, that is a different matter,' said Lady Birchwood.

'Oh?' Lord Caldicot gave her a cold look. 'How, exactly?'

Lady Birchwood's mouth opened and closed a few times. It was, Rosalind thought, almost becoming a habit whenever she had to argue with Lord Caldicot.

'Do you think, because a woman is poor,' he said with a touch of disdain, 'she has no right to defend her virtue?'

Rosalind had the impression that was exactly what Lady Birchwood did think. Many of her class did. It was why all the housemaids at Dorrington Hall had been so glad when she'd punched the pernicious Peregrine and caused him to fall down the stairs. Because, for years, he'd been preying on them and nobody had done a single thing to stop him. Not Lady Dorrington, not Lord Dorrington, nobody.

'Very well,' said Lord Caldicot, turning to look at Rosalind, and clasping his hands behind his back. 'Not only will you *not* be leaving my employ, but as from tomorrow I would like you to start teaching my ward how to defend herself from importunate males. Just in case neither you, nor I, nor anyone else who cares for her welfare is on hand to come to her rescue.'

'That,' cried Lady Birchwood, 'is the most outrageous and ridiculous thing I've ever heard!'

'You forget, madam,' he said, 'that my ward is a considerable heiress. I have already noticed that she is attracting the attention of the very worst sort of men. Men who would not scruple to attempt an abduction.'

'No!' Lady Birchwood's hand went to her throat. And since she'd mangled that last biscuit so completely, the crumbs that had stuck to her fingers now found their way into the lace at her neckline.

'And anyway,' put in Rosalind, 'I don't really know anything that I could actually *teach* her. I mean, I just sort of…lashed out. In a panic. And got in a lucky punch. And if we hadn't been at the top of the stairs, I don't think I could have knocked him down, or anything like that.'

He gave her a searching look. 'In that case,' he said, 'you will oblige me by accompanying me to my study, straight away, so that I may give you some pointers. And then you may pass on what you have learned, to my ward. For I have reason to believe,' he said to Lady Birchwood, 'that she is in particular need of protection.'

'Then we should hire someone…' said Lady Birchwood.

'And how would we explain that? Do you want to frighten the girl? Wouldn't you rather equip Miss Hinchcliffe with the weapons necessary to protect her, so that she may enjoy the rest of the Season without worrying about possible danger?'

Lady Birchwood scowled at him.

'I suppose,' she eventually said, though very grudgingly, 'that since Miss Hinchcliffe is the kind of person who *is* prone to violence,' she said, wrinkling her nose as though she'd smelled something nasty, 'we may as well put her proclivities to good use. Since you refuse to dismiss her.'

'It is the most practical solution,' said Lord Caldicot, smoothly.

Then he turned and, with his back to Lady Birchwood, winked at Rosalind.

Chapter Nineteen

He went to the door and opened it, and held it open until Miss Hinchcliffe got to her feet and crossed the room.

Beyond her, he could see Lady Birchwood subsiding into a mound of frustrated spite on her sofa. But there was nothing more she could do. Not today. He'd completely spiked her guns.

Miss Hinchcliffe kept her head down and said nothing all the way to the hall, where she paused and looked around frantically as though searching for something.

'My valise,' she said. 'I left it in the drawing room. I had better go back and get it.'

'No need.' More than that, he didn't want her going back and facing Lady Birchwood alone. 'I shall get Timms to take it back to your room. I dare say he will be only too glad to do so.'

She frowned. Her confused frown. God, he was

starting to notice the difference between the degrees and intentions of those frowns of hers!

'Rather like the staff at your previous post,' he continued, brushing away that stray epiphany, 'the ones here won't want you to leave. Apart from anything else,' he hastened to add, when she gave a little shake of her head as though she wanted to contradict him, 'they know that if you leave, there will be nobody left who has the knack of calming her down when she flies into one of her pets.'

She said nothing, but only made a strange little noise, as though clucking her tongue at him. Which was better, to his way of thinking, than allowing her to sink into a slew of self-deprecation.

He went ahead of her, opened the study door and once again held it open until she'd taken the hint that she had to do as he'd bid her, in spite of her reservations.

'I cannot really teach Susannah how to defend herself, you know,' she announced, the moment he'd closed the door on them.

'I know,' he said gently, reaching for the ribbons of her bonnet to begin untying them.

She slapped his hand away. 'I am perfectly capable of undoing my own bonnet, thank you!'

'I know. But for some reason, the fact that you haven't yet done so gives me the uncomfortable feeling that you are still thinking of bolting.' And the fact that she'd lost her temper so far as to slap his hand cheered him no end. Because it meant that her spirit was recovering.

'I was not,' she said, yanking at the bows of her bonnet ribbon, *'bolting.'*

'Nevertheless, I feel easier in my mind now that you are removing your bonnet. It makes me more hopeful that you will not try to leave again. For any reason.'

She lifted it from her head and turned to set it on a table just inside the door. He would guess that this was as much to avoid having to look at him as for any real need to put it down in that particular spot.

'I… I must thank you for defending me from… Lady Birchwood's accusations,' she said, keeping her back to him. 'Even though you, of all people, must know that she had a fair point.' She turned to face him, her hands clasped at her waist, her brow furrowed, this time in…yes, contrition.

'I do have a tendency to resort to…to *violence*,' she said with a tremor, as though struggling with some strong emotion. 'I have a shocking temper…'

'Nonsense,' he said briskly. 'I have never met anyone with more patience than you! Nobody has ever managed to remain calm and unruffled in Susannah's orbit for long. If you really had a problem with controlling your temper it would have been Susannah you tossed out of the window.'

'I didn't *toss*…' she began to object, though, he

thought, rather mechanically. 'Besides,' she added, wringing her hands, 'I have…sometimes…wanted to throw a glass of water into her face…'

'I am not a bit surprised. But you have never done so, have you? In fact, the only times you have ever resorted to any kind of action have been when you have been in danger. And then you have *defended* yourself. Not, I repeat, *not* gone on the attack.'

She considered what he said for a moment, her frown turning to one of consideration, as though she was running through all the instances of action she'd had to take. 'You make me sound…' she said.

'Spirited,' he declared, bracingly. 'And long-suffering.'

She frowned again, this time as though she disagreed. 'But, if you really believe *that* of me, then why did you…compel me to break my word to Lady Dorrington and speak of that…vile… *Peregrine*.' She spat his name out like a lump of unpalatable gristle.

'I had to get to the truth,' he said, a touch uncomfortably. He'd simply *had* to get to the truth. Because the thought that she'd lied to him, from the start, that his vision of her had been a false one, had been so abhorrent that, well, it had felt as though he'd run, full tilt, into a brick wall. A thing that hurt, particularly for being such a stupid thing to do. For what man in his right mind did such a thing as run into a wall? Only one who was an idiot. Or blind. And for a horrid moment or two there he'd suspected he might have been both, if he'd misjudged her so badly.

'And I only had to ask Lady Birchwood a few of the most rudimentary questions to see that she was just grasping at any excuse to be rid of you. She never approved of me hiring you, to start with. Then, when Susannah made it plain she felt she'd need you to stay with her during her Season, she must have felt it added insult to injury.'

'Not approve of you hiring me? But why? Susannah needed a governess, back then...'

'Yes, but up to that point, one or other of her aunts would have managed the business. They all regarded the fact that I stepped in and consulted an agency, rather than relying on someone in the family to recommend someone, and then proceeded to interview all the applicants myself, as a piece of impertinence. As interference in the management of family matters.'

'But...you are Susannah's legal guardian. How could she...?'

'It is probably largely because she's known me from my boyhood. She still sees me as an overgrown, impudent, jackanapes. Not only her. All her sisters cannot resist reminding me of how I invariably got into trouble on the few times I was invited to either this house, or Caldicot Dane, to pay homage to the venerable head of the family. Caldicot Dane, in particular, was run on such rigid rules that, well...'

'Yes,' she said with feeling. 'That was one of the reasons why I felt so safe there.'

'I can see your point. I cannot imagine anything havey-cavey ever going on beneath that particular roof. Which is a good thing. And something I wouldn't want to change when I eventually go down and take up the reins. But… I was just a scrubby schoolboy who would much rather have been out of doors shooting rabbits or climbing trees than sitting in a drawing room being told to mind his manners while all the adults talked and talked about…well… nothing I could ever get interested in.'

'Well, as someone who has climbed a few trees herself,' she said with a wry grin, 'I can see no reason why you should not have been allowed to do so.'

'Exactly! But the thing is, I got so bored that… Well, let me give you an example. I once spent a whole afternoon in the library, where I was supposed to be improving my mind, building a maze from the books for some rats I'd liberated from the rat catcher that morning. Only, being rather intelligent creatures, they spurned the sport I'd planned for them. The moment I let them out of their boxes, they went in search of something more to their taste, which just happened to be terrorising the people gathered in the next room drinking tea. All of whom were extremely dignified sorts. There was a general, I seem to recall, as well as a bishop and a Member of Parliament…'

To his relief, he saw her clap one hand over her mouth to suppress a spurt of laughter.

'The next time I went there, on the occasion of His Lordship's birthday, they made an attempt to keep me out of mischief, by effectively confining me to the schoolroom. Naturally I broke out, stole supplies from the kitchen and camped out in the grounds. It was only a day or so before they found me, that time...'

'That time?'

'Yes, the next time I went to Caldicot Dane I—' He broke off, aware that there were some sorts of mischief he was certain she wouldn't approve of. 'Suffice it to say that I continued to embark on adventures calculated to scandalise all of Susannah's aunts, which, erm, reflected my age and developing interests. So you see why,' he said, clearing his throat, 'she formed such a low opinion of my character and morals.'

'Yes,' she said, rather cautiously, 'you do sound as though you were a very...energetic sort of boy. And, having spent some time at Caldicot Dane myself, I can see how...stuffy it must have felt.'

'Precisely! Well, eventually one of them, probably one of the aunts, suggested that I was too much for my mother to manage—you see, my father had died by then and we were living in reduced circumstances, not that I really noticed. A great manager was my mother. I was never conscious of going without anything. But Lord Caldicot, that is, the previous one, arranged for her to go and live in a cottage at Weymouth and bought me a commission in a regiment serving overseas.

'In truth, he couldn't have done anything better for me. Army life suited me to a nicety. But I digress. I was supposed to be explaining why Lady Birchwood thinks so poorly of me and to try to help you understand why it infuriated her so much when you turned out to be such a treasure, instead of being totally wrong for the job.'

He went to his desk and leaned against it, spreading his hands on the surface behind him. 'She'd wanted you, I suspect, to be living proof that I am still irresponsible and useless. The dance last week was merely the last straw, causing her simmering resentment to come to the boil. It was entirely my fault,' he said ruefully, 'that she wanted to dismiss you. I deliberately provoked her, at that ball. Well, not just her, if you must know. I wanted to offend all of them!' He was sick of them all waiting for him to do something outrageous. Something that would prove he wasn't fit to hold the title that he'd inherited.

'All of…who?'

He pushed away from the desk and took a few steps across the room. 'Every last one of those matchmaking mothers,' he said as he reached the fireplace and braced one hand on the mantel, 'and their desperate daughters and the prosy old bores who pretend they have nothing to do with what their wives and daughters get up to, but who supply them with all the ammunition they need to gun down hapless men with titles and fortunes.'

That was the worst of it. They still wanted to marry their daughters to him, in spite of looking down their snobbish noses at him. Because of the title. They wanted the title for their daughters and the only way they could get at it was through him. 'It was a selfish act on my part,' he admitted, looking down into the grate. 'Because I exposed you to their spite.'

'Well, thank you for explaining all that to me. But it isn't the whole story, is it? I mean, I have made an enemy on my own account, haven't I? You reminded me, back there in the drawing room, when you spoke of an enemy spreading malicious gossip about me—who gave Lady Birchwood a mangled version of events surrounding the way I left my previous post?'

'Well, yes,' he said, straightening up and turning round, 'I do think that somehow Baxter was behind the unpleasantness you suffered this morning. However, he would not have had any success with Lady Birchwood had I not made you the target of some of the most spiteful people it has ever been my misfortune to meet.'

'I wouldn't wonder,' she mused, 'if he isn't just the sort of man who would be friends with *Peregrine*.' She said his name in that gristle-spitting way again.

'Or at least, the sort who frequents the same sort of hells,' he agreed. 'And they are both the sort of men who can charm a certain type of lady into believing in them. It was true, what Lady Birchwood said, about Fullerton being received everywhere. Just like Baxter, he comes from a respected family. So between them, they could have poured their poison into the ears of some female susceptible to their brand of charm, who could have run straight to Lady Birchwood to tell her the version of events *they* wanted known.'

'You know, in a way,' said Miss Hinchcliffe, going over to the chair before his desk, and sinking down wearily on to it, 'I can hardly blame Lady Birchwood for wanting to get rid of me. I am hardly a shining example of decorous female behaviour, am I?'

He went back to the desk, and hitched his hip on to it, as he'd grown into the habit of doing whenever they had one of their little meetings in here. He thought he'd persuaded her that she'd done nothing so very wrong. But her conscience was clearly still troubling her. There was nothing for it. He was going to have to tease her out of the sullens.

'I must admit,' he therefore said, 'that I am *shocked*, positively shocked, at the number of injuries you have done to men during the course of your young life.'

'No, you aren't,' she said, scowling up at him. 'You thought it was funny. You could hardly keep your face straight when I told you about punching Peregrine.'

He held up one hand, in a gesture familiar to a fencer, to acknowledge the hit. 'It was hearing how he landed on the butler that nearly did it for me,' he admitted. 'I could just picture it. That stout young rascal, tumbling head over heels, spraying blood all down the stairs, only to land on an incoming butler. Priceless!' It was what he'd been itching to do ever since he'd deduced that some rogue or other must have attempted something of the sort before she'd come to work for him.

'It isn't,' she said repressively, as he succumbed once more to the laughter that hearing the tale the first time had provoked, 'a laughing matter!'

'Oh, but it is. I could never have imagined how many adventures one innocent-looking governess could have. To think that when I left the army, I expected life to become a dull round of boring routine. And though mostly it is, I can always rely on you to relieve the monotony by doing something outrageous.'

'I don't! I mean, not on purpose.'

'Which makes it all the more delightful. Though I should love to know exactly how many bodies you have left strewn in your wake. I am sure the stories connected with each and every...*accident*...would be well worth the hearing.'

'None! I have not killed anyone!'

'I confess,' he said, with a rueful shake of his head, 'to being a trifle disappointed.'

'Well, I confess,' she said, her eyes narrowing, 'to thinking you can be rather...' She pulled herself up, biting down on her lower lip.

'Beastly? Yes, I think you have said so before. It comes, I dare say, of having been a serving soldier most of my adult life. I always had to do whatever was necessary, which meant there was no time to have scruples. Added to which, I am not the slightest bit squeamish. So, if there are no more bodies weighing down your conscience, you may freely confess to all the broken bones, lost teeth, bruises...'

She pulled her lips into a firm line, but to his concern, instead of scowling at him, she began to look rather upset.

'It isn't my fault. Things just happen...and when they do, though I have *tried* to curb my temper and behave in a more ladylike fashion...'

'Well, don't! Don't change anything about yourself!'

Her eyes widened.

'That is,' he put in hastily, wondering if he'd betrayed his feelings for her in too direct a manner, 'I mean, as I told Lady Birchwood, you need to be able to defend yourself against the kind of men who would take advantage of you. And if you didn't punch them, or kick them, or throw something at them, well, who knows what they might have done to you.'

She tilted her head to one side. 'Yes. That is a fair

point. And thank you for saying it. But as for teaching Susannah how to fight...' She shook her head. 'I wouldn't know where to begin. You have been amused to paint me as some sort of...avenging harpy, going about fighting evil wherever I find it, but it isn't anything like so...noble. In fact, I think of the way I... lash out as something...instinctive. A habit. A bad habit, that I developed in the orphanage. You see, I hadn't been there for very long before I learned that if you didn't stick up for yourself, you would go hungry. Because the bigger children always pushed the smaller, weaker ones aside whenever mealtimes came round. And I was *always* hungry.'

'It is completely understandable,' he told her. 'I know just how hard it is to break habits developed in childhood. I can lecture myself until I am blue in the face, but I can never totally suppress that part of me which is still a little boy who doesn't want to sit in the schoolroom, who wants to break out and explore the world outside the stuffy confines of Caldicot Dane.

'You know, I didn't literally mean you should teach Susannah to box, or shoot, or anything of that nature. I was just trying to persuade Lady Birchwood that those very qualities in you she so dislikes could be seen as an advantage. Rather than just throwing my weight around and decreeing that my word in this house is law, which would have set her back up even more.'

'But your word in this house *should* be law.'

'You are just about the only person who thinks so,' he replied bitterly.

'I am sure that is not the case.'

'But Lady Birchwood makes it her business to undermine me at every turn! I shouldn't have let her take charge of hiring staff for the Season,' he mused, 'that was a mistake. It encouraged her to make out that she still has…rights over things here. She constantly reminds everyone how often she visited this house when her brother was the Marquess. And wastes no opportunity to bemoan the fact that I am only his uncle's son, rather than his own. A very inferior uncle at that, who married a woman of gentry stock!

'And do you remember how tediously she went on and on about her own come-out ball, which her father, the Fourth Marquess, threw for her, in this very house, while she was supposed to be welcoming Susannah's guests to *her* come-out ball?'

Rosalind nodded ruefully. On that occasion, she'd taken up a position on the landing, from which she could observe, without herself being seen, he recalled. And even back then, he'd wanted to invite her to come down and join in. Before he'd truly known what a delightful person she was.

'Well, never mind all that,' he said, pushing himself off the desk and walking over to the window. Because the way she looked at him, the way she spoke to him with such…trust, made him want to take her in his arms and kiss her. But if he did that, it would shatter that trust. She'd think he was just like all the other men who'd tried to take advantage of her.

And he'd be the next victim she felled with her powerful right hook. Unless she was left-handed.

He turned round. 'Are you left-handed, or right-handed?'

She frowned in confusion at the sudden change of subject. 'What has that to do with anything?'

'Only that I had a sudden…whim to know which arm you threw punches with.'

'I… Well, I write with my right hand,' she said. 'But I honestly couldn't tell you which hand I punched Peregrine with. It was so long ago, and I have tried to…to blot it out of my memory.'

'Stand up,' he said, suddenly seeing a way he could legitimately interact with her, in a physical way, right here, right now. He couldn't kiss her. After all she'd told him, that would be an act of sheer villainy. But he could spar with her. In fact, now he came to think of it, every encounter they'd ever had in private had been in the nature of a sparring match. Verbally, anyway.

She stood up, even though she still looked a bit confused, so he went round the desk to remove her chair, so as to clear a bit of floor space.

'Now, imagine, if you will, that I am Peregrine,' he said.

She pursed her lips. 'Really, my lord, I don't think this is the least bit appropriate.'

'Haven't you learned by now that I don't enjoy doing what is appropriate? Being appropriate is no fun.'

'And pretending to be a man like Peregrine is?'

'Just humour me,' he said. 'I suspect you must have a powerful right hook if you managed to knock a man right down the stairs. Let alone another one out of a window, just by throwing a book. And I'd like to feel it.'

'I couldn't punch you!'

'Well, no, of course not, not if you haven't any science. I box regularly, so I know how to block any attack you might make.'

'Then what is the point?'

The point was...to hell with what the point was! He couldn't do what he really wanted with her. And he couldn't dance with her, in here, not without benefit of music, she'd think he'd got windmills in his head. But this sort of flowed on from the conversation they'd been having.

'Now,' he said, stooping into a crouch, 'I am creeping up the stairs, trying to get you into an alcove,' he said, inching closer and spreading his arms wide as if to catch her. But instead of raising her fists, she just began to breathe more deeply. And her lips parted.

'This isn't going to work, Miss Hinchcliffe,' he warned her, 'if you look at me like that.'

He stepped right up to her. He was so close now that the toe of his boot slipped under the edge of her skirt. As she breathed out, her scent brushed his lips. The look of intensity in her gaze took his breath away.

She was blushing. Breathing heavily, but making no attempt to repulse him.

He began to bring his arms round her. He ought not to do it. He knew it was wrong. But the temptation was so great…

And then she moved. Her hand shot out so swiftly that it took him completely by surprise as she gave him a hefty shove in the chest. Then, her face flaming, she whirled round and fled from the room.

Leaving him standing there, staring at the open door and rubbing at his breastbone where he felt certain, by tomorrow, there would be a bruise.

He was, most definitely, a marked man.

But, since he'd been gazing into her eyes, or at her lips, he still had no idea whether she'd led with her left or her right.

Chapter Twenty

Rosalind ran all the way upstairs and didn't stop until she'd reached her room, gone in and slammed the door behind her.

She'd almost let him kiss her! What had she been thinking!

That she'd *wanted* him to, that was what. So much so that she'd just stood there, willing him to come closer, though how he could have done so when their breaths had been mingling in a way that, had it been any other man, she would have thought it indecent.

Why didn't she think it was indecent with him? What was it about him that overturned all her ingrained dislike and distrust of men and made her wish she was eligible and pretty, and, oh, all the things she was not?

She slumped against the door, letting it take her weight.

Would he believe the excuse that she'd been grateful to him for the way he'd come to her rescue? For persuading her that she *didn't* have trouble controlling her temper? For the way he'd...teased her, rousing her temper so that she'd started to feel more like herself than the weak, wilting watering pot she'd become when she'd thought she'd have to leave Kilburn House for ever. And never see him again.

For saying that he didn't want her to try to change herself. Which had meant that he liked her just as she was.

For confiding in her about his youth and his own background which wasn't all that dissimilar to hers, since his mother was from gentry stock, and his... struggles to fill the shoes of the former Marquess, who sounded to her like a complete fathead.

But none of that was the complete truth. She just... wanted him. In a way she'd never felt about any other man. Indeed, in a way she'd never thought she possibly *could* feel about a man. She'd always thought men were best avoided. They let her down, or caused trouble, or were just generally unreliable. But somehow, Lord Caldicot had crept into a category all his own. She couldn't see him letting her down, or causing her trouble, or being unreliable...

How on earth was she going to get through the days ahead, feeling the way she did about him, and, worse, knowing that he must know how she felt? He must think she was a sad, desperate, spinster, that was what. He must *despise* her.

It turned out that she managed to muddle through by never looking him in the eye. By making excuses about being too busy whenever he requested another private discussion about Susannah, so that she could avoid ever being on her own with him. And by forbidding herself from gazing at him, whenever they were in the same room, in case anyone else noticed her feelings. Because she was sure they must be written on her face.

It was hardest when they went out to a ball. Tonight, for example, she'd found it well-nigh impossible not to watch whatever he was doing. Whether it was talking to the other men present, or dancing with eligible debutantes. No matter how hard she tried to keep her eyes on Susannah, they just kept on straying back to him.

It was a huge relief when Lieutenant Minter came over to ask permission to take Susannah out on to the terrace, while new sets were forming up on the floor.

'You are not going to dance, then?' Rosalind looked from the Lieutenant, to Susannah, who was already taking his arm,with a determined look on her face.

'We would only annoy Lady Birchwood again, wouldn't we,' Susannah pointed out. 'And she would take it out on *you*, like she did before. I was so upset when I heard that she tried to dismiss you, it made me…' She bit down on her lower lip, then tossed her head as though casting whatever thought had troubled her to one side. 'But nobody could object to us going outside for a stroll, provided you accompanied us, could they?'

Rosalind pursed her lips, because she thought that people would probably think the exact opposite. That a man could not get a girl into trouble on a dance floor, the way he could if he took her outside. Even if he did make sure he had a chaperon in attendance. It hinted at…intimacy.

Nevertheless, she never could find it in herself to be unkind to poor Lieutenant Minter. And going outside would also mean she wouldn't have to sit watching Lord Caldicot dancing with Lady Susan Pettifer. Out of all the girls with titles, wealth and connections, why on earth did he seem to spend so much time with one who was renowned for her spiteful tongue?

But, perhaps most crucially, Susannah now had the kind of mulish set to her mouth which meant she'd made up her mind. And even though she'd just said she regretted acting in a way that had contributed to Rosalind almost losing her job, that was no guarantee her mood of contrition, and thoughtfulness for another's welfare, would persist, if Rosalind attempted to thwart her will. So, taking all things into consideration, she might as well accept the inevitable.

So, outside the three of them went. It was a mild night, so she did not need to go and fetch a shawl first. And the sky was clear. She went and leaned against the parapet separating the terrace from the grounds, while the younger couple kept on walking. It was a night with far more opportunity for romance, she reflected, than the last time she'd come out on to a terrace very similar to this one. Not only were the stars twinkling enthusiastically, but the moon was also smiling down on the scene.

She sighed. If only Lord Caldicot…but no. If he were to come out here, she'd have to *talk* to him. Which she'd successfully managed to avoid doing ever since the almost-kiss in his study. And if they talked, he'd probably get her to admit how she felt. And then he'd have to point out, in the kindest way possible, that she could never be anything more to him than…

She tilted back her head, blinking furiously up at the moon which was wavering before her watering eyes.

No, he wouldn't be kind. He'd be direct. Forthright. And wasn't that what she liked about him? No… flummery.

He…wait a minute, what on earth was the matter with Susannah? She appeared to be shouting, or at least, speaking to Lieutenant Minter in an agitated manner. Rosalind stepped back from the parapet and turned to look at the young couple.

Lieutenant Minter was glowering at Susannah. Glowering!

While Susannah had her hands on her hips, and was pouring out a torrent of words that, although she could not overhear them, sounded...indignant.

Oh, dear. Rosalind had been so wrapped up in her own concerns that she'd entirely neglected her charge. And it looked as if the young man must have over-stepped the bounds of propriety, because all of a sudden Susannah stopped berating him, slapped his face, turned on her heel and came marching back along the terrace, tears streaming down her face.

'I want to go home,' she sobbed, flinging herself on to Rosalind's chest.

'Yes...yes, of course,' Rosalind murmured sooth-ingly, as she wondered how on earth she was going to remove a sobbing girl from a ballroom without raising eyebrows.

Lieutenant Minter came over. 'I shall order your carriage and collect your cloaks,' he said grimly, be-fore marching back into the house, solving Rosalind's concern without her having to ask for his help.

Susannah sobbed a bit harder and buried her face in Rosalind's neck.

'There, there,' she said, helplessly, patting Susan-nah's heaving shoulders. And then, 'I must say, I am surprised by the Lieutenant. I never thought he would step out of line. I thought he respected and admired you too much.' She'd begun to think that Lord Caldicot might not be the only man in the world who could treat a woman with respect.

'He is a beast!' Susannah raised her tear-stained face to Rosalind's. 'I never want to see him or speak to him again!'

At which precise moment, the Lieutenant appeared, carrying their cloaks. And though he must have heard Susannah, he took no notice of her outburst, merely draping her cloak round the girl's shoulders.

'The carriage should be ready by the time you reach the front steps,' he said woodenly. 'You can reach it by going along the terrace, down the steps, and through the servants' hall. Nobody needs to see her in such distress. I know it would pain her for anyone to see her when she is not in looks.'

Which she wasn't. Susannah didn't cry prettily. When she cried, she gave it her all. Which meant that her complexion went blotchy and her nose went red.

'Ooh!' cried Susannah, stamping her foot and whirling round indignantly. 'Must you be so…hatefully…*organised*? And how…ungallant of you to mention my looks!'

He looked down at Susannah's furious little face, pain etched across his features. 'I will inform our hosts that you have taken Lady Susannah home as she is suffering from a sudden headache,' he said to Rosalind. He reached out his hand, as though to touch Susannah's hair, then withdrew it, balling it into a fist.

'I *am* suffering from a headache,' Susannah spat, raising a resentful face to his. 'Thanks to you!'

Rosalind didn't think this was the time or the place to find out precisely what the Lieutenant had done to upset Susannah so. Nor to point out the fact that not two minutes after she'd said she never wanted to speak to him again, she'd done just that. As she'd learned from her own grandfather, when a person lost their temper, consistency, along with logic, frequently flew out of the window.

When they reached Kilburn House, Susannah went flying up the stairs to her room, scattering a trail of gloves, scarves and one dancing shoe in her wake. Rosalind trailed behind her, picking up each item and following her to her room. From beyond the closed door she could hear the sound of furious weeping.

Taking a deep breath, she knocked, then, without waiting for an answer, she went in.

Having dropped the bundle of random accessories Susannah had discarded, in a pile by the door, she crossed the room and sank down on her usual chair.

After only a short while, Susannah raised her head from the pillows and turned her tear-stained face in Rosalind's direction.

'Go away,' she sobbed. 'I do not want one of your…
uplifting homilies! I do not want to be coaxed out of
the sullens as though I am a child! My heart is broken—*broken*, do you hear me? And there is nothing
anyone can do about it!'

'Oh, dear,' said Rosalind, inadequately. 'Should I
perhaps ring for Pauline, then, to help you undress?
And bring you some warm milk?'

'I just told you,' Susannah screamed. 'I am not a
child to soothe with glasses of warm milk! Leave me
alone!' she sobbed.

'Very well,' said Rosalind, getting to her feet. To
be honest, she didn't feel up to dealing with Susannah tonight. She already had enough to perplex and
trouble her on her own account.

Although, she mused, as she made her way next
door to her own room, not once had she felt the slightest bit angry with the girl. Or inclined to slap her, or
throw something at her.

Perhaps Lord Caldicot was correct about her. Perhaps she wasn't as bad-tempered as various people,
throughout her life, had told her.

In some surprise, she sank on to her favourite chair,
at which point she realised that Susannah was not
the only one with a headache. She rubbed at a spot
above her right eye, where it felt as if someone was
stabbing her with a red-hot needle. How long had this
been coming on? Days, probably. She'd put her gen-

eral feeling of malaise, and her low spirits, down to a combination of all that crying when she'd thought she'd lost her job here and then the overwhelming humiliation of almost letting Lord Caldicot kiss her.

But now she wondered if she was, in truth, sickening for something. She felt...hot. And cold at the same time. And a bit...well, queasy.

She went over to the balcony to open the doors, wondering why it was that the maids insisted on shutting them every time she turned her back. There was little enough fresh air in London at the best of times, but sometimes, in the evenings, a slight breeze did get up and made the rooms feel a bit fresher.

She was walking away, wondering whether to return to the chair from where she could reap the benefit of what air was coming into the room, or go over to the bed and flop on to it and pull a pillow over her head to muffle the pain which was starting to build and spread across her whole forehead, when she heard a sound that made a chill run down her spine.

The sound of something grating against her balcony railing.

Followed by the muffled grunt of someone clambering on to it.

She whirled round, her heart pounding, knowing that there was only one person who would use this route to gain entry to the house, rather than knocking on the front door.

And she was right.

It was Cecil Baxter.

Chapter Twenty-One

Mr Baxter looked rather the worse for wear. That was Rosalind's first thought. His hair needed cutting and the attention of a comb, and his clothes should have gone to the laundry at least a week ago.

But it was his face that really alarmed her. His complexion was mottled purple, his eyes glittering strangely.

Instinctively, she took a step back, her eyes scanning the room for something she could use as a weapon. Although hadn't she vowed to stop acting without thinking first? Especially when a man was poised on the edge of a balcony. If she rushed over and pushed him off, which was what she wanted to do, who was to say he wouldn't land on the terrace, rather than in the shrubbery this time?

She'd felt dreadful when she'd thought she'd killed him. She hadn't meant to hurt him at all, only to… to…well, she didn't know what she'd thought. She'd just *reacted*, as Lord Caldicot had said, to what had felt like a threat. It hadn't been, but how was a girl to have known that? Well, what was a girl to think when a man sneaked into a house through a window, at night, rather than entering through the front door, at a respectable hour for visiting?

But anyway, after hesitating this long, she would never be able to claim that she hadn't *meant* to hurt him, would she, if she ran over and pushed him off the balcony now? She wouldn't just be lashing out in self-defence.

'You…' he breathed, as he finally got both feet on to the balcony, so that she no longer had much of a chance of ejecting him right back out the way he'd come in, anyway. 'You…jade.'

'No flowers to offer me this time, Mr Baxter?' she found herself saying, rather absurdly.

'Flowers are wasted on your type,' he hissed, prowling towards her in a way that made her retreat even further from him.

The backs of her legs connected with her reading chair. Unwilling to be trapped in it, with him looming over her, she skirted round it, so that it became a barrier between them.

'You have a mean, twisted heart,' he snarled, 'that no man will ever be able to melt. And what man would want to?'

She found herself unable to answer that, since

she agreed with the second part of it, if not the first.
Though her heart was not twisted, she suddenly saw
very clearly, but already melted.

'Nothing to say?' Mr Baxter bent slightly, took hold
of one of the arms of her chair, and then flung it aside,
his face twisted into an ugly sneer.

'I don't know what you hope to gain from coming
in here, being nasty,' she said, taking a couple of hasty
steps away from the overturned chair, to avoid trip-
ping over it. She tried to move away from the window,
which had already proved to be the most dangerous
place to linger. But something about the look on his
face when she did that made her heart speed up uncomfortably. And about the same time, it occurred to
her that he was deliberately herding her in the direction of the bedroom part of her room.

'Well, you'll soon find out,' he sneered, making
her feel more frightened than she could ever recall
feeling in her life. 'You have thwarted me from the
start. Caused me bodily injury. And kept me from
the one sure way out of my difficulties. I had that little pigeon,' he said, waving one arm in the direction
of her bed, though she thought he probably meant to
indicate the room which lay on the other side of the
wall beyond it, which belonged to Susannah, 'ready
for the plucking, until you shoved your oar in.'

'It is my job,' she protested.

Oh, dear, why had she ever thought it would be a

good idea to try talking her way out of trouble? Every time she said something it only seemed to make him angrier. Though at least she'd refrained from pointing out his use of mixed metaphors, which she was certain would have enraged him. Men detested having their defects pointed out to them by women.

But his response was not encouraging. 'Hah!'

He was so close to her now that the explosive bark of cynical laughter blasted her face with the mingled fumes of stale beer and onions. And she'd retreated so far that there was nowhere else to go. One more step and her back would be pressed against the bedpost.

All sorts of thoughts flitted through her mind.

Lord Caldicot saying she'd never be able to land a punch on him because she had no *science*.

Her earlier declaration that if a woman showed weakness, a certain type of man would take advantage of it.

The knowledge that when the family went out for the evening, most of the servants leaped at the opportunity to do so as well, so that even if she should scream for help, the chances of anyone hearing her and rushing to help her were slim.

'Mr Baxter,' she said, as calmly as she could, all things considered, 'you can gain nothing by coming in here and threatening me. You really should leave, before somebody discovers you.'

'And who is to discover me, eh? The last of the

menservants on the premises took himself off to join the others at the Jolly Footman as soon as he'd let you in...'

Just as she'd thought!

'And if I know anything about female staff, they will all be up in the attics, tucked up into their snug little beds...'

Yes, she'd thought the same, which was why she'd hesitated before ringing for Pauline, assuming she'd be taking the opportunity to snatch a well-earned nap.

'And I have learned from you,' he said with a sinister chuckle, 'that a person can get away with murder in this house, when the master and his family are out at a ball. After all, that is what you tried to do, isn't it?'

Then, just as she was opening her mouth to retort that she hadn't got away with murder, because here he was, large as life and twice as nasty, he reached out to grab her neck.

Rosalind just had the time to let out a brief scream before his dirty fingers closed round her throat, choking it off.

She clawed at his fingers, but they were stronger than hers.

She clawed at his face, but he didn't seem to care, which was probably because she kept her nails so short that they couldn't do much damage.

Finally, she thought of using her legs, to kick out at

him, but all that achieved was to put her off balance so that they both tumbled to the floor on to the rug she kept next to her bed. His grip on her neck slackened slightly as they fell, but only briefly. And every breath she struggled to take now was rancid with the odour of greasy clothes and stale sweat.

Why on earth hadn't she just pushed him off the balcony when she'd had the chance? Lord Caldicot would have dealt with the body, even if he had fallen on to the terrace…

'What on earth,' cried the last person Rosalind might have expected to come to her rescue in the nick of time, 'is going on in here?'

'Susannah,' cried Mr Baxter, whipping his hands away from Rosalind's throat, though he still straddled her body, keeping her firmly pinned to the floor. 'She…she tried to kill me, my darling. What else could I do?'

'*She* tried to kill *you*?'

Rosalind tried to turn her head far enough to be able to look at Susannah, who still seemed to be hovering in the doorway. Or to speak, but it was all she could do to breathe, let alone force any words through her throat. And because of the angle at which she was lying, all she could see was the coverlet, hanging down from the side of her bed, and her slippers, set neatly side by side.

'I cannot,' said Susannah, in a bewildered voice, 'believe that. She wouldn't!'

'You don't know her,' said Mr Baxter. 'You don't know what violence she's capable of!'

'I didn't know you were capable of violence either,' said Susannah, sounding shocked. 'Especially not to a woman.'

'She's no woman, she's a hellcat!'

'Cecil,' said Susannah, in the petulant tone that usually came just before she lost her temper. 'Let go of Miss Hinchcliffe at once and get up off the floor.'

Amazingly, he did as he was told, and as he began to get to his feet, Rosalind rolled to one side, her hands to her bruised throat as she sucked in air greedily.

Mr Baxter stepped over her and she heard him scamper over to where Susannah was still standing, by the open door.

'My darling, I came to take you away from this place. To free you from her toils. So you can escape from the repressive rules that tyrannical guardian has set over you.'

Susannah made a strange sound. 'Cecil, you...smell awful!'

'I am sorry, my love,' he said in that oily voice he'd used on Rosalind in the library. 'But they have made things so hard for me, lately, that I've been unable to live as I would wish.'

'You have debts, then?' Susannah's voice sounded strained. 'You *have* been hiding from your creditors?'

'How clever of you to work that out.'

Rosalind began to feel as if she could sit up, now, if she did so very slowly and carefully. So she tried it, and, though the walls seemed to be rippling in and out of her vision and the floor heaved in an alarming fashion, she managed to get into a position from where she saw Mr Baxter take hold of Susannah's hand.

'Our only hope now,' he was saying, tugging Susannah away from where Rosalind lay on the floor, in the general direction of the window, 'is to elope. I know it is not the done thing, but can you not see that my case is desperate? They have kept me from you ever since your guardian refused me permission to marry you. You cannot imagine what lengths they have gone to, to keep us apart.'

'Elope? No,' said Susannah, trying to pull her hand free. 'I don't want to elope. It would be most uncomfortable.'

So, she *had* taken in some of the practical problems Rosalind had spelled out to her, when they'd been discussing eloping before, she reflected with satisfaction, as she got to her hands and knees. Whatever else she might be, Susannah was by no means stupid.

'It is the only way we can be together,' said Mr Baxter, getting one arm round Susannah's waist and compelling her in the direction of the window.

That, Rosalind reflected, was a mistake. The moment anyone attempted to compel Susannah to do anything, she invariably dug in her heels.

'I am not,' said Susannah, beginning, as anyone who knew her well would have known she would, to struggle in earnest, 'going out of that window!'

'I have provided a ladder,' said Mr Baxter soothingly. 'Surely a girl with your pluck can manage to climb down one little ladder.'

Not, Rosalind reflected, shuffling forward, a girl who was as scared of heights as Susannah.

'I am not going down a ladder,' said Susannah, 'and if you really loved me, you wouldn't ask it of me!'

'Then I will just have to carry you,' he said, stooping down to take Susannah by the knees and tipping her over his shoulder.

Susannah let out a piercing scream. One that he couldn't stifle, since both his hands were occupied in keeping her in place. And as he began to walk over to the window, the source of Susannah's terror, her screams became louder and she struggled more frantically.

Rosalind could see that if she didn't do something to stop him from getting to the ladder, they were both likely to end up plummeting to the terrace. And though it would serve Mr Baxter right, she could not allow him to harm poor Susannah.

She dismissed the bizarre notion of chucking her

slippers at him, which were the only throwable objects in reach. She needed something much harder.

Underneath the bed, she knew, was a very hard object indeed. Her chamber pot.

She groped blindly for it, grasped it and, with her other hand, grabbed the bedpost, somehow managing to pull herself to her feet.

Then, with the last of her strength, she tottered across the room, her porcelain weapon primed for action.

Just as she raised it, to strike in the general direction of the back of Mr Baxter's head, he flinched and turned. He must have caught sight of her reflection in the glass panes of the window, Rosalind realised, as he swiped at her, the same way he'd swiped at her armchair before. This time, he knocked the chamber pot clean out of her hand. It flew across the room and smashed to pieces when it struck the wall.

But at least he'd slackened his hold on Susannah when she'd obliged him to use one of his hands to defend himself. He now held her with only one arm.

And Susannah was so determined not to go anywhere near that window that he had no hope of restraining her any longer. She squirmed out of his hold and landed on her hands and knees on the floor.

Leaving Mr Baxter standing right by the open balcony doors, glaring from one to the other of them, swaying first one way, and then the other, as though he couldn't decide which of them to deal with first.

Just like, Rosalind thought, rather hysterically, a bull being baited by two small, but determined terriers.

Chapter Twenty-Two

Michael was getting that feeling again. The feeling that something wasn't right.

It had started as soon as he'd noticed that both Miss Hinchliffe and Susannah had disappeared. When he'd asked a flunkey where they were, the man had told him that they'd gone home because the young lady had the headache. By that, he'd meant Susannah. But that didn't ring true. If anyone had reason to have a headache, it was Miss Hinchliffe. She'd been looking distinctly peaky for the last few days.

Ever since he'd nearly lost his head and almost attempted to kiss her, damn fool that he was. She'd trusted him so much that she'd just stood there, allowing him closer. Which had shocked her. So much that she'd fled the room.

She'd been avoiding him ever since. And he couldn't blame her. Hadn't she just told him all about how she'd treated that pestilential Peregrine? She'd knocked *that* scoundrel down the stairs. He was lucky that shoving him away was the worst she'd done to *him*. She ought to have slapped his face, at the very least.

If only she wasn't his employee. If only he had the right to kiss her! He wouldn't even dislike attending balls so much if he could dance with her, without raising eyebrows.

But anyway, he was now getting the horrid feeling that this headache they'd come up with between them was just a smokescreen. That if he didn't get back to the house and put things right between them, he'd find her packed and gone.

And this time there might be no stopping her.

Although…wouldn't that solve the problem caused by her being in his employ? Yes! For once she was a free agent, he could…court her without any nasty overtones of impropriety. Which was exactly what he wanted to do, he realised. Court her.

She'd taken the carriage to convey Susannah back to Kilburn House, naturally. Not that he cared. It would be as quick to walk there, particularly as his state of mind was not going to allow him to stroll. Because, once Susannah had married and Rosalind was free, he would not have to stay in London, dancing attendance on women he could not imagine spending five minutes alone with, never mind the rest of his life!

* * *

Nobody answered his knock when he went up the front steps. He frowned. Lady Birchwood didn't seem to have hired a particularly reliable set of servants for this London Season. According to his account books, he paid a man a generous wage to act as night porter, so the fellow ought to be there to let him in. But from what he could tell, it looked as though the whole house was deserted. He wouldn't be a bit surprised to learn that all the staff had sloped off to the pub, just as they'd done the night Baxter had tried climbing in through a balcony window and received his just deserts. Though, if that was the case, how had Miss Hinchcliffe and Susannah fared when they got home? Where could they have gone if they hadn't been able to get in? If Miss Hinchcliffe had been in charge of this household she'd have kept the staff up to the mark, he was sure. In fact, she wouldn't have hired this motley crew in the first place.

Michael scowled at the infuriatingly unopened front door as he wondered how *he* was going to get in. Then, taking a step back, he noticed a light glowing through the window of the basement area. Might he be able to get in through the kitchen door?

The level of indignation he felt as he began to go down the area steps made him wonder if he finally *was* settling into the role of Marquess. After all, when he'd been merely Major Kilburn, he wouldn't have thought twice about going into anyone's house via the servants' entrance. And, though this was the first time he'd tried to enter this particular house by way of the kitchen door, he certainly wasn't unfamiliar with the areas below stairs, was he? As a boy he'd felt more at home down there, where the cook would give him biscuits and the grooms would let him look at the horses, than above stairs where his aunts and uncles, as well as his parents, would all expect him to sit still and *behave*.

Nobody answered when he knocked on the kitchen door, either, dashing his hope that there might at least have been a cook enjoying a doze before the fire, whom he could rouse. But when he tried the handle, it turned easily and the door swung inwards.

And now he wasn't sure whether to be relieved he'd managed to get in, or annoyed that *anyone* might have done the same. Baxter, for example. In spite of it all, his lips quirked into a wry grin. If only the fellow had known how lax security was in this house, he could have saved himself a great deal of effort, not to mention serious injury, last time he'd been here.

He stood for a moment or two, looking round the kitchen. It looked like the same table where the old cook, Mrs Watson, had plied him with biscuits, though she was long gone. On that table stood the lighted lamp he'd glimpsed from the front steps. A kettle was simmering on the stove, steam dulling the surfaces of the copper pans hanging from the over-mantel.

The staff who had deserted their posts, he reflected sardonically, would be able to make themselves a lovely hot drink when they got back.

He wondered whether he ought to have a word with Lady Birchwood about the staff. Or speak to Timms, perhaps, he reflected as he walked across the room to the door leading to the hall, about the non-existent security arrangements in place. He could accept that staff hired for a Season couldn't be expected to feel all that much loyalty for employers they might never see again, once they'd returned to their own estates for summer. But to all go out like this was practically an invitation to the local housebreakers to walk in and help themselves.

On the other hand, if he made too much of a fuss, that same lack of loyalty might induce them to simply seek employment elsewhere. And then they'd have to go through all the inconvenience of hiring new people, which could be rather tricky since they'd probably have gained a reputation for being difficult employers. He tossed his hat on to the nearest table he found once he was in the hall and was just pulling off his gloves when he heard from an upper floor the sound of a blood-curdling scream, followed by the crash of breaking crockery, then a series of muffled thuds.

All thoughts of staffing problems vanished. For it

sounded as though it was not merely from any part of the upper floor, but from Miss Hinchcliffe's very room that those ominous sounds had come.

He took the stairs two at a time, his heart thudding painfully.

He threw open the door to Miss Hinchcliffe's room, not knowing what horrors might be waiting for him on the other side, only to see his worst fears made flesh.

Miss Hinchcliffe was lying, half on one side, unmoving, beside an overturned chair.

And Baxter was stalking steadily in Susannah's direction, though she was darting about in her attempts to evade him. She was the one he'd heard scream, he realised as she did it again.

Later, he supposed he should have gone straight to Susannah's aid, but at that moment, all he could think of was Miss Hinchcliffe, lying so still. So pale.

He went to her, bent over and saw livid marks on her neck. Marks that showed Baxter had throttled her.

He couldn't let the cur get away with that!

Rising to his feet, he crossed the room in two strides, grabbed Baxter by his collar, yanked him back, turned him round and punched him, hard, in the face.

He went down in an untidy sprawl of limbs.

'Lord Caldicot!' Susannah bounded over, wrapped her arms round his neck and burst into tears. 'You… s-saved m-me!'

'Yes, yes,' he said, impatiently removing her arms from about his neck. 'I only wish to God I'd been in time to save Miss Hinchcliffe, too.'

'She was so…so brave,' sobbed Susannah, dropping to the floor the moment he let go of her, as though she had no bones in her legs. 'When Cecil tried to… to make me g-go out of the w-window,' he dimly heard the chit say, as he sank to his knees next to Miss Hinchcliffe's unnaturally still body, 'she w-went under her bed and g-got the chamber pot.'

Which was so typical of her. She wouldn't have thought twice about using whatever weapon she could get her hands on to save an innocent girl from the depredations of an ugly fellow like Baxter.

'She would have brained him with it, I think,' Susannah said, as he slipped one arm about Miss Hinchcliffe's shoulders, raised her limp form across his lap, and tucked her against his chest, while gazing into her deathly white face, 'only that he smacked it out of her hand, then made as if he was going to strike her.'

'Did he? Did he dare to strike her?' If he had, then he was a dead man.

'N-no. He would have done, I'm sure, only that she fainted just as he lunged at her.'

At that, Miss Hinchcliffe's eyes flew open. 'I did not faint,' she croaked, indignantly. 'I *never* faint. I tripped over the chair.' Then her hand flew to her neck. Her poor, bruised neck.

He wanted to cheer. She wasn't, as he'd feared for a few dreadful moments, dead. Even though her face was a ghastly shade that reminded him of finest hot-pressed writing paper.

'I b-beg your pardon, Miss Hinchcliffe,' said Susannah, while he was swallowing back a most unmanly rush of tears, 'but it wouldn't have been surprising if you had, after his attempt to throttle you. Indeed, it was very brave of you to try to go and fetch a weapon with which to brain him, when you could hardly breathe…'

'He tried to throttle you?' With hands that trembled, he brushed a stray lock of hair from her forehead.

As she nodded dumbly, Susannah took up the tale once more. *'He* said *she'd* tried to kill him when I came in and discovered him with his hands round her neck. I think…' She swallowed back a sob. 'I think he must have gone mad!' And then she began to sob in earnest.

He didn't have the time, or the patience, to deal with hysterics. Not when Miss Hinchcliffe was lying, unmoving, in his arms, looking up at him so…passively.

She must be seriously injured to be lying there, making no attempt to struggle, or slap his face, or utter a stern rebuke, or anything.

'Susannah,' he said curtly, 'I know you've had a shock, but Miss Hinchcliffe is in a far worse case.

So I want you to pull yourself together, run down to my study, and fetch some brandy. Mixed with a little water it might just help to revive her.'

'Oh,' said Susannah, switching off the flow of tears and sitting up straight. 'Yes, poor Miss Hinchcliffe. But for her...' She wiped her face with the back of her hand. 'Though wouldn't it be better if *I* sat with her, while you went and got the brandy?'

No! There was no way he was going to let go of her and run the risk of her slipping from this life while he was away. And just to confirm him in his conviction that he ought not to leave her, Miss Hinchcliffe slid one hand up the front of his waistcoat and curled her fingers into his lapel.

Nothing that any woman, no matter how experienced in the arts of love, had ever done had moved him so much as that timid little gesture of appeal.

'You need to distract yourself from the unpleasantness you suffered at that villain's hands,' he said to Susannah without taking his eyes from Miss Hinchcliffe's face. 'I promise you, running down the stairs, and back up, while doing something to mend matters, will do you a whole lot more good than sitting there working yourself up into hysterics.'

'W-working myself up?' Susannah scrambled to her feet. 'She is right,' she said, pointing to Miss Hinchcliffe. 'You *are* beastly. But I *will* go and get some brandy. For *her*,' she snapped, whirling out of the room in a froth of expensive lace and pique.

'I thought I'd lost you,' he said, his voice hoarse with emotion, 'when I saw you lying there so still.' Then he took the opportunity of being alone with Miss Hinchcliffe to rain kisses across her forehead and cheeks. He would rather have kissed her on the mouth, but she was having enough trouble breathing as it was without him blocking up that essential lifeline.

'I'm sorry, but I cannot help kissing you,' he managed to say. 'Slap me, if you like. I deserve it for taking advantage when you are so weak and helpless.'

'Not weak,' she croaked. Then gave a funny sort of smile. 'Safe,' she mouthed. And then, with a little more conviction, *'Safe.'*

'Are you telling me I make you feel safe? Is that it?' She nodded, shyly.

'You don't mind me holding you in my arms? You don't want to push me away, as you've done to every other male who's had the temerity to make an attempt on your virtue?'

She raised her brows, as though he'd said something extremely stupid.

'Does that mean what I think it means? That you… that you…' He gazed down at her, his heart racing. She just looked back up at him…with what looked like affection shining from her eyes. 'I *will* keep you safe from now on,' he vowed. 'Always, do you hear me? If you'll let me.'

She looked up at him then, a question in her eyes.

'What,' she whispered, 'are you trying to say?'

'That I want to marry you, of course!' He stroked her cheek, noting that it wasn't so dreadfully pale any longer. In fact, there was a distinct flush to it. 'I don't know why it hasn't occurred to me before. No other woman measures up. And I don't want any other woman the way I want you.'

'Mad,' she whispered, raising one trembling hand to briefly press her palm to his cheek. 'Quite mad.'

'Madly in love, I think,' he agreed.

'Excuse me,' came Susannah's petulant voice from the hall doorway. 'I have brought the drink you ordered, so you need to put Miss Hinchcliffe down so that I can help her drink it.'

'Don't be so silly, Susannah,' he replied curtly, reaching out his hand for the glass. 'I am perfectly capable of getting that brandy down Miss Hinchcliffe myself.'

'It isn't proper,' Susannah pointed out. 'Nor is kissing her the minute my back is turned. You have no right to…to make free with her!'

'Of course I do,' he said impatiently. 'I'm going to marry her.'

'Oh!' Susannah was so surprised to hear this that she lowered the hand which was holding the glass just enough that he was able to snatch it from her and raise it to Miss Hinchcliffe's lips.

'I cannot possibly go on calling you Miss Hinchcliffe if we are going to be married,' he remarked as he started tipping the contents of the glass into her parted lips. 'What is your given name?'

'Rosalind,' she whispered, between sips.

'And you must call me Michael,' he said.

'Lady Birchwood,' said Susannah, with what sounded to him like relish, 'is going to be livid!'

'That I am going to marry the lowly governess,' he replied, 'or that we are going to have to get the governess off a murder charge not one week after she attempted to throw her out of the house on the charge of excessive use of violence.'

'It wouldn't be murder,' Susannah objected. 'Besides, she never got near him with the chamber pot. I can vouch for that. It was you who knocked him down.'

'Yes,' croaked Rosalind, 'but he isn't dead.'

As though to prove her point, Baxter chose that moment to let out a moan.

All three of them turned to look at Baxter's body, with varying degrees of disgust.

Rosalind made as if to sit up. 'I am feeling stronger now, I should...'

He tightened the hold of his arm round her shoulders. 'You should stay exactly where you are, for now. While we decide what to do about...*him*.'

Susannah gave a little sob. 'Lieutenant Minter will never forgive me!'

'For what, precisely?' he said, wondering why on earth the girl should bring that name into this situation.

'For saying he was lying to me, in order to make me forsake what I thought was my true love,' she admitted, flicking her eyes briefly at Mr Baxter, who'd gone quiet again.

Rosalind must have seen the confusion on his face, because she explained, 'Susannah told Lieutenant Minter he was wasting his time courting her, because her heart was already engaged.' She paused and swallowed. 'To a man forbidden to her by her family. And the Lieutenant declared he would be content just to be her friend.' Her voice, at first rather raspy, began to fade away entirely. So he lifted the glass of brandy to her lips again.

'Yes, and then,' Susannah chipped in, since Rosalind seemed to need to rest her voice, 'when I became so worried about not seeing Cecil, Lieutenant Minter agreed to find out if some ill had befallen him. And then tonight, tonight...' Her face puckered. But instead of giving way to tears, this time she took a deep breath, swallowed hard, and continued.

'He told me that Cecil had run up debts all over

town, and fobbed off his creditors by saying he was expecting to come into money. By which he meant, the Lieutenant told me, marrying me and gaining control of my fortune. But since word had got out that you had forbidden the match, he'd gone into hiding, so that his creditors wouldn't find him and have him thrown into prison for debt. I… I accused the Lieutenant of making it all up! I said if he thought he could make me forsake Cecil by making up a lot of lies, so that he could win me over, he had another think coming!'

'Ah,' said Rosalind. 'That was what you were arguing with him about tonight.'

'Yes,' said Susannah miserably. 'But now… But now…' She gulped. 'Oh, I would never have thought he could be so…' she looked at the still, unkempt, bloody form of Mr Baxter '…so downright nasty!'

'He revealed his true colours,' Michael told her gently. 'Even I had no idea how, er, *nasty* he really was. I only knew he had a reputation for being, er, unsteady. And I thought you deserved someone better. Someone who would care for you for your own sake, not for your money.'

Susannah, scrambled in a most undignified manner over to where he and Rosalind were sitting and flung her arms round his neck. Again.

'I am so sorry I didn't trust you!'

'Er…there, there,' he said, wishing he had at least one hand free to push her away. But he wasn't prepared to let go of Rosalind, not now he had her in his arms.

'How could you trust His Lordship,' said Rosalind, having apparently recovered her voice again, 'when you didn't know him? And all your life, your various aunts and cousins had been telling you what a selfish, irresponsible person he was? Not a patch on your father.'

Susannah sat back, suddenly. 'Yes. They *did* do that. So that when he finally did come home, and was so…cold and distant with me, when he wasn't being stern and disapproving, I… I… Well…' She petered out, looking up at him with chagrin.

'It is hard,' put in Rosalind, 'knowing who to trust, isn't it?' And then she looked up at him, with a wry smile. 'I have never been able to rely on any of the men in my family, nor the ones I've met during the course of my work. Until I met your guardian.' She sighed then, gazing up at him with what looked like… worship. 'Men of his calibre,' she added, 'are very thin on the ground.'

'But I *should* have trusted you,' said Susannah, sitting back on her heels. 'And Lieutenant Minter. You are both…so…' she screwed up her face '…honourable. I thought that meant dull. But…'

Michael realised that if he didn't put a stop to this flow of confidences, they were going to be stuck on the floor all night.

'Glad though I am that you have finally realised the worth of a man who only wants the best for you, we have got to decide what to do with the *un*worthy one lying in a pool of his own gore over there.'

Susannah gave a disdainful sniff.

'And you don't need to worry about Lieutenant Minter too much, you know,' added Rosalind. 'He is fathoms deep in love with you. You will only have to apologise and tell him that you have seen his worth, and he will be so happy that he will probably burst his waistcoat buttons.'

'Oh, I wish he was here now,' cried Susannah. 'He would know just what to do! Why, he is always talking about the sort of stratagems he's had to adopt to defeat the enemy, you know, when at sea.'

Michael toyed with the idea of telling her that officers in His Majesty's army had to do that sort of thing on land, as well. But thought it was probably better not to dampen her enthusiasm for the fellow, now she'd decided to have some.

He was on the verge of telling her that one of them was going to have to go and fetch a constable, or something of the sort, when he became aware of the sound of muted voices, coming from the other side of the bedroom door.

Female voices.

'If I am not mistaken,' he said, 'it sounds as if some of the maids who have been asleep in the attics have woken up and come to find out what is going on in here. So we'd better come up with a story, quickly, unless you want everyone to know that this fellow almost abducted you?'

But it was too late. The door burst open and, with an air of valour, three housemaids came tumbling into the room, two of them brandishing pokers and the other one, a silver hairbrush.

Chapter Twenty-Three

'Oh, miss!' cried Susannah's maid, Pauline. 'Oh, miss!'

She had been taking a nap, Rosalind could tell, because she'd evidently put her hair in curling papers. There was still one tangled in a strand of hair that had escaped her cap.

The other two maids, who'd ranged themselves behind her, peeked over her shoulders, their eyes widening as they saw, well, an apparently dead body on the floor by the window and their master clutching the skinny, plain governess in his arms. It was hard to tell, as their heads swung from one tableau to the other, which they found the most shocking.

'If we'd only known it was a housebreaker,' said Constance, stepping round Pauline to take a closer look at Mr Baxter's body, 'we would have come sooner. Only when we first heard the screams, we just thought—' She broke off abruptly as Pauline dug her sharp elbow into the girl's ribs.

Yes, Rosalind could easily guess what they'd thought. That Susannah had been brought home early, because of some misdemeanour, and that the screams were just her indulging in a fit of bad temper. Also, they'd taken their time making themselves presentable. To try to look as though they'd been sitting up, patiently waiting for their mistresses to come home, and hadn't needed to tidy themselves up after lying on their beds.

'A housebreaker,' said Lord Caldicot, looking across at Baxter's form, thoughtfully. 'Yes. That is exactly what this is.'

'Oh, but…' said Susannah.

'And he tried to choke Miss Hinchcliffe to stop her calling out for help,' he continued, cutting through whatever Susannah had been about to say and shooting her a warning look while he was at it, 'when he climbed in through the window, not expecting to find anyone at home. Though why,' he continued, in withering accents, 'he went to all the trouble of procuring a ladder and climbing in by this window I cannot imagine. He might just as well have strolled in through the front door, since the night porter, a man I pay to be at his post to prevent such things, is conspicuous by his absence.'

'I suspect,' said Throgmorton, the third of the trio,

with a disapproving sniff, 'they all went to the Jolly Footman.'

'Well, may I suggest,' said Lord Caldicot, in that same magnificently disdainful tone, 'that one of you go straight there and fetch some of the jolly footmen back? And dispatch at least one of them to fetch a constable, who can dispose of this…miscreant.'

All three maids dispersed at once, practically tumbling over each other in their eagerness to be the first to report on all the excitement the men had missed by going out.

Susannah gave an impatient huff, planting her hands on her hips.

'They've just gone off and left us to deal with… him,' she complained.

'It seems to me that you two are extremely capable,' Lord Caldicot said, giving Rosalind a bit of a squeeze, 'of dealing with anything or anyone who attempts to cross either of you.'

Susannah tilted her head to one side. 'Lord Caldicot,' she said with a shake of her head. 'It almost sounds as though you are *proud* of me!'

'Don't let it go to your head,' he said, though he was smiling as he said it. 'I dare say you will do something to make me cross with you again directly.'

Susannah chuckled. 'Or you will come over all tyrannical again and make me cross as crabs with you.'

Although Rosalind was glad the pair of them were

getting on so well, she couldn't stop worrying about what Mr Baxter might do when he woke up.

'I hate to have to remind you both,' she therefore said, 'but Mr Baxter is still lying there.' And might wake up at any moment.

'I think,' said Lord Caldicot, 'that when the authorities come, it may be as well to go along with the suggestion the maids gave. After all, if the truth were known, that he'd tried to abduct Susannah, people will really enjoy making a scandal broth of it. Susannah, I know you haven't always trusted me, but trust me on this. That is *not* the sort of story a girl wants hanging over her head like the stench of bad fish.'

She pouted. 'I want him punished for this. For hurting Miss Hinchcliffe, too!'

'So do I,' said Lord Caldicot, grimly. 'But I think once he is taken into custody, there will be plenty of other people clamouring to press all sorts of charges. And that we could keep your names out of it.'

'That's not enough,' she said. '*I* want to…to *hurt* him!' She strode over to the body and glared down at it, her fists clenched.

'No, Susannah,' said Rosalind, stretching out her hand. 'If you gave in to the urge to have your revenge, you would be as bad as he is.'

'I would not!'

'In fact,' added Rosalind, 'what we really ought to be doing is fetching a doctor.'

'Oh, no, you don't,' said Lord Caldicot hastily. 'Not after what happened last time,' he added, lowering his voice so that Susannah, who was standing with her back to them as she glared down at Mr Baxter, could not hear. 'I am not going to give him the chance to escape a second time.'

'I know,' said Susannah, suddenly. 'We should tie him up.'

'That,' said Lord Caldicot, 'is an excellent idea.'

'I will go and find some ropes with which to bind him,' said Susannah, rather gleefully, and darted from the room.

'At last,' said Lord Caldicot, gazing down into her face. 'I thought we would never have any peace. How are you feeling, now? Can you breathe any better yet?'

'Yes, much better, thank you. And really, he only got his hands round my neck briefly. Susannah must have heard the sound of him throwing the chair across the room, and, knowing it was not the sort of thing I'd do, came to find out what was going on—'

'I don't care why she came in here,' he broke in.

'But…'

'Please, stop talking. Though I am glad you are able to, of course. But what I'd really rather be doing is kissing that mouth, not listening to what it can say.'

'What, like this? I mean, with Mr Baxter lying over there…'

'Absolutely! In fact, it is rather fitting, since the

very first time I wanted to kiss you was the last time you rendered the blighter unconscious.'

'You…you wanted to kiss me…then? But…but why?'

Instead of explaining, he simply lowered his head and did what he'd been threatening to do. Or promising to do, she wasn't sure. She only knew that she'd never expected the evening, which had started out so badly, could have ended like this.

She felt as if she was floating. She felt as if she was dreaming. She was just plucking up the courage to raise her arms and link her hands behind his neck, when the door burst open. Again.

'What,' came the aggrieved tone of Lady Birchwood, 'is the meaning of this?'

Lord Caldicot groaned. And lifted his head.

'I heard all sorts of garbled talk,' continued Lady Birchwood, 'from Throgmorton as she went dashing out of the house just when she ought to be attending to *me*,' she said indignantly, 'about housebreakers and scandalous conduct, but never, ever, could I have imagined that you would be so shameless as to fling yourself at His Lordship like this. You, Miss,' she cried, pointing at Rosalind, 'are a disgrace!'

'No, she isn't,' said Lord Caldicot, getting to his feet, while keeping his arms firmly round Rosalind, with the result that he lifted her off the floor and held her in his arms, cradled to his chest. 'On the contrary, she saved your niece from being abducted by that villain.' He jerked his head at the body lying on the floor.

At that moment, Susannah came bounding back in, with what looked like the tasselled cords from all her bedroom curtains. 'It's true,' she said, skipping over to Mr Baxter. 'Even though he tried to strangle her, she went for him with the chamber pot.'

'The chamber pot?' Lady Birchwood looked even more appalled than ever as her eyes lit on the shattered pieces of the offending item.

'Come and help me tie him up, Aunt Birchwood,' said Susannah, dropping to her knees. 'If you know how to tie knots? Do you?'

'I?' Lady Birchwood reached out and took hold of the door frame as if she needed something solid to hang on to. 'Why on earth would I know how to tie knots?'

'Do you,' Susannah asked Rosalind, hopefully, 'know how to tie knots?'

Rosalind was about to answer that of course she could, when Lord Caldicot let out a low sort of growling noise.

'You are going to have to manage him on your own,' he said firmly. 'Miss Hinchcliffe has suffered enough. I am going to take her away.'

'Yes,' said Susannah with a grin. 'So you can kiss her more thoroughly, I dare say.'

'I have hardly managed to kiss her at all,' he said,

sounding aggrieved, as he shouldered his way past Lady Birchwood.

Lady Birchwood let out a shriek. 'Put her down! This is scandalous!'

'No, it isn't,' he replied. 'I'm going to marry her.'

'Marry her? You can't! What will people think?'

'I don't care.' He came to a halt and gave Lady Birchwood a level look. 'Ever since I sold my commission and returned to England, I have been trying to atone for the mistakes my predecessor made. *He* was the one who was gudgeon enough not to remarry and secure the succession after Susannah's mother died, yet *I* have been the one trying to find what people term a *suitable* bride to fill the position. Mainly because you all made me feel that, since I was not fit to fill his shoes, I should at least find a woman who could make up for my deficiencies. But do you know what?'

He didn't pause to allow Lady Birchwood to make any response, but plunged straight on. 'Your brother was *not* the paragon you all made him out to be. And *I* am the Marquess of Caldicot now. And I am going to be a marquess on my own terms. Starting with marrying the one woman with whom I can see myself spending the rest of my life. The woman, in fact, that I love.'

'Bravo!' cried Susannah, though Lady Birchwood

made a sort of choking noise, and tottered away to sink despondently on to a chair.

'The family honour…' Lady Birchwood began to wail.

'Oh, for heaven's sake!' Lord Caldicot turned to her, with Rosalind still held in his arms. 'It's not as if I was threatening to marry an opera dancer! Miss Hinchcliffe comes from a decent family, even if she has fallen on hard times. Her grandfather is General Smallwood! Not that it makes any difference to me, my darling,' he said, looking down at her with a slight frown. 'I don't want you thinking that…'

She reached up and placed one finger over his lips.

'I think,' she suggested, 'that you had better not waste your energy on arguing. Not right at this moment. I am not a small, delicate wisp of a woman. And since you seem so reluctant to put me down…'

'Good point! I can deal with Lady Birchwood's arguments later.'

With that, he turned from the room, strode along the landing, went down the stairs and into his study.

Even once there, he did not let her go, so that when he sat down on the chair in front of his desk, she ended up sitting on his lap.

'Now,' he said, studying her face intently. 'Where were we before we were so rudely interrupted?'

'You…' she said, her cheeks growing rather warm,

'had just declared your intention to marry me, in spite of what anyone might think. You had also said,' she reminded him hopefully, 'that you were planning to kiss me.'

He sucked in a sharp breath, looking rather alarmed.

Got to his feet, then set her down on the chair and began pacing back and forth, running his fingers through his hair.

Why, in heaven's name, why? Was he having second thoughts about her? Had he just said all those things about marriage, and kissing, to annoy Lady Birchwood? And was only now realising what it would really mean if he carried through on his threats to scandalise her?

All of a sudden his expression cleared. He went to the desk, picked up one of the ledgers, came back to her and held it out.

'Here,' he said. 'Take this.'

'Why?'

'So that you can hit me with it, of course,' he said, as though it was obvious.

'Why would I want to do anything of the sort?'

'Because I am about to attempt to take liberties with you,' he said. Then frowned. 'Actually, no, I'm not. It has just occurred to me, you see, that I *told* you I wanted to kiss you and that I told everyone else that I intended to marry you. Without once, ever, asking you what you want. Perhaps,' he said, eyeing the ledger warily, 'you ought to just whack me with it any-way. I fully deserve it after the way I…mauled you about and dragged you down here, not to mention the way I kissed your face when you were in no fit state to defend yourself…'

She stood up so abruptly that the ledger fell to the floor, reached out for the lapels of his coat and tugged, hard.

'I am *never* too weak to defend myself,' she de-clared. 'Could you not tell that I had no objection to anything you were doing, or saying?'

'Well, I…er…*hoped* you didn't. But then I won-dered if I was just fooling myself, because it is what I want, so much.'

She shook her head. 'It is what I want, too.'

'Really?' His face lit up.

'Don't you remember, we made a deal to always be honest with one another?'

'I certainly do.' A brief shadow flitted dimmed his expression. 'Only, I haven't always kept to that deal. I never admitted, for instance, how much you were becoming to mean to me…'

'Never mind. I concealed my growing feelings for you, too.'

'So you have them? Feelings for me, that is?'

'How could you doubt it?' she asked, nudging the accounts ledger aside with one foot, then running her hands up his lapels until they rested on his shoulders.

'Last chance,' he said with a rather wicked look-ing grin, 'to escape.'

'I don't want to escape,' she breathed, her heart hammering in her chest as he lowered his head, pur-posefully. 'Never, ever... Mmm...'

She couldn't say any more—because he was, at last, kissing her in earnest. And suddenly she no lon-ger felt headachy, or queasy, or as if she was sickening for something. On the contrary, she felt wonderfully, vibrantly alive, for perhaps the first time in her life.

Dimly, in the background, she could hear the sound of someone pounding on the front door and booted feet running across the hall and up the stairs, but Lord Caldicot, no, Michael—she could hardly think of him by any other name now that he was holding her like this, kissing her like this—paid no heed. So she decided it would be rude to suggest he ought to be overseeing whatever was going on.

Besides, she was rapidly losing the ability to think. Michael's kisses were unleashing feelings she'd never dreamed she could feel.

She needed to get closer to him. She wanted to feel him, every bit of him. His shoulders, his sides, even his legs. She didn't have enough hands! She'd have to run her own legs up and down his, she supposed, to satisfy that particular craving...

All of a sudden there came the sound of someone knocking, rather insistently, on the study door.

'What!' Michael lifted his head to glare at the door, only to see Timms peeping round it.

'Begging your pardon, my lord, but I thought you would wish to know that the…er…felon has been removed from the premises.'

'I don't know what the devil gave you that idea. If I cared two pins for that heap of refuse I would have overseen his removal myself!'

'Yes, my lord. Indeed.' Timms inclined his head. 'And may I be the first to congratulate you,' he said, his eyes sliding over Rosalind's dishevelled form. 'On behalf of all the staff, Miss Hinchcliffe,' he added with a decided twinkle in his eye.

'Yes, well now you've said your piece you can take yourself off,' said Michael, rather ungraciously.

'Really,' Rosalind protested, as Timms retreated, shutting the door behind him. 'The poor man was only doing his job.'

'It is a great pity,' he said bitterly, 'that he wasn't doing it earlier, rather than enjoying himself with his underlings, in that pub.'

'But if he hadn't neglected his post,' Rosalind pointed out, 'we might never have reached this point.'

'Hmmm,' he said, as though considering the rights and wrongs of it all. 'Well, never mind what *might* have happened,' he said, testily. 'The fact is, I've had enough of interruptions for one night. I feel as if I've wasted *weeks* trying to persuade people I don't really care about that I'm fit to inhabit the role that has been thrust upon me. Now that I've got you in my arms, that's all I care to think about. Just you. And me.' He hugged her tightly.

And kissed her again.

They managed another few moments, during which time his shirt became detached from the waistband of his breeches and his knees buckled, and somehow they ended up tumbling to the hearthrug, which, she discovered, was every bit as soft as she'd suspected when she'd watched Susannah employing it, before there was another knock on the door.

'What is it now? Whoever it is, they had better watch out,' he snarled, striding to the door and flinging it open.

Susannah stood there, a broad smile on her face. 'I've just had the most wonderful idea,' she said.

'Don't want to hear it. Can't you see I'm busy?'

She peeped round him, to where Rosalind was desperately trying to rearrange her clothing so that it didn't look as if he'd just been ravishing her on the hearthrug.

She giggled. 'You aren't setting me a very good example, are you?'

'Much you would care if I was,' he snapped, 'you minx.'

'Yes, but I was thinking, you will want to throw

an engagement ball, won't you? And I have seen the most ravishing outfit…'

Michael dealt with her by shutting the door in her face, then turning the key in the lock.

'What are you laughing at?' He looked at her in confusion.

'Because it has just occurred to me, that the only way we are going to get any privacy to indulge in…' she felt her cheeks heat '…anything truly scandalous is to elope. And that, for once, Mr Baxter has done us a good turn.'

'He has?'

'Yes. Don't you remember? He left a ladder propped up outside my window!'

'No eloping for us,' he said firmly. 'I am going to throw you the most extravagant and public wedding money can buy, so that nobody can doubt how proud I am to have you as my bride.'

'Are you? Truly?'

'How can you doubt it?'

'B-Because there are so many prettier, more eligible women you could have chosen.'

'That's as may be,' he said, stalking over to where she was sitting, in a confusion of blushes and dishevelled clothing. 'But none of them dared argue with me the way you do. None of them could make me laugh. Or keep me wondering what audacious thing they might do or say next. None of them,' he added, sinking down beside her with what looked like a purposeful glint in his eye, 'made me long to throw propriety out of the window and kiss them senseless.'

'No other man has made me feel the way I feel about you, either,' she confessed shyly. 'But…'

'But what?'

'Well, I haven't been raised to fill a position in society…'

'I sincerely hope you aren't going to tell me that you have no idea how to be a marchioness.'

'Well, no, I don't.'

'May I remind you of what you said to me, when I admitted I didn't feel capable of being a marquess? You said that I was one and so other people would have to get used to me being a marquess my own way.'

'No, I didn't!'

'Well, words to that effect. Which is why I'm going to say them to you. Once you are my marchioness, people will have to accustom themselves to you doing things your way. One thing you've taught me is that you need not change to try and fit in with what you think other people expect of you. In fact, I expressly forbid you to change at all. I love you just as you are!'

And then he put paid to any further arguments by kissing her again.

And all at once she stopped caring about what anyone else thought. Michael loved her just as she was! And as long as *he* loved her just as she was, nothing else mattered.

* * * *

If you enjoyed this story,
be sure to read Annie Burrows's
other brilliant stories

"Invitation to a Wedding"
in Regency Christmas Parties
The Countess's Forgotten Marriage

And make sure to check out her
The Patterdale Siblings miniseries

A Scandal at Midnight
How to Catch a Viscount
Wooing His Convenient Wife

MILLS & BOON®

Coming next month

THE DUKE'S GUIDE TO FAKE COURTSHIP
Jade Lee

He touched her face. A slow caress of his thumb across her jaw. Fire sizzled in its wake, and her breath caught and held. Certainly she had experienced flirtation before, but this man had seen her worth faster than anyone else. He looked at her with admiration mixed with desire, and she wanted to leap into his fire just to feel the burn.

Madness. And yet she wanted it. Even more so when he leaned forward as if to kiss her. But she couldn't allow that to happen. It would be leaping into something she could not control, and that was dangerous territory—especially for a woman.

So she leapt free. A quick jump and a grab and she was swinging herself away from him for all that they were still tied together.

'Miss Richards?' he said as she pulled herself up and away. 'Is everything well?'

'Yes,' she said, horrified to realise that her breath was short with panic. It took her a moment to slow it down, to steady her heart, and to dry the slickness from her palms. 'Yes,' she repeated more strongly. 'We must go back down.'

It was a lie. There was no need to go down for more than an hour except boredom. But he didn't question her. Instead, he took one last look at the world around them before reaching up and pulling himself from the crow's nest.

She watched his strong arms, noted the size of his hands, and admired the ease with which he managed his body. No wonder he was an English mandarin. He exuded power with every movement.

Then he smiled at her, gesturing for her to begin the descent. Normally she would warn him to be extra careful. The descent was harder than the climb, always. But she didn't have the breath. And for the first time in years she felt awed by a man.

Continue reading

THE DUKE'S GUIDE TO FAKE COURTSHIP
Jade Lee

Available next month
millsandboon.co.uk

COMING SOON!

We really hope you enjoyed reading this book.
If you're looking for more romance
be sure to head to the shops when
new books are available on

Thursday 16th January

MILLS & BOON

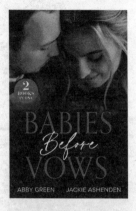
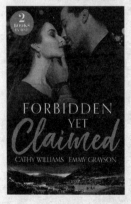

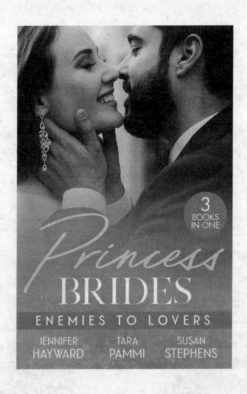

LET'S TALK
Romance

For exclusive extracts, competitions and special offers, find us online:

f MillsandBoon

X @MillsandBoon

◉ @MillsandBoonUK

♪ @MillsandBoonUK

Get in touch on 01413 063 232